A French Girl in New York

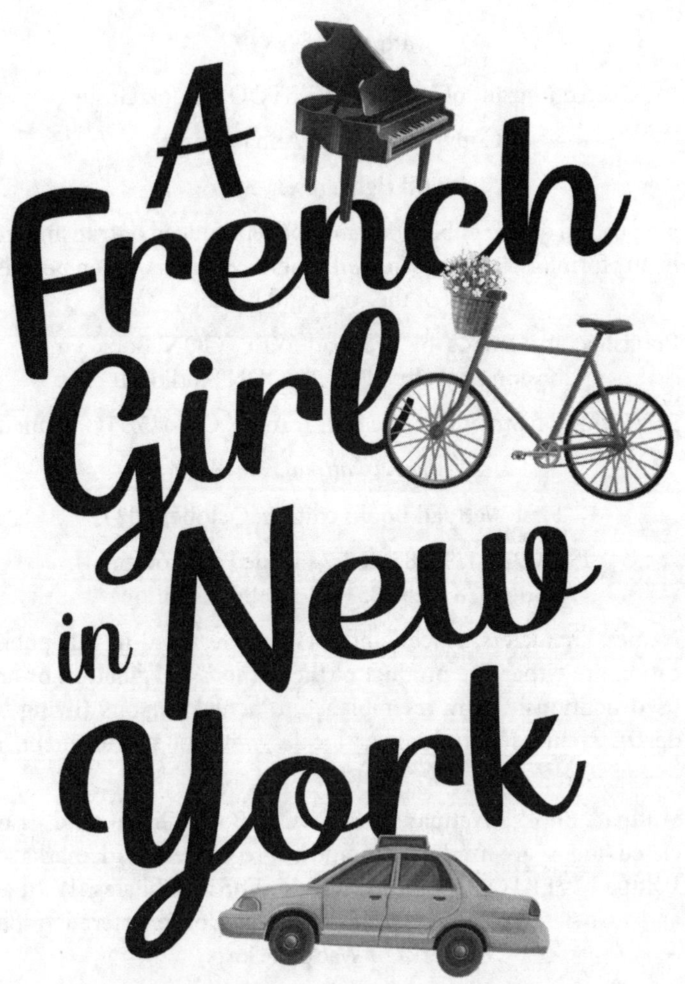

A French Girl in New York

ANNA ADAMS

wattpad books

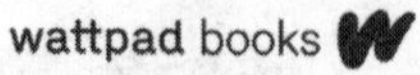

An imprint of Wattpad WEBTOON Book Group

Published in Canada by Wattpad WEBTOON Book Group, a division of Wattpad WEBTOON Studios, Inc.

36 Wellington Street E., Suite 200, Toronto, ON M5E 1C7 Canada

www.wattpad.com

First Wattpad Books edition: October 2024

ISBN 978-1-99885-462-2 (Trade Paper original)
ISBN 978-1-99885-463-9 (eBook edition)

Library and Archives Canada Cataloguing in Publication information is available upon request.

Printed and bound in Canada

1 3 5 7 9 10 8 6 4 2

Cover design by Niko Dalcin and Patrick McCormick
Icon Illustrations by Chelsea Charles
Typesetting by Delaney Anderson

To my mom, Régine

Chapter One

Maude Laurent pressed her face against the window as her school bus entered the French capital city of Paris.

At last!

For Maude, a sixteen-year-old who had never left her small French town, the view unfolding before her was like an exquisite masterpiece.

The sun shone brightly, its rays bouncing off the majestic Eiffel Tower. *La Dame de fer*. The Iron Lady. Maude saw the tower as the iron goddess. Below, the river Seine flowed to the rhythm of the city, transporting enchanted tourists eager to appreciate the capital's historic monuments alongside its modern graffitied beauty in colorful Bateaux Mouches.

As the bus parked close to the Place du Trocadéro, Maude photographed each moment in her mind.

To Maude's classmates, who jumped out of the school bus and raced to the plaza, Paris was well worth a dozen actual pictures to post on social media.

Maude watched with longing as Astrid and Samia, two girls from her class who never spoke to her, struck a pose with the Eiffel Tower in the background and yelled "Besties forever!" They both stuck out their tongues right before Samia clicked several times on her phone.

"How do I look?" Astrid grabbed Samia's phone. "Don't post this one," she ordered, deleting the first photo. "We both look good in *this* one."

Samia readily agreed and ran her fingers over her screen, posting the image to PixeLight. "Let's do a video next."

Maude sighed. She wished she had her own phone. Any phone! She could only access the internet and her secret PixeLight account through the town's local library. Her foster family had made it perfectly clear that Maude's technological deficiency wasn't their priority. Besides food and shelter, Maude's general well-being wasn't of much concern. Instead, she had worn-out sneakers from the second-hand store and leggings that bore a not-so-tiny hole on the left thigh that only her oversized faded yellow parka could conceal.

That morning, she'd tied her pretty, natural hair in a bun, and as the sun danced on her chocolate-brown skin, Maude hoped its rays made her face look livelier than it usually did in October when subjected to Carvin's harsh northern wind. She inhaled and smiled with contentment. She was in Paris!

"Stephane, take a video of us," Samia called, giggling and pulling to her side a tall boy with dark hair, wearing a hoodie and Nikes.

Maude stared at Stephane dreamily and wished he could see her like he saw those two. She often daydreamed that he'd finally notice her, sweep her into his strong brown arms, and give her a passionate kiss worthy of a Hollywood movie.

But he never saw her, and she'd never found the courage to speak to him in the carefree manner the other girls did. There had been one historic instance when he'd asked for the time in science class. Petrified by his gorgeous brown eyes, she had stammered, "It's forty-five." Just forty-five, no hour, no a.m., p.m., nothing. The conversation hadn't moved past that point, much to Maude's despair.

"Ooh, let's sing 'Burning Bridges'!" Astrid suggested. Samia proceeded to screech the first verse of the song.

Maude turned away, rolling her eyes. She couldn't stand Lindsey Linton's latest hit, but that was all anyone sang these days. Maude, who only listened to opera, had once vowed to avoid popular music altogether. She liked that she had this in common with the famed opera star, and her personal heroine, Cordelia Tragent, who had partly attributed her early success to growing up in a pop music–free household. Maude had even attempted to compose short opera songs, but they never matched the beauty of her favorite Italian arias.

However, Maude's oath was regularly put to the test by the latest crazes. Once everyone around her had begun to sing "Burning Bridges," it had become extremely difficult to ignore the song. So much so that she knew its simple lyrics by heart.

The class moved on from the Eiffel Tower to the Louvre.

After visiting the museum, their teacher, Ms. Clement, gave them free time.

"I want you all back here in front of the glass pyramid at seven. Don't be late or you'll get detention for two weeks. Got it?"

"Astrid, why is the teacher looking at me?" Stephane asked with a grin, holding his arms up playfully.

"Because you're the one with the most detention hours so far," Ms. Clement answered sharply, before Astrid could. "You might even break a school record this year."

"I'll do my best to break the record then. Wouldn't want to disappoint you," Stephane answered smoothly.

"Seven o'clock sharp," Ms. Clement reminded them as they began to walk away in groups.

Maude wandered off alone. She was so incredibly happy, mesmerized by the beauty surrounding her. She was just thrilled to be walking around aimlessly in Paris. She visited the small shops on Île Saint-Louis, even though she had very little money to spend. She strolled along the Seine, peering at the elegant houseboats, and smiled at the artists painting portraits of tourists. After two hours' rambling in the city, leaving Place Georges-Pompidou and heading toward Notre-Dame, Maude was thinking about how hungry she was. Being surrounded by a variety of food only made choosing harder, and she was having a difficult time deciding whether she wanted to eat sweet crêpes full of strawberry or peach jam, a French hot dog in a baguette, or a delicious croque monsieur filled with ham and melted cheese.

That was when she heard it.

At the café right in front of her, Le Cavalier Bleu, a musician, surrounded by a crowd of happy customers, was at the piano singing "Milord," one of Edith Piaf's most famous songs.

Maude's vow to avoid popular music flitted out of her head. She felt drawn inside the café. No one ever sang in cafés in Carvin.

In the back corner of the room, a smiling young man wearing a red cap turned backward filmed the entire scene with his smartphone.

Maude went up to him and asked in French, "What's going on?"

"*Je ne parle pas français,*" he said with a heavy American accent.

She hesitated. He didn't speak French. She'd practiced speaking English a million times in her room and in class, but never with a native speaker. She slowly repeated her question in English, and he answered.

"Oh, apparently, it's always like this here. Anyone can play the piano. I'm just visiting, but a friend mentioned this place to me. I'm Chad, by the way. You should follow me on PixeLight under the name 'Chad the Expat.'"

Maude strained her ears and focused on what he said. He spoke really fast!

"I'll do that, erm, once I'm back home. I don't have a phone," she added apologetically.

"Sorry." Chad looked at her as if she'd announced the death of a grandparent. "Do you play the piano?"

"Yeah." She hesitated, searching for her words. "But, um, I've never played in front of anyone."

"No one knows you here. Perfect audience if you ask me."

At that moment, the current pianist finished his song and stood up.

"You should play," Chad insisted. "You know you want to. Come on, I'll film you and send you the video. That's the best way to improve."

Maude found herself nodding slowly. She did want to improve. She'd never get into the world famous Conservatoire de Paris or the National Academy of Arts if she only ever practiced on her own in the auditorium at her local library. And after all, she would be back in Carvin again that night. The magic of Paris took over and Maude walked to the dark upright Pleyel piano, her legs feeling a bit heavier with every step she took. She kneeled at the bench, adjusting it to her height, and then took her rightful place. The crowd grew silent.

She placed her hands and pondered what to play. An opera aria wouldn't do in a Parisian café. No, even an Italian song from her favorite opera wasn't right. She'd have to break her vow and sing something the crowd liked, she decided.

Unfortunately, the only song that came to her mind was "Burning Bridges." The lyrics tiptoed insistently in her mind until she gave in.

I'll make it my own, Maude decided. She stripped the pop song of its fast, electronic elements, its bass, its guitar, its autotune effects. All that remained was the piano score.

Slowly, she hummed while playing *la, re, fa* with her left hand. Suddenly, her voice rang out, loud and clear, as she began the first verse of "Burning Bridges" in a clear, warm mezzo-soprano voice.

"I want out

"Wanna shout

"Can't go back

"On to the next track."

The crowd fell silent. As she sang the lyrics, it felt as if she was discovering them for the first time. They spoke to her in a way they never had before. Why should she go back to Carvin? She could stay in Paris and pursue the opera career she'd always wanted. Who would miss her?

She had spent the most wonderful day in this city. Her mind revisited her enchanted discovery of the Louvre, her walk through its wide colorful halls, eyes staring in awe at every painting, Neoclassical or Romantic. As her fingers slid across the piano, the *Mona Lisa* beamed at her as she transformed the hit pop song into a beautiful classical melody.

"The past is gone

"My image, undone

"Took a torch
"Raised it high
"Said good-bye
"To all the lies."

On the final word, Maude's voice reached a high note that Lindsey Linton had autotuned in the original version. As a mezzo-soprano, Maude was more comfortable singing in the middle of her range, but she'd spent hours training her voice to leap into the higher notes with agility. When Maude sang the word *lies*, she didn't stop there; she repeated the lyric, singing higher and higher until she held the final syllable for four whole beats.

"Lies!"

Her foster family had never told her who her parents were or how they'd died. They said they didn't know, but Maude knew they were lying. She recalled a parent-teacher meeting in sixth grade. Her English teacher had praised Maude for her good grades in every subject but had expressed concern to the Ruchets about their foster child's poor grades in English. Mrs. Ruchet had snorted. *"I guess she doesn't take after her father, who was perfectly fluent in English!"* She had stopped abruptly under Mr. Ruchet's warning glare. Maude, who had never heard Mrs. Ruchet talk about her parents before, treasured this information, and since that moment she had immersed herself wholeheartedly in the English language, its literature, its grammar, and its history. She would learn to speak it fluently, like her father. Whoever he was.

"Took a torch
"Poured the gas
"Burned the bridges of my past
"Took a torch
"Poured the gas

"Burned the bridges to the last."

Every bone in her body awoke to true happiness at the thought of leaving her foster family, of burning those bridges to create a new life in Paris.

Her voice trembled with emotion that only added breathtaking beauty to her performance. She ended her song, the song that now possessed her whole being, and slowly turned around. No one in the audience, which had gradually grown as she played, said a word. Then, suddenly, a great round of applause broke out. Those who were seated rose to their feet. The owner had abandoned his tray and was clapping enthusiastically.

Maude smiled, her heart pounding in her ears, and, as her eyes circled the cheering crowd, she paused. Chad had filmed the entire scene and looked at her with amazement.

Her smile abruptly faded as her gaze fell on the clock right behind him. It was five minutes past seven.

She had to leave!

That was easier said than done. The crowd had gathered around her, and the owner was offering her free drinks.

"I've never had so many happy customers!" he exclaimed in amazement. "You have to stay longer. You can't leave without getting a free drink. Don't make me beg," he urged as he saw her about to protest.

"No, really I have to go," Maude insisted, trying to make her way to the exit.

People were gathering around her on all sides, congratulating her. With all her heart she wanted to stay, but the clock had struck seven and she had to go back to her lonely existence with the Ruchets. She smiled hastily at the customers, all the while peeling away from the crowd and finally managing to make it to the street and away from the crowd. Just as she was about to head to the Métro station, she heard someone call, "Singer! Girl! You with the yellow parka."

She turned and saw Chad from the café running toward her.

"Give me your PixeLight handle. I'm going to tag you in my post. What an amazing performance!"

"Thanks! But I'm going to be late. My handle is atMaude-LaurentCarvin. Gotta go! Bye!"

"Wait!" he cried.

But she'd already hurried away and entered the subway station, certain she'd never hear from him again.

When she arrived at the Louvre, she was thirty minutes late, and Ms. Clement spluttered furiously, wagging an indignant finger.

"We've been waiting for you for ages! Even Stephane made it on time. You don't even have a phone. I was worried sick. You're getting fourteen hours of detention and your foster parents are going to hear about this, young lady!"

"See, I didn't break the school record. Maude did," Stephane said triumphantly. Maude sighed as she sat on the bus. At least Stephane knew her name.

As the bus crawled out of the city Maude thought about her performance. She'd done it! She had performed in public for the first time. Detention didn't faze her, now that she knew what she wanted.

She was more certain than ever: as soon as she turned eighteen she'd move to Paris to become an opera diva.

Chapter Two

Life in Carvin couldn't be further from life in Paris. At Carvin's center was a small château, now housing the municipal offices, and an impressive eighteenth-century cathedral in Dutch Renaissance style. But what Carvin possessed, what made it undeniably a town in this northern region, was its Grand Place, the main square where everything interesting that could happen, happened. It might have seemed like an ordinary plaza with a couple of hairdressers, banks, opticians, and a few restaurants, had it not been for Mrs. Bonnin's incredible bakery.

Early Saturday mornings, Maude's first errand was to buy croissants for the Ruchet family. It wasn't her least favorite task, as she enjoyed walking through the deserted town when the only other person up was Mrs. Bonnin. Maude was extremely fond of the baker.

That day, two weeks after her trip to Paris, soft gray clouds covered the sky. The air was damp, the streets were wet, and droplets of rain fell from the lampposts into Maude's frizzy hair as she glided through the leaves that were changing shades and covering the town in a new, light-brown, autumnal blanket.

As Maude pushed the door to the bakery open the bell announced her arrival with a jolly jingle. Mrs. Bonnin hurried to the counter to greet her favorite customer.

Mrs. Bonnin was a pretty, plump woman who always greeted her customers with a smile, even on occasions when she had no reason to smile. She was also the town gossip. All small French towns have one, and she was very good at it. Indeed, the location of the *boulangerie* in the center of town was perfect for the mission she felt she had been called to fulfill. From behind her counter, at what she called her "observation post," Mrs. Bonnin eyed every new couple lovingly holding hands, and would unashamedly observe a week later the same couple having screaming matches on the terrace of La Torche café. Mrs. Bonnin had told Maude she'd once been the object of every wild story in the small town but now felt immensely bored with her life. She couldn't stand the humdrum of her calm, uneventful existence, and longed for amusement. That was why she dedicated her time to learning about other people's mishaps and commenting on them to her friends. She never did it to hurt anyone; she just couldn't help herself, and nobody in Carvin really blamed her for it, seeing as she had more interesting news than the local newspaper. She knew the life and history of everyone in Carvin.

Everyone but Maude. Maude had once found the courage to ask her, but all Mrs. Bonnin knew was that one day, sixteen years ago, Mr. Ruchet had come home with a delightful, beautiful, smiling brown baby. Mr. Ruchet, who had refused to give any sort of information about this newborn, became the object of the wildest speculations. It had been the talk of the town for three months, dying down only after a fresh, new, explosive scandal surfaced: the mayor's embezzlement.

"You, my darling, are still as skinny as ever." Mrs. Bonnin admonished Maude. "You're not leaving here without a good breakfast."

"I can't," Maude replied regretfully. "Mrs. Ruchet is waiting for me. She needs me to deep clean the living room and kitchen before her friends come over."

"Thirty minutes won't kill her. She could lift a finger herself from time to time. Sit, sit. Take your pick!"

Maude obliged and took a seat at one of the bakery's round tables. Her favorite words in the world were Mrs. Bonnin's invitation to "take her pick." But how could Maude choose from the splendid treasures displayed all over the bakery on rotating platters and colorful shelves? Freshly made fruit cakes, croissants, fluffy baguettes, cupcakes dripping with warm Nutella, and tartlets bursting with ruby-red strawberries were all wrapped up with the sweet scent of melted chocolate that filled the bakery.

Maude politely chose a croissant. She always left the best pastries to the paying customers. Mrs. Bonnin sat across from her with a steaming cup of coffee.

"You'll never guess which market vendor is having an affair with Pascal!"

"I love a good guessing game," Maude chirped. "Let me see. Marianne, the fruit vendor?"

"She's really close to the fish guy. There's something fishy there, if you ask me." Mrs. Bonnin's eyes twinkled with pride over her own joke.

"Oh, then who's left at the market? Let's see. Noooo, the cheese girl."

"As I live and breathe."

"Your proof?"

"I saw them strolling across the Grand Place at *eleven* last night. Saw them with my own two eyes. She laughed at one of his dumb jokes *and*"—Mrs. Bonnin leaned closer to Maude for dramatic effect—"she stood inches from his face though he'd eaten half a Maroilles cheese pie. Imagine the smell!"

"Ewww." Maude clapped her hands over her nose. As a girl from northern France, she loved Maroilles cheese just as much as the next person, but she would never stand inches from a person who'd just eaten the odorous cheese. Unless that person happened to be Stephane, of course.

"Gotta go check the next round of baguettes isn't burning," Mrs. Bonnin cried, jumping up from her seat. She dashed to the back of the bakery.

Just as Maude took a bite of her buttery croissant, Morgane, a girl from her school, walked in with her mother, Jocelyne. The two could pass as twins, not least because they both wore long, flowery skirts and matching jean jackets. Thick chestnut-colored hair framed their oval faces, and both wore square-rimmed glasses. There was one ostensible dissimilarity: wrinkles lined the elder's forehead while bright-red pimples spotted the younger's.

Maude was fascinated by the workings of genetics. She thought wistfully how lucky they were that they looked alike, and couldn't help but wonder if she looked anything like her own late mother. The girl peered at Maude, her eyes widening behind her glasses, and she hastily whispered something to her mom.

"That ain't her," Jocelyne answered gruffly.

Maude, busy demolishing her croissant with a voracious appetite, barely noticed the exchange. But Morgane insisted just as Mrs. Bonnin emerged from the back.

"Look!" Morgane fished out her phone from the pocket of her jean jacket and shoved it in front of her mom's eyes.

The sound from the video resonated throughout the bakery: it was Maude's voice singing "Burning Bridges"!

Maude bit her tongue in surprise. "Ow!" she cried, her eyes tearing up.

"What's that?" Mrs. Bonnin asked, at the same time as Maude waved her hands to signal to Morgane to put the phone away. Too late. In three shuffled strides Mrs. Bonnin was at the girl's side, peering at the phone with her beady, curious eyes.

"What the . . . ? Maude, is that you?" the baker shrieked.

"I don't think so," Maude said, preferring to avoid honesty when she did not know how much of her face appeared on the video. "It can't be. I'm right here." She was unsure how much Mrs. Bonnin knew about the internet.

"It's not live, Maude," Mrs. Bonnin retorted.

Drat, Maude thought, burying her face in her hands. Mrs. Bonnin was decidedly sharper than she'd anticipated.

"Would you look at all those views?" Mrs. Bonnin cried, snatching the phone away from Morgane. "There's like thirty million."

"What?" Maude's head shot up. She pushed her chair back and leaned closer to Mrs. Bonnin, who hid the phone under her chef's cap.

"I thought you said it wasn't you."

"Okay, so, what happened is . . . maybe I sang in a Parisian café two weeks ago," Maude admitted. "A random tourist might have posted the video. But I thought he had, like, a hundred followers tops."

"What rock have you been living under?" Morgane said, taking her phone from under Mrs. Bonnin's cap. "*Chad the Expat* is a huge influencer with over five million followers, including me."

"But if she's got thirty million views then that can only mean one thing," Morgane's mother observed.

Mother and daughter cried at the same time, "The video's gone viral!"

"Mom, we have to go tell everyone we know!" Morgane threw an arm around Maude, snapped a quick selfie before Maude could protest, and flew out of the bakery, followed by her twin-mother.

"I've got to go. Mrs. Ruchet's waiting for me," Maude said hastily.

"Wait!" Mrs. Bonnin raised an authoritative finger.

"I'm sorry I didn't tell you, Mrs. Bonnin. Honestly, I didn't know anybody would hear about this."

Mrs. Bonnin did not listen. She disappeared behind the counter and emerged with a bag full of goodies.

"Take this."

"Mrs. Bonnin, honestly, you can't always give me a bag of food every time I come here."

"There's a Maroilles cheese pie in it. Eat it when no one else is around. And don't let Mrs. Ruchet find it."

Maude knew it was futile to argue. She gratefully took the bag of food and left. But instead of heading back home she made a run for the library.

She stumbled through its glass doors and paused for an instant, trying to keep her mind from racing.

It was here, in this very library, that she'd learned to sing opera and play the piano on her own, behind the locked door of that little auditorium on the right. She'd pored over scores since she was eleven, learning all there was to know about classical piano and opera.

Every lunch break the kindly librarian had let her in when no one else was there so she could practice secretly. Her foster family didn't even know she sang.

But now the whole world knew?

A dreadful thought niggled at her mind. What if they hated her?

It was almost enough to make Maude turn around and flee. But she wasn't a coward. She marched to the closest computer and logged in to her PixeLight account.

She was about to type *Chad the Expat* in the search bar, but a blinking icon on the upper right-hand side of the screen caught her attention.

She clicked on it.

Immediately, a list of names rolled down like the end credits of a film.

Sten-T29 followed you

Lisa402 followed you

OrengeFeather218 followed you

And the list went on and on.

She headed to her profile to check the total number of followers.

"Twenty million followers," she gasped.

She closed the page, but she knew it wouldn't change anything.

She was an internet celebrity!

Chapter Three

Dazed, Maude made her way back home. Luckily, her foster family's house wasn't far. Encumbered by her bag of food, she proceeded past the vinegar factory on her street and its cylindrical containers. For once, she paid little attention to the pungent smell stinging her nostrils as she arrived in front of the Ruchets' two-story house. The medium-sized brick house was sandwiched in a row of red, coron-style houses, reminiscent of Carvin's coal-mining past.

As soon as she entered Maude heard a moan, followed by a whiny, "Why, why, why does my life have to be so hard?" Then, "Maude, come here immediately!"

Maude dropped her bag in the kitchen and joined Mrs. Ruchet in the living room. The eight-year-old twins, Leo and Louis, played loudly with Legos close to the fireplace.

Marie-Antoinette Ruchet was an imposing woman with short, curly blond hair tangled wildly around her face. She spent most of her days sitting on the couch, her legs propped on a dark-green cushion in front of her, watching soap operas on television, all the while hating the actresses for being so thin. Her dark eyes accompanied a constant pout, which occasionally turned into a smirk when Maude didn't plump her cushion like she was supposed to. Her foster mother had been especially difficult these last two days as she had started her umpteenth new diet. Maude couldn't help but smile, remembering watching Mrs. Ruchet munch on nothing but red vegetables and fruits for the last few days. She swallowed nothing but tomatoes, radishes, capsicum, strawberries, and cherries, and forced herself to drink tomato juice.

"What's this story I heard from Jocelyne? You singing and dancing in a Parisian cabaret?" she asked Maude with undisguised animosity.

"I don't even know how to dance! And it was just a plain, simple café," Maude protested.

"Are you talking back? I told Robert we shouldn't let you go on that school trip," Mrs. Ruchet continued over Maude's protests. "But that gossiping baker insisted, and bribed me with free quiches. You came back with fourteen hours of detention but it felt like I was being punished. I had to watch the twins after school all on my own for two weeks."

"Mrs. Bonnin helped you," Maude pointed out.

"Don't interrupt me when I talk!" Mrs. Ruchet barked. "First the detention, now this. Singing and dancing in the Moulin Rouge. Why can't I ever get any rest? I'll rest when I'm in my grave." Mrs. Ruchet moaned, stretching her legs over her dented cushion.

"The Moulin Rouge is miles away from where I was," Maude mumbled.

"I told you to be quiet! I just want to know why you're always repaying our kindness with misbehavior. Why do you give me so much trouble?"

Maude remained silent, but ramrod straight.

"Answer me when I ask you a question!"

"You *just* told me to be quiet," Maude answered, dispassionately.

"Don't get cheeky with me! I can't even look at you right now. Just go to your room!" Mrs. Ruchet ordered. Then, remembering her earlier orders, she barked, "Come back in thirty minutes to tidy up the house before Caroline and Virginie arrive."

Maude sighed, left the living room, and trudged up the stairs to her room in the attic.

Once inside, she took a deep breath then exhaled slowly. This room, brightened by multiple lamps, was the only place in which she found solace, surrounded by posters of her favorite opera divas, her bookshelves full of English books and scores, and a bunch of kitsch cushions.

In any other room she was regarded as a housekeeper, and spent much of her free time cleaning, cooking for the family, and looking after the couple's unruly twins. Deep down, she felt it would be a nice change to have people to talk to apart from the Ruchet twins, who viewed her as nothing more than an annoying nanny. She had craved friendship and a family for as long as she could remember. She had even foolishly thought that kindness, meekness, and obedience would win Mrs. Ruchet over. Boy, had she been wrong!

Maude knew that Mrs. Ruchet would use the video as an excuse to make her do more chores, even though it was a harmless video, creating a buzz that would die down in a day or two. At least, Maude hoped it would.

But it didn't.

Over the following days the whole town talked about only one thing: Maude's overnight success. Then, sitting at the computer in the library, she checked her PixeLight account one day.

Messages from fans flooded her inbox! Delighted, Maude read them one by one until she realized some of the messages were from record companies. They not only wanted to speak with her but promised to make her a star!

She squealed—though not too loudly, because she was in the library.

Maude spent hours researching the first label, Star Records, based in Paris. Pouring over every page of the website, she could picture herself singing opera in its sleek Haussmannian buildings in the 9th arrondissement. Among their artists, Maude noticed they had signed another opera singer for a full classical album.

"I'm going to be an opera star!" Maude exclaimed in a loud whisper.

She immediately answered the message and made a video chat appointment for the next day with a Mrs. Frébert.

Finally! She could go back to Paris much sooner than she had ever anticipated.

The next day, Maude sat in front of the screen in the library's meeting room. She had tried to look her best. Gone was her yellow faded shirt. Without asking, she'd borrowed one of Mrs. Ruchet's blouses. Luckily, Mrs. Frébert would not see her worn leggings.

The video icon popped open, and Maude answered with a wide smile.

"Hello, hi, Maude," Mrs. Frébert said in French.

"Hi, it's lovely to meet you." Maude's voice had an excited tremor, and she was relieved the woman could not see her sweaty palms. Her correspondent was the image of composure, dressed casually in a light-pink T-shirt and barely any makeup, but with undisputable class.

"The pleasure is all mine really," Mrs. Frébert continued. "Everybody's been talking about you. You're quite the sensation."

The words all sounded flattering, but the woman's smile didn't quite reach her eyes.

"Thank you," was all Maude said.

"Why don't you tell me a little more about yourself?"

"There's not much to say, really. I grew up here in Carvin, and I discovered classical music at eleven. I've been playing the piano since then." Maude continued with her story about Paris, her encounter with Chad, how she sang the cover. As she ended, she said, "I'm so glad you contacted me because I dream of becoming an opera singer."

"Wait, opera?" Mrs. Frébert's manicured hands crossed under her chin. "But you sang a pop song."

"In an operatic manner," Maude said.

"But we would make you a pop star. Nobody wants to listen to you sing opera."

"The video went viral," Maude pointed out.

"And that's all very nice but you can't make a lasting career out of it. You need to capitalize on this to launch your pop career. Forget opera."

The words were like bullets hitting Maude's heart.

"Forget opera?" Maude repeated. "I'm sorry, Mrs. Frébert, but I'm not interested. Opera's always been my dream."

"Then we're not interested either. I hope you find what you're looking for," Mrs. Frébert said with an annoyed sigh.

Mrs. Frébert hung up. And Maude was left with nothing but acute disappointment. For a moment she'd thought she'd be able to leave Carvin, that she'd go to Paris and finally live her dream.

• • •

The messages didn't stop in the days that followed. Many came from spammers, but others came from big international record labels in London, New York, and Los Angeles, promising to launch her career as a pop singer or in a girl band. Maude was flattered, shocked, excited, and confused. But it was all pointless. After all, she would never be allowed to leave the Ruchets' house to go abroad. And besides, her sights were set on opera. Not pop!

She checked their websites, and despite her curiosity, deleted all the messages, including an email from Glitter Records, several from DisCover Records, and another from a man named Terence Baldwin from Soulville Records. Maude was satisfied she had put an end to it all until it all caught up with her . . .

One cold November afternoon, the twenty-eighth, to be exact, Maude was at the optician's on the plaza running an errand for Mrs. Ruchet when she looked out the window and saw a tall black man in a smart brown topcoat walking through the Grand Place, with a young woman she guessed was his daughter, so similar were their mannerisms.

They both stopped, unsure of where they were headed. The girl pointed left, while he pointed right. Spotting the open bakery, he headed toward it.

Maude took in every detail of the two strangers. The man had a kind face, framed by gray hair curling against his temples. The crease on his left cheek showed that he smiled easily at life, and the absence of wrinkles on his forehead suggested that he never let worries bother him too long. His daughter had flawless ebony skin and long, beautiful box braids. Her dark-brown eyes were kind, and her pace gentle. Her coat was simple but chic, and her low-heeled boots made her elegance look effortless.

The man strongly resembled the photo of Mr. Baldwin from Soulville Records that Maude had seen. But it couldn't be him. He lived in New York.

Zipping up her coat and pulling her hood over her head, Maude left the shop and followed the two strangers from afar until she saw them enter Mrs. Bonnin's bakery. She hurried around the back and entered through the bakery's back entrance. Hunched in the oven room, she peered discreetly into the shop and saw Mrs. Bonnin greet the strangers.

"*Bonjour*," the man greeted the baker in hesitant French. "My name's Terence Baldwin. This is my daughter, Cynthia. We're looking for this address"—he held up a card with a typed address—"and Maude Laurent."

Maude jumped back and pressed her back against the wall. What was Mr. Baldwin doing in France? Overcome with curiosity, she peeled herself off the wall and peered back into the shop.

Mrs. Bonnin, who Maude was sure had barely understood his "Bonjour," wondered aloud in French, "Who is this man? Why did he mention Maude?"

Maude knew Mrs. Bonnin couldn't speak a word of English and certainly couldn't give this stranger directions if her life depended on it.

The baker held up both her hands, signaling him to wait. She put on her warm coat, mittens, and tucked her hair in her hood. She grabbed her keys to lock the main entrance behind her. *Not that her bakery would ever be robbed*, Maude thought, *because nothing ever happens in Carvin*. The local police were rarely busy.

They were headed for her house; Maude was sure of it.

She raced out of the bakery, jumped on a stray bicycle, and cycled back home as quickly as she could. Drops of sweat pearled on her forehead as she rushed inside.

"Maude, where were you?" Mrs. Ruchet whined from the living room. "Weren't you supposed to make a cake for tea this afternoon?"

"Doing it now!" Maude cried.

She hurried to the kitchen, blindly throwing flour, eggs, sugar, butter, and milk in a bowl. Mixing the batter, Maude rushed back and waited near the main entry. Dreading that the Ruchets would open the door, she checked through the peephole frantically so she would see the party arrive.

Mrs. Bonnin was walking so fast that the Baldwins had trouble keeping up with her. Maude could see the baker's lips twitch as she muttered excitedly to herself, all the while glancing at the pair from time to time. Terence turned to her.

"Thank you," he said politely. "Thank you so much. You're very kind." He turned to the doorbell, then took a quick look over his shoulder and startled. Maude could tell he'd expected the baker to leave at that point. She just smiled at him, waiting for him to ring it.

Maude groaned. Why couldn't Mrs. Bonnin mind her own business for once? If Maude spoke to the Baldwins in front of her, the whole town, including the Ruchets, would know the details of the conversation before sunset.

"Dad, do you think this woman's going to stay here while we talk to Maude?" Maude heard Cynthia ask. The plastered smile on her face could not quite conceal her nervousness.

Maude saw her father shrug as he rang the doorbell.

Maude swung the door open so forcefully, that, of course, the inevitable happened.

The bowl crashed to the floor. The loud noise rang through the house, and glass and batter splattered all over the tiles that Maude had washed that same morning and onto Maude's feet and Terence Baldwin's polished black shoes. Cynthia giggled. She had been spared, as had Mrs. Bonnin.

Before Maude could utter a word, an irate voice called from the living room. "What's going on? Who's at the door?"

Mr. Ruchet, somewhat more prone to movement than his wife, appeared in the doorway. He was a lanky man with thinning hair and sallow skin. He frowned as he surveyed the extent of the disaster, rubbing his chin as he often did when thinking.

"What is this mess?" he said. "Clean this up, Maude. This is such a waste. Now what will we have with our tea?" Then turning and addressing his uninvited guests, he asked, "Who are these people? Mrs. Bonnin, what are you doing here?"

"Mr. Ruchet," whispered Mrs. Bonnin, bending toward the door. "These people speak English. No French. And they want to see *Maude*."

Mr. Ruchet looked at the strangers, looked back at Mrs. Bonnin, and told her in a firm tone, "Thank you for bringing them, Mrs. Bonnin. *I* will take things from here."

He stared at her coldly. Clearly he thought Mrs. Bonnin had overstayed her welcome.

She turned to Mr. Baldwin, smiled at him, and said loudly, "*Au revoir*, Monsieur. Good morning!" she said proudly.

Looking quite content with herself, Mrs. Bonnin waddled away.

Mr. Ruchet turned to the Baldwins and invited them inside. They strode into the living room where Mrs. Ruchet sipped a cup of tomato juice gloomily. The look on her face was pure gold. She hated to be disturbed! Maude rushed to the kitchen, reemerged with a mop, and surveyed the situation with a sinking heart. She'd be in trouble for sure. She began to clean up the batter she'd dropped but stayed near the door so she could listen to the conversation.

Mr. Ruchet, as a former international human rights lawyer, spoke English very well, though with a strong French accent that, he often boasted, made American girls swoon every time he pronounced *the* as *ze*.

The host and the new arrivals sat down, and Mr. Ruchet said in English, "You have come to see Maude?"

"Yes," Mr. Baldwin said slowly. "My name is Terence Baldwin, and I'm a music producer from Soulville Records in New York. Here's my card."

"And what can you possibly want from *Maude*?" asked Mr. Ruchet, spitting out Maude's name. "Is this about that video everyone's been talking about?"

Maude wiped up the last of the batter, then tiptoed back to the living room, stealing a peek inside.

Mr. Baldwin pretended not to notice the other man's disdain and spoke calmly. "Maude's a very talented musician."

"Maude?" snorted Mrs. Ruchet, choking on her drink. She coughed loudly. Maude knew she didn't know as much English as her husband, but she understood a little.

"What my wife means," started Mr. Ruchet, "is zat you are probably, most certainly mistaken. Ze young girl has no talent at all. She is no musician and lacks talent in every artistic domain."

Terence looked at Mr. Ruchet fixedly and said, "Have you watched the video?"

"I'm a lawyer, a servant of the law. I have no time to scroll on Pixel Tights."

"PixeLight," Cynthia corrected, suppressing a smile.

"She's talented in ways I've rarely seen. My father-in-law and I never agree on anything, but even he could see that she could be a star. I'd like to sign Maude to Soulville. If Maude can move a grumpy old man—and believe me, he's grumpy, especially since his heart attack—and a twenty-year-old like my daughter here, that means one thing: her music is a bridge between generations."

Mrs. Ruchet almost dropped her tomato juice.

"Look," Terence Baldwin continued firmly, opening his briefcase. "I came all the way here for a reason. My company would like to sign Maude. I have a contract right here for three singles that we'd release over the course of six months. And if they're hits, we'd record a full album. Of course, as her guardians, you'd get a percentage of all her earnings and—"

"How much would we get?" Mr. Ruchet interrupted quickly.

"As her guardians, you're entitled to ten percent of this advance and royalties." Terence pointed to a section of the contract.

The Ruchets leaned in and yelped with giddiness at the number. Mrs. Ruchet's large, wolfish smile revealed teeth coated with thick tomato juice.

"Mr. Batwing," Mr. Ruchet coaxed. "Sit down comfortably while Maude prepares a cup of coffee for ze two of you. Maude!" Mr. Ruchet yelled.

"It's Baldwin," Cynthia corrected.

"I don't need coffee," replied Mr. Baldwin. "But I'd like to speak with Maude and perhaps discuss—"

"I'm sorry, there's nothing to discuss," Maude said, appearing at the entrance of the living room and speaking in English. She refused to remain silent a minute longer. "I don't want to become a pop star. I want to be an opera singer."

"Precisely. That's your strength," Mr. Baldwin said. "We would have you create music that's a mix of classical and pop music."

Maude contemplated his offer. This was a far cry from Mrs. Frébert's advice to abandon classical music altogether.

"I've composed a few arias, but I've never written a pop song in my life," Maude said, thinking this additional piece of information might deter Mr. Baldwin.

"You've worked on opera songs?" Terence scratched his chin thoughtfully, then a flicker of elation illuminated his eyes.

"We could pair you with a really talented pop singer! I have someone in mind, but we'll see."

"Maude," Cynthia added enthusiastically, "there's more. You'd train with the incomparable Cordelia Tragent."

"You know Cordelia Tragent? The famous soprano?" Maude squeaked, experiencing a tiny thrill at the mention of the famous opera singer.

"She's retired now, as you probably know," Mr. Baldwin said. "But she's a vocal coach with a precise teaching method. She uses the training of opera singers to strengthen the voices of students wanting to become pop artists. And she helps opera singers sing pop. Her technique has been a wild success."

Maude's heart raced. Meeting her idol, working with her? This was a dream come true. Almost.

She'd still have to sing pop. At least partly.

"Would I have to go to New York?" Maude asked.

"Yes, for six months," Mr. Baldwin said gently. "Mr. or Mrs. Ruchet can accompany you if they wish. A lot of ze, er, I mean *the* young musicians we sign have one of their parents stay with them. It's greatly encouraged as it provides structure and guidance."

"Ze *whole* family can't move to New York, Mr. Batling," said Mr. Ruchet with a smirk. "Maude will go alone."

"I haven't decided if I'm going yet," Maude responded.

"If Maude were to come unaccompanied," Cynthia chirped, "we'd take care of her. She would stay with our family. I have a sister. She's the same age as Maude. She's sixteen, right? That's what her PixeLight profile says. They'd be in the same class! And I have a silly little brother who'd be happy to have her too."

"We've welcomed young musicians in our home many times while they were producing their albums," Mr. Baldwin added. "My wife and I would care for Maude as if she were our own. I can guarantee that."

"Maude," Cynthia said gently, placing her hands on her knees. "I know this is a lot to take in. But as your publicist, I'd personally manage your image. I'd go beyond that and make sure that your career is everything that you want it to be. We'd have so much fun together, I promise." Cynthia's eyes shone with so much sincerity and warmth that Maude immediately responded with a smile.

"I'll have to think about it."

"What she means, is that she'll say yes," Mr. Ruchet said.

"I'll think about it," Maude insisted.

"We want you to say yes because *you* want to," Cynthia assured her. "We're staying in town for the rest of the week. Come back to us with any questions you may have."

Cynthia and Terence rose, and after polite handshakes, they left.

That night, Maude couldn't sleep. She tossed and turned, mulling over her options. How had one little cover song prompted such huge repercussions? In a little over a week she'd spoken to two big label representatives, and one had traveled overseas to meet her. Still, she'd never imagined going outside of France so soon, or ever for that matter. She'd just fallen in love with Paris and what did she know about New York? She'd be in a whole new country, a different culture. What if she couldn't speak English properly? What if her three singles failed? She'd come back to Carvin and everyone would mock her. But then, there was Cordelia Tragent. Soulville didn't want to erase classical music from her career like Star Records had intimated. It was a huge opportunity.

Maude got out of bed, slipped on her slippers, and tiptoed quietly down the stairs. As she approached the kitchen she saw the light was on and heard voices. Her foster parents were up.

". . . this is what we could afford with the money from the advance," Mrs. Ruchet was saying.

"But there's something else to consider, *ma chérie*," Mr. Ruchet whispered.

Maude leaned closer to the kitchen door to hear Mr. Ruchet's deep voice.

"Her father lived there for a while. There's a huge Nigerian community in New York, what if she finds out—"

"How could she? She doesn't know anything about Aaron," Mrs. Ruchet interrupted. "She doesn't even know she's part Nigerian. She won't find out a single thing. Now, how can we hide the money we're going to get from her album from the taxman?"

Maude brought her hand to her mouth, hoping they didn't hear her gasp.

Aaron. Aaron Laurent. Her father. He'd lived in New York!

She'd never gotten this close to finding out anything about

her family. She needed to know more; she needed to find out who her parents were and how they'd died. Finding more information about a Nigerian man with a French name couldn't be that difficult.

Maude's mind was made up. She was going to New York.

Chapter Four

"Ladies and gentlemen, we have arrived safely at JFK International Airport. We hope you enjoyed your flight. The whole crew wishes you a pleasant stay in New York City."

Maude snapped her book on Nigerian cultures shut and looked out the window of the Boeing excitedly. She'd finally arrived in her father's city.

One worry kept nagging at her. After having typed her father's name, *Aaron Laurent* into Google, she'd found nothing about him whatsoever. True, *Laurent* didn't sound like a Nigerian or a British name. She'd decided that her father must have been half French, which was why she had been born there. He'd probably lived in New York for some time in his youth. She'd find information about him, even if she had to knock on every door in the city.

Maude had been excited to fly for the first time, though she hadn't expected sleeping on a plane to be so uncomfortable. Nothing was as daunting as the takeoff, and seeing the airport from way up high in the endless sky.

However, the quality of a flight depends partly on the behavior of a passenger's neighbor, and Maude had come close to snapping at the man sitting next to her. With every jolt the plane gave the middle-aged man would jump and shriek in a high-pitched voice, the entire eight hours from Paris to New York. Thankfully, she'd watched movies, read, and discovered that she loved airplane food. She'd also gone through her English phonetic and grammar lessons again, including the dreaded list of irregular verbs her British tutor had given her. From the moment she'd learned she was going to New York Maude had taken intensive English courses to improve her oral and writing skills. For days she'd listened only to Purcell's operas, temporarily abandoning her beloved Italian arias. It had all been worth it, she thought happily as she took her carry-on luggage from the overhead bin, if she could discover who her parents had been.

After getting off the plane and navigating immigration, Maude wondered what she would say to Mrs. Baldwin. Mr. Baldwin had warned her he wouldn't be at the airport, and that his wife was going to meet Maude. She had rehearsed a couple of greeting phrases her tutor had taught her but felt none would do the trick.

"Pleased to meet you, Mrs. Baldwin," she muttered under her breath. Talking to herself, she continued, "No, no, that won't do. It sounds too polite. Not that I want to appear impolite." She shook her head. She was getting flustered! "Maybe something like 'How do you do?' I don't know. It sounds kind of stuck-up, Queen of England–like. I'm in New York, not Buckingham Palace."

Maude stopped in her tracks and fell silent.

They hadn't seen her yet, but she knew who they were.

A few feet from her, a small boy of about ten or eleven with abundant dark coils and an eager grin waved a sign with her name crookedly sprawled over it: MAUD. Behind the boy stood a tall woman with a kind face, a heartwarming smile, and glowing dark skin, wearing her hair in an Afro tied in an elegant red scarf. Victoria Baldwin. Maude noticed her beauty and wondered if her class was something she'd been born with or had acquired with time and discipline. Her eyes then flitted to the person standing next to the woman.

She immediately recognized Cynthia. The eldest Baldwin smiled as she gently tried to calm her excited little brother down. Her long braids were wrapped in a lazy bun, making her beauty look effortless.

The girl next to Cynthia, her sister presumably, was enthusiastically craning her neck, searching the crowd. She wore her hair in gorgeous Bantu knots, which gave her an artsy, chic look. She had the assured stance of a girl who felt good about herself without having to crush others. Although she was very stylishly dressed in a beautiful brown coat and high-heeled boots, Maude was sure she would look just as breathtaking in simple worn-out jeans and a T-shirt.

Mr. Baldwin's entire family had come, Maude suddenly realized, a wave of shyness coming over her.

They, on the other hand weren't shy at all.

Mrs. Baldwin strode toward her and before Maude knew it, the whole family surrounded her, all talking at once, asking how her flight had been, what food she'd eaten, which movies she'd seen, not even giving her time to answer.

"Maude! Hi! I'm Ben. You *are* Maude, aren't you?" asked the boy waving the sign under her nose to make sure she didn't miss it.

"Er, yes, that's me. I think," she answered, looking at the sign. "You forgot, um," Maude focused. She always confused her *e*'s and *i*'s in English. "It's Maude with an *e*." *Great*, she thought, *that's a nice way to greet your hosts. I should've stuck with* How do you do?

"How do you do?" she blurted.

The whole family paused, then burst out laughing.

"Oh, Cynth, you were right!" the tall stylish girl exclaimed, laughing genuinely. "Her accent is so sweet. All the boys at school are going to go wild over you, Maude."

"You mean to tell me that all the boys aren't mad about *you*, Jazmine?" her sister asked in a mocking tone.

"Please, Cynthia," her mother implored. "Don't encourage your sister's vanity or else Maude won't be able to stand her for six whole months."

"Neither will we," the boy whispered loudly to Maude.

The family burst out laughing again, including Jazmine, who slapped her brother's head playfully. "Seriously, though, we should probably get Maude's luggage, boxes, and things," Mrs. Baldwin said.

"I already have my luggage. It's just this suitcase and it isn't heavy," Maude said, pointing to her carry-on.

"*What?*" cried Jazmine in disbelief. "You mean to tell me that you left France, the home of fashion, for six entire months with only one suitcase?"

"Come on, Jaz. Not everyone takes five *entire* suitcases for a two-week trip to the Hamptons, you know," Cynthia teased, rolling her eyes.

"Neither do I," said Jazmine, smiling sheepishly. "Those were four suitcases, big sis. And let me remind you that two of those were yours."

"Yes, but they were filled with the objects necessary to the harmony and peace of my being," replied Cynthia.

"Yeah, yeah. Yin and yang, yoga and everything. We know the drill. My twenty different outfits were also essential to the harmony of *my* being, you know."

"What can I say? I travel light," Maude explained, shrugging. Besides, she couldn't possibly tell them that her suitcase was mostly filled with piano scores. She didn't own much, and she certainly didn't own five suitcases worth of cool clothes.

"Ah, finally, a girl who gets me," Ben said, sighing in relief.

"Don't feel too relieved, Ben," his mom warned. "We'll be taking her shopping this weekend."

"But first," she added, "welcome hug."

As if on cue, the whole family wrapped their arms around Maude and squeezed her so tight she couldn't breathe.

Maude wasn't used to having so many people pay attention to her; it made her feel a little uneasy. She had craved friendship all these years, but was she so unused to friendly interaction that she felt uncomfortable in a group hug? What would they think if they knew that the main reason she was here was to find out who her father was? Well, okay, maybe she also really wanted to meet Cordelia Tragent as well.

While in the cab headed to Manhattan the Baldwins talked a mile a minute, wanting to know everything about her. Terence and Cynthia hadn't said much about Maude, and all the family really knew was from the video they'd seen of her.

"Isn't it amazing?" Jazmine sighed. "Being discovered just by singing in Paris. Paris! I love that city with all my heart, but I couldn't live there. I love New York too much. You'll see, Maude, you'll have so much fun here you won't ever want to live anywhere else in the world."

Maude didn't tell her that Paris had her whole heart and soul, and let the family continue to chatter. She couldn't speak half as fast as they could anyway.

"Do you know Edith Piaf?" Cynthia asked, her eyes sparkling. "She's one of my favorite singers."

"You know French music?" Maude asked, surprised.

"Of course! Mom and Dad have always encouraged us to listen to music from all over the world."

"My foster parents, the Ruchets, always said that Americans never cared about anyone but themselves, especially musicwise," Maude said. To herself she mumbled, "That's one more thing they lied about."

"Dad said you knew all the classical composers?" asked Jazmine, squeezing her arm excitedly. Maude nodded.

"You'll have to duet with Cynthia. She's a great violinist." Jazmine leaned closer to Maude and whispered, "She's started her third year at Juilliard and works with Dad. And she's only twenty. She's an overachiever."

"I heard you, Jaz," Cynthia said.

"Oh come on, Cynth. I don't see why you don't like us mentioning Juilliard. It's something to be proud of."

"I'm not ashamed. It's just, well, what if I always introduced *you* by saying that you're in a rock band?"

"I wouldn't mind," Jazmine said. "The more people hear about the Screaming Angels, the better."

"You're so proud when you mention everything I do musically but I have other—"

"I'm so *sorry* for being proud of my big sister. You know what, Maude, forget what I just said. Cynthia is a terrible violinist. When she plays she makes all the dogs in the neighborhood bark, and—"

"And cats cry," chirped Benjamin.

The family laughed.

"Oh forget it, you two," Cynthia said, annoyed. "Thank god we're almost home."

As Manhattan whizzed past her eyes, its beauty, vastly different from that of Paris, amazed Maude.

Where Paris's buildings were human height, New York was a city built for titans.

The skyscrapers tickled the skies and towered over her like tropical trees in a jungle. The city was filled with an excited, electric buzz, with people crisscrossing in every direction, like they were moving through a gigantic ant farm. Looking through the window of the speeding car, wrapped in awed silence, Maude felt deliciously small.

She couldn't believe how wide the streets were. The cars were huge! It was a wonder that bike delivery workers found the courage to cycle next to them, especially in this cold January weather. Even the fire escape stairways on the buildings were an invitation to ascend to higher ground. The crescent-shaped Tribeca Bridge whizzed past her eyes along with 7-Elevens, hair and nail salons, spas, and shiny grocery shops.

New York City was full of noise, life, shops, colors, shadows, and lights. Maude could feel the energy flowing through her veins. She already felt connected to the city's vibrancy somehow, and her heart began to beat with the city's deep rumble.

This was the city where her father had lived! And she was going to walk in his footsteps. At that moment, Maude wanted to be a part of what she saw, not just watch it. She wanted to step into the scenery and play a role in the city so many singers had sung about. This was the second time in four months that she'd been in a city, and she couldn't help but sigh at all that she had missed during her life in Carvin. Carvin's entire Grand Place could fit in the intersection between Chambers Street and Greenwich Street.

Jazmine heard Maude sigh and asked if something was wrong.

"Nothing's wrong. This city's amazing. I wonder if I'll ever get used to it."

"Of course you will," she reassured Maude. "You'll probably get lost a couple of times in the subway but you'll get the hang of it. And we'll go to school together, and I'll introduce you as the little sister I've asked my parents for every Christmas since I was three. Instead I got a brother, but, hey, when he's dressed up, you can't tell the difference."

"Little sister? She's sixteen, just like *you*, Jaz," Ben said, shaking his head.

"Yes, but she was born September seventh, while I was born in August. So that makes her de facto my little sister," replied Jazmine. "I saw that on your PixeLight account. Could you follow me back?" Maude smiled, amused at the idea of being a complete stranger's sister.

"Don't smile, Maude," warned Ben. "You have no idea what you're getting into. Seniority is very important in this family. Believe me, I know. Nobody ever listens to what I say."

"Yeah, and you'll get to unload your new big sister's luggage too. It's a good thing it isn't heavy," Cynthia added.

Before Maude could protest, Ben retorted, "I don't mind doing it for my new sister since I'm sure she'll be the nicest of the three."

Amid this cheerful chatter about seniority and little brothers' civil rights, the taxi arrived in front of the brownstone where Terence Baldwin waited on the doorstep.

Maude followed the family inside and into a spacious living room designed in a quiet, unobtrusive Japanese style that was sophisticated as well as cozy.

"Welcome home," Terence Baldwin said warmly. "Let's get you settled. Remember, you start school in three days."

Maude nodded, a bit weary from the journey. Then she remembered. "I've got a gift for you all!" She rummaged in her luggage and pulled out a red tin box filled with sweets.

"They're traditional sweets from the northern part of France," she said proudly. "They're called *bêtises de Cambrai*. Bêtise means, *mmm*, it's kind of like a blunder because the recipe was the result of a mistake."

"Just like Coca-Cola!" Jazmine exclaimed.

"The best things in life often come from mistakes," Terence said. He took the box before Ben could, scratched off the tape around the lid, opened it, and popped a candy into his mouth. "Tastes like a peppermint. Thank you for bringing happy mistakes into our lives," he said, bowing ceremoniously, while Ben grabbed a fistful of candies and stuffed them in his mouth.

Maude giggled, thinking back to the batter she'd spilled all over Terence's shoes. So much had changed since then!

"About room arrangements, we have two proposals," Victoria explained, also taking a bêtise. "You can either share Cynthia and Jazmine's room, which is big enough for you three—"

"Isn't it pathetic that my two grown sisters can't live in separate rooms?" asked Ben mockingly.

"I tried," sighed Cynthia. "Jazmine just couldn't handle it. So we stayed together, although I put my foot down about bunk beds."

"I was *nine*, Cynth. I've totally outgrown the bunk beds now, thank you very much."

"—or you could have your own room," Victoria finished.

Maude, who wasn't used to sharing her room with anyone and felt uncomfortable intruding on the two sisters' comradeship, said she preferred being on her own. Jazmine's mouth scrunched up in disappointment.

"See, Jaz," her brother said. "You scared her, just like I knew you would."

Maude followed Victoria upstairs. When she entered her new room, her eyes widened in disbelief.

It wasn't just that the room was huge.

On the gigantic, bouncy-looking bed laid a little rectangular box; the kind of box Maude had dreamed about for the longest time. Maude sat on the bed and opened it.

A shiny, brand-new cell phone!

"Your French number won't work here, so we thought you'd need an American number, and the phone came with it. That way we can contact you easily while you're in New York," Victoria said simply.

"Yeah, I won't use my French phone here. I left it in Carvin," Maude said, trying very hard to sound like she was used to having phones wherever she traveled. She waited for Victoria to leave before kicking off her shoes and jumping on the bed.

"I have a phone!" she squealed. She sprang off the bed onto the soft, white-carpeted floor where she danced, barefoot, enjoying its warmth, until she bumped into something hard.

Right behind her, in the left corner of the room was a big object covered by a large white sheet. Maude pulled it away to reveal an upright white Yamaha piano with a lovely dark stool.

Her very own piano!

Maude touched its keys softly, afraid it might vanish in front of her eyes. She caressed the white, polished instrument while softly humming the tune to "La Vie en Rose." Her thoughts drifted to the next few days. In two days she would be attending a meeting at Soulville Records to meet Mr. Baldwin's associates, Mr. Brighton and Mr. Lewis, and the main crew she was going to work with. Then she would be heading to her first day at her new school. And after that was to be her first singing class with Madame Tragent.

Life was beautiful.

Chapter Five

Saturday afternoon, Maude discovered the joys and downsides of taking the subway during the weekend in Manhattan.

Confident that she had the skills, or at least the will, to discover the subway on her own, she'd declined the Baldwins' assistance and had walked around in Tribeca all morning before her meeting with Soulville in the afternoon. After all, she had managed to take the subway in Paris all on her own. Once.

The New York subway would be a piece of cake.

She took the express 2 line at Chambers Street certain she'd be at Times Square in ten minutes and four stops, just like the MTA app on her brand-new phone said, though she'd left an hour early. Maude was fascinated by the subway. Everything was close by in Carvin, so she either walked or rode her bike to get around.

Even the novelty of being squeezed between two angry-looking women in a packed train had its charm, Maude thought giddily. Though she felt she really shouldn't have bought coffee that afternoon, and held it tight, not wanting to spill it on the brand-new clothes that she was so very proud of.

New clothes.

She and the Baldwin girls had gone shopping at Century 21 the day before.

Maude recalled the huge department store and her wonder at its floor to ceiling clothes, shoes, and accessories. And the number of French people who were there, too, just like her!

Not only had she felt elated, but she also felt like a whole different person in the new clothes Victoria had insisted on buying for her. She accepted only when Victoria agreed that Maude would pay her back once she'd received her advance. With the Ruchets, she had never had clothes of her own, and wore whatever Mrs. Ruchet bought for her from the thrift store. She now had a lovely new winter cropped-sleeved white coat, black gloves, and scarf, and amazing leather boots that Jazmine and Cynthia had insisted she get. She felt like a princess, and was certain she'd keep that coat until the day she died. Even if she outgrew it, she'd carry it with her to her grave! Her first new coat and such a fine one too. What a relief she wouldn't face all those fancy people in Times Square with just her worn-out parka.

As the doors to the station shut, the speaker crackled. A male voice droned to the whole train, *"Due to congestion, this train will be running local, stopping at every station on the two line."* A few people in the train groaned, while Maude wondered what *local* could mean.

She quickly discovered what it meant as the train moved at a snail's pace from one station to another, including several that hadn't appeared on her app.

Maude joined her fellow passengers in a belated groan, which lasted as long as her train took to crawl from Franklin Street to Canal Street and then to the next stations. It was taking forever. Maude was sure that she wouldn't make it to her meeting on time.

Forty-five minutes later, when the train finally got to Times Square, Maude hurried out. She jostled along the station's long tunnels full of people, still holding the coffee cup, which had lost its lid and grown cold. She still had ten minutes to get to Soulville Tower on time.

Suddenly, a young man appeared out of nowhere, trying to run past Maude. As he passed her, his shoulder bumped into her roughly. Her cup of coffee splattered all over her brand-new white coat. "No, no, no," she moaned. Her cherished possession! Her first elegant piece of clothing!

The young man stopped in his tracks and looked at her, irritated. He headed back in her direction reluctantly, hands in his beige trench coat, his face partially hidden by his upturned collar. He was tall, with wavy dark-blond hair sweeping his broad shoulders. He wore a cap low over his face, though not low enough to shield his obvious annoyance.

Maude was both furious and panicked at the same time. She couldn't go to her meeting in this state! What first impression was she going to make? And the jerk who had just bumped into her hadn't bothered to apologize. The fact that he was annoyed made her angrier.

Maude was at a loss for words in English and went straight to the language in which she could easily express her anger.

"Oh, mais c'est pas possible! Tu te rends compte de ce que tu viens de faire! Comment est-ce que je vais aller à ma réunion maintenant? On venait de m'acheter ce manteau! Quoi ? En plus, tu te marres!" she shrieked. Did he have any idea what he had just done? How was she supposed to go to the meeting now. She had just bought this coat and this guy was *laughing*?

In fact, the stranger was laughing uncontrollably, obviously amused at the girl with her stained coat, yelling at him in a foreign language. It just made her angrier.

Maude couldn't believe it. *New Yorkers are quite something,* she thought.

She had just spent forty-five minutes in the midst of the slowest subway ride, and now she had to deal with this? She looked at him angrily, and before she knew it, threw the rest of her coffee in his face.

His face froze midlaugh.

Maude smiled, pleased to see his astounded expression, lifted her head haughtily, and stomped off before he could say another word.

She rushed out of the station, all the while thinking fast. So fast in fact that she had no time to admire the famous square's blinking lights, let alone its lively commercials, crazy energy, tourists, or costumed characters galore.

Nose over her phone, she followed the map to Soulville Tower on Broadway, rushing past the Disney Store and a costumed Minnie Mouse who wanted to take pictures with her.

She couldn't possibly walk into that room with a coat that looked like she'd just rolled in mud. As she got closer to the building, she took it off. The cold air bit into her, and she shivered. Although some coffee had spilled on her beige blouse, she could still cover it up with her scarf.

She breathed in deeply, entered the gigantic building, and got into the elevator, her heart pounding in her chest. She would be right on time if the elevator didn't break down. Luckily, nothing happened, as she would've lost it if it had, and she arrived on the twentieth floor. As she asked the receptionist for directions to the conference room, she took in the wide lobby. Her eyes lingered on an ancient Steinway concert grand piano reigning majestically in the center of the room.

After thanking the receptionist for his help, she reluctantly tore her eyes away from the magnetic object and hurried into a conference room where several people were chatting around a large oval table. At the far end of the table Terence Baldwin was talking to a kind-looking brown-haired man and another small, bald man in an expensive-looking gray suit who wore a dissatisfied smirk on his face.

When Terence saw Maude, he smiled broadly at her, cleared his throat, and spoke.

"All right, everybody, gather around. Almost everyone is here, except Matt. He called to say he's running a little late and to go ahead and start without him. You've heard of Matt Durand, Maude haven't you?"

Maude's mind went blank. She had no idea who he was.

"You probably know his hit 'Love Doctor.'"

"Of course!" Maude hit her forehead. How could she have forgotten her classmates' obsession with that song two years ago?

Mr. Baldwin beamed and continued.

"For those of you who don't know her, this is Maude Laurent, the talented French singer we'll be working with to produce three singles in the next six months."

Maude thought she saw the bald man's smirk deepen as Terence introduced her, and she felt a little uneasy.

"She has a classical background that I think will really enrich her music once she learns about other, more modern, music styles." Then, facing Maude, Terence said, "That's why you'll be working with Matt, Maude. He's a singer, composer, and songwriter, and knows everything there is to know about music," Terence continued, his eyes shining. "He's a younger, seventeen-year-old version of me, musicwise at least. He's taking a break from his singing career and will help you compose, here, several days a week. He'll do the heavy lifting, but not without your input. Your role will be to infuse his compositions with your classical touch. With your knowledge of classical music and his pop background, you two will be great together. As soon as your first song is ready, we'll start recording with the musicians and sound engineers. We're all in this together, and I think this will be a great experience."

"I also have to say that we've got some pretty exciting things in store for Maude," Cynthia said. "As Maude's publicists, my team and I will work on expanding her social-media presence with some cool, relatable brand campaigns. Of course, you'll have to post more regularly."

Maude gulped. She'd never imagined her interactions with her PixeLight account would have to increase from the odd video she occasionally posted.

"In terms of endorsements," Cynthia continued, "we've got a few interesting prospects. Including an offer from the number one teen skin product, Cleanskin, and one from Relish Cookies that will definitely receive a lot of engagement."

The crowd in the room clapped but the small, bald man held up his hand, bringing the applause to a stop.

"That was all very nice, Terence and Cynthia," he said. "However, I think you forgot a few things in your presentation. First, you didn't introduce me. I'm Alan Lewis, Terence's associate, and an important shareholder in this company. I want you to understand that this is very serious business. We'd previously considered signing another young singer to this label before Terence met you. He convinced us to sign you instead. You aren't allowed to fail, Maude Laurent," Alan said, looking at her with narrowed eyes. Terence seemed annoyed at the interruption but remained silent.

Maude looked at the man and replied calmly, "I understand what you mean. And I hope you realize that I'm a hundred percent in."

"I *wish* you'd said you were a hundred and ten percent in," he said dryly.

And Maude *wished* she could wipe the smirk off his face. But she didn't say anything. How could she promise 100 percent when she wanted more than anything to use classical as her musical style, not pop? Could she convince them that classical was the way to go?

"Why don't you give us a little taste of what you've got?" the man said, crossing his arms.

Frowning, Maude looked at the dark Yamaha piano in the room. She didn't like his tone or the way he ordered her to play, as if she was a jukebox playing on demand. She wasn't intimidated by him one bit. She'd give him a "taste" as he put it. She lifted her head proudly and walked to the piano. She knew exactly what to play.

In Carvin, when the twins had been particularly difficult to handle, Maude would play Beethoven's *Tempest*, as it perfectly suited her stormy mood. When playing this piece, she imagined herself in utter despair, stranded alone on a ship in the middle of a stormy, raging ocean, with no one to help her, waves crashing around her, the sky in complete darkness.

Maude sat down and her hands slid across the piano keys; the low-pitched notes sounded like thunder rumbling under her fingers. She saw the waves smashing the boat to pieces—wood, masts, ropes raining all around her as the boat disintegrated to nothingness. The loud roar of the ocean covered her pleas, enjoying the devastation of the poor soul. The salty water mixed with her tears. The boat jerked from side to side. The wind howled a long, strident complaint that pierced her ears.

Maude poured her anger into the *Tempest*. Her afternoon had been awful, her coat ruined by a jerk who hadn't even had the decency to apologize. She thought about it all, her heart beating loudly as she saw the boy's laughing face, which reminded her of Luc, a boy in her class in Carvin who had always loudly made fun of her clothes, roaring with laughter at her worn-out shoes and torn-up jeans and faded shirts. In her mind Luc's face merged into the boy from the subway's and finally, Mr. Lewis's smirk. She no longer saw the room around her or the people who were in it. She barely felt the piano as her fingers flew over the keys.

However, slowly, in the middle of the fast-paced allegretto, hope prevailed, light shone through the threatening clouds as she played the light, high-pitched notes of the sonata.

But the peaceful moment in the *Tempest* was just a lure. It wasn't real. The storm came back with a vengeance. Even more menacing, joyfully rejoicing over the lone mortal's false hope and eating her alive, it swallowed her in a giant gulf, her frail mortal form disappearing from the face of the earth. That was how, at the end of the *Tempest*, the storm subsided, satisfied with the immensity of the destruction that had just taken place.

Maude finished, staying seated, and elegantly folded her hands in her lap before surveying her audience. Terence beamed with fatherly pride. Alan's smirk was gone; he clearly understood the message Maude was sending him.

Terence's longtime friend and associate, Travis Brighton, smiled at him and made a thumbs-up sign.

Alan cleared his throat.

"That's a good start, but you still have a lot of work to do," he declared, looking at Maude with narrowed eyes. He turned to the door and a newcomer who had silently crept in while Maude was playing.

Alan grinned broadly.

"Look who just got here! Matt! Where have you been, buddy? We've all been waiting for you."

Maude turned around and gasped as she recognized the boy from the subway, leaning against the door frame.

Matt's eyes danced with silent amusement at her astonishment. Maude looked haughtily away, angry with herself for letting him see her reaction.

"What happened to your jacket, man?" Mr. Lewis asked surveying the stained trench coat. "Oh, let me guess. You drove another one of your girlfriends up the wall, right," he joked, showing his large white teeth in a ridiculous grin and nudging Matt with his elbow as if they were best friends.

"Yeah," answered Matt smoothly, looking directly at Maude. "This one was in a real fury. I'm sure they could hear her yelling at me in *France*."

Except for a contemptuous snort, Maude remained silent.

"Ah, knowing you, I'm pretty sure she had a good reason," Terence said, raising his eyebrows.

Maude thanked him silently.

"Maude," he called. "Come meet Matt. He's the songwriter I've been telling you about. He's French just like you, but he's been living in New York for such a long time, I wonder if he hasn't lost all of his refined European manners. Assuming he ever had any."

Maude barely hid her surprise. Matt was French! Which meant he had understood every single word she had spewed at him in the subway!

Cold rage swept over her afresh as she got up, meeting Matt's amused gaze with a dark glare.

Matt appeared to falter under her stare.

He's probably more used to girls batting their eyelashes than using their eyes to throw daggers at him, Maude thought, annoyed.

While his senses were always alert musicwise, Terence didn't seem as aware of the subtleties of human behavior, so he continued to talk animatedly about the projects he had in mind for them both.

When he was done, he said, "Why don't we all go have coffee together?"

"I'm sorry, Mr. Baldwin, but I have to meet Victoria so that she can show me my new school and my new locker," Maude reminded him. "Can you believe I'll have a locker? I didn't have one in French high school."

"Oh right. School. Right, you do that. Yes, Vic and Jazmine really want to show you around before you start," he said. "Enjoy the tour!" He turned to follow the rest of the crowd to the elevator.

Maude stayed behind, and, thinking she was alone, looked fondly at the Yamaha piano. She hadn't played many pianos in her life, but each one she had touched was different. This one had light keys that felt like water under her hands.

"It's a beautiful instrument, isn't it?" Matt observed from the other end of the room.

Maude turned. She was surprised to see he was still there, and wondered uneasily how long he had been watching her.

"A piano is like a friend to me," she explained slowly, carefully choosing her words. "We're in sync. It never betrays me or makes fun of me. I cannot say the same about human beings."

She grabbed her coat and headed for the door. Matt shrugged. "You know, I've never even seen your video. I don't like seeing anything about the artists I work with. I'm not influenced that way. Also, I'm on a social media cleanse these days."

Maude rolled her eyes. "You mean if you'd known I was internet famous you wouldn't have acted like a jerk."

"What is internet famous really? Trends change every day. So no, I probably would've acted the same way." His smile grew. "I needed to keep a low profile. I'm on a hiatus from my career. Taking a break. For personal reasons." He paused, as if to see what effect his last words would have on Maude. When they didn't have any, he continued. "Didn't want anyone to recognize me."

"I'm not really interested, and you still haven't apologized," Maude pointed out, though a part of her brain remained on the personal troubles that had prompted his hiatus. An inquiry tumbled out of her mouth before she could stop herself. "What were you doing in the subway anyway? Since you're so famous and all shouldn't you be driving around in a limo?"

His eyes became as somber as the gray autumnal sky of Carvin, and Maude regretted asking the question. "I needed to see a musician," he said. "He's in that subway station a lot. A really talented guy, and he meant a lot to someone I cared about."

"Did you just go through a breakup?" Maude mocked him. "Is that why you're on a social media cleanse? And a hiatus. You were in the subway and ruined my coat because you're nursing a broken heart. Excuse me, but I've got to go."

Maude saw his face fall, but he quickly pulled himself together.

"Look," Matt said, blocking the exit route. "We were both stupid this morning. Times Square is crazy. A little like you. You're an *incredibly* talented musician. I hope you realize I don't say that often. We're going to spend a lot of time together working on your singles, roaming the city, discovering its musical beats for inspiration. Why don't we just put this behind us and be friends?"

He held out his hand, waiting for her to shake it. Maude looked into his eyes and was disturbed by how intensely gray they were. She stretched out her hand and, as he took hers in his, felt her heart race ever so slightly and an electric wave of attraction coursed through her body. In his eyes she read bafflement and a hint of fascination. She dropped her hand swiftly, ashamed of having appeared the slightest bit swayed by his charm.

He was just a famous, pampered, obnoxious celebrity used to getting his own way. And he still hadn't apologized! Saying that she was *crazy* wasn't even close to an apology! He was no better than her former classmate who took pleasure in making fun of her. Well, she wasn't in Carvin any longer, and she refused to perpetuate the tradition of being someone's personal laughingstock. She wouldn't forget how those same gray eyes had shone that morning when he'd laughed at her while she was angrily shouting at him in a language he understood perfectly, and had not even bothered to help her.

Maude lifted her head a little higher and with a frosty glare, said, "We'll work together since we must. But there is no way you and I can ever be friends."

With that, she proudly swept past him and headed to the elevator.

Chapter Six

Her first Monday at school in Manhattan left Maude wondering if she hadn't landed on another planet. She was in English class and Jazmine, who sat next to her, had spent the last half hour scribbling furiously, passing slips of paper to her friends.

Maude was just plain puzzled.

It wasn't the numerous American flags in the hallways and classes that confused her, nor was it the sheer number of students stealing glances at her and whispering "PixeLight" and "cover." Simply, she had not understood a single sentence the teacher had uttered after she had said, "Good morning, class. Take out your copies of *Jane Eyre*."

After that, it was all a blur. The teacher spoke so fast it was impossible to understand a word she said. Thankfully, Maude had already read Charlotte Brontë's *Jane Eyre* in English, and it was one of her favorite books. As for the teacher's analysis of the story, she would have to rely on Jazmine's notes.

She heaved a deep sigh of relief when the bell rang.

"So, what did you think of your first English class?" asked Jazmine as they headed out of the room. "Oh wait! Let me film you." She fished her phone out of her pocket. "Cynthia wants you to post a story today on PixeLight."

"You can't film me now," Maude moaned. "Unless Cynthia wants the whole world to know I didn't understand a word the teacher said."

"Ah, you'll get the hang of it in no time," Jazmine reassured her, putting her phone back in her pocket. "In the meantime, I'll give you my notes so you won't fall behind. Although I admit, I was a bit distracted today."

"Why? What's going on?"

Jazmine was searching the crowded beige painted hallway and didn't answer. Clusters of students rushed past them, retrieving books from lockers and either kidding around or whining about the workload.

"Ah, there they are," she said. "Let me introduce you to my friends."

A small group stood near Jazmine's bright-yellow locker: a brown-haired jock in a football jersey, a blond girl in a cheerleader outfit, and a redheaded girl leaning against the lockers, all talking animatedly.

This is like the movies, Maude thought. As they approached, she noticed the boy staring at Jazmine with plain admiration. Admittedly, she looked breathtaking even dressed simply in a long white wool sweater and a pair of black pants.

"Guys, this is Maude Laurent, the musician you've all seen on PixeLight. Maude, this is Brad, Lily, and Stacey."

Then before Maude could say a proper hello, Jazmine jumped on Brad, pushed him against the lockers, and proceeded to have a long, noisy, make-out session.

Maude grinned sheepishly at Stacey and Lily.

"So." Maude cleared her throat. "It's nice to meet you! You're in the band with Jazmine, yes? I heard you had a great concert last Friday. I wish I could've been there, but I was still so jet-lagged."

"Don't worry about it," Stacey said enthusiastically. "We'd love to see you at the next one. Whenever that happens."

"It's the last one for a while," Lily explained. "We're temporarily out of action while we look for a new guitarist to complete the Screaming Angels, also known as the best rock band ever, right, Stace?"

"We're a great band," Stacey agreed, flipping her dark-red hair behind her shoulder. "We'd be even better with my cousin Carter as our new guitarist," she added.

Talk about the band made Jazmine pull away from Brad immediately. He sighed and wrapped his arms protectively around her as she turned to her friends.

"And I told you a million times: the selection of our new guitarist has to be made democratically. We should organize auditions to meet the rare gift that will be our fourth band member." Jazmine smiled with excitement. "So that means your cousin will have to audition too."

"I think Jaz is right," Lily said. "Although I do think Carter's a great musician—and so hot!—it's better to hold auditions. Besides, we don't want Jazmine breaking your cousin's heart and forcing him to leave the group like Joe did."

"Jaz is with me now," Brad said. "She's not about to hook up with a guitarist."

"We're not exclusive, remember?" Jazmine pointed out, with a tight smile.

"You broke the other guitarist's heart?" Maude asked, amused, while Brad grumbled, looking upset.

"Don't look like you find it so funny, Maude. You remind

me of Cynthia with that face. I didn't break anybody's heart. Joe and I flirted a little, but it's not like I told him I loved him or anything. He was already imagining us getting married and having kids!"

"It's a good thing he's gone then," Brad mumbled, with a deepening grimace.

Jazmine pretended not to notice and said, "We should be heading for lunch, shouldn't we?"

"Which way is the canteen?" asked Maude.

The four teenagers stared at her puzzled, then burst out laughing.

"What?"

"I think you mean *cafeteria*, right?" asked Stacey between giggles.

"Oh," Maude said sheepishly.

"*Canteen* in American English doesn't mean the same thing as in French. Here, it refers to a cafeteria in a military camp. I know school promotes discipline and everything, but it's not boot camp. Not yet, at least," Jazmine said laughing. "Come on, don't frown." She put her arm around Maude's shoulders sympathetically. "You say all the wrong things with *just* the right accent. It's cute! No one can hold it against you."

"What do you mean by 'all the wrong things'?" cried Maude, raising a questioning eyebrow.

"Let's not get into this right now. I'm starving. Let's all go to the *canteen*," Jazmine joked as they walked.

"Seriously, Jazmine, I want to know," Maude insisted.

"Oh wait, I forgot to grab my science book," said Jazmine, ignoring the question.

"I'll come with you. We'll meet you at the *cafeteria* in ten minutes," Maude called as she and Jazmine hurried back to their lockers.

"So what other wrong things did I say? You have to tell me, Jazmine, or else I'll say them again."

"Apart from the fact that you keep on calling me Jazmine instead of Jaz like all my friends do, you did say 'how do you do' at the airport, but that was—" Jazmine stopped.

"What's wrong?"

"Oh no, Lindsey's headed this way."

"Lindsey who's that?"

"Lindsey Linton."

"What? She goes to high school? *This* high school?"

"Yeah, and I wish she didn't. She wants her fans to think she's a 'normal' teenager."

Lindsey Linton, an extremely well-dressed, skinny girl with a sharp, angular jaw, walked toward them. Her long blond ponytail bounced energetically behind her while her heels echoed loudly in the empty halls. She stopped in front of them, her hands with their perfectly polished nails resting on her hips. Instantly, Maude detected something chilling and off-putting about the singer.

"So, Jazmine, is this your new project?" asked Lindsey, looking Maude up and down.

"Maude Laurent, you know who she is. Didn't you see her video?" Jazmine said, slamming her locker door shut.

"I did, I did." Lindsey pursed her lips. "Really, classical music makes my hit so much more boring than it should be."

Maude bit her lower lip. "To each its own."

Lindsey turned to Maude and said sweetly, "I guess I'll be seeing you in Madame Tragent's class tomorrow since Jazmine's dad managed to get you in. She usually takes nothing but the best, but seeing as you're Terence Baldwin's charity case, she couldn't say no to the poor little French orphan he's taken in, could she?"

Maude's face grew hot with anger. "*Tu sais quoi?* You know what? My video's got more views than your original one. So I guess Madame Tragent must really like charity cases if she's allowed your sorry, shallow self in her class," she retorted.

Lindsey's fake, plastered-on smile wavered, and her eyeballs popped out of their sockets while Jazmine stifled a giggle.

"*I'm* her most famous and most talented student. You'll figure that out soon enough tomorrow evening."

"I guess I will," Maude answered coolly. "I can hardly wait." She walked away, Jazmine following her, still giggling.

"Oh, Maude, did you see her face? I couldn't have said it better myself! That girl is so full of herself."

"It's a good thing I didn't say *canteen* or anything like that in front of her right?" Maude said slowly smiling, her anger gradually subsiding.

"Right."

"Or that I didn't insult her entirely in French, right?"

"Right. Um, you switch to French when you're angry?"

Maude sighed deeply, not wanting to get into the whole coffee debacle right now.

"So, you and Brad the joke are cute together!" she said, changing the subject.

"I think you mean *jock*. And I'm going to end it this evening."

"What? But you seemed to really like him five minutes ago. And he obviously likes you," Maude observed, thinking that *jock* and *joke* sounded so similar that it was too bad they didn't mean the same thing.

"He's getting too attached. Soon he'll be calling me his

girlfriend, and I don't like him enough for that. He's just too . . ." She hesitated. "I don't know. Too *jocky*, if that's even a word. He's only interested in football and doesn't know a thing about music. He's not mean, he's just not my type."

"Then what is your type?"

"I don't know. All I know is this: he has to be at least as handsome as Brad, as cultivated as Joe, and as rich as Lindsey. At any rate, I don't want to be in a relationship. For now, I just want to have fun! Speaking of fun . . ."

Maude followed Jazmine's gaze, and couldn't contain her giggle.

A tall, dark-haired, scrawny boy with caramel-colored skin was walking in their direction. He held a sky-high stack of books that tilted dangerously from one side to the other. His big round-rimmed glasses slid down his nose, and he hesitated, caught in an impossible dilemma: give in to the irresistible urge to push his glasses back up or keep his stack of books in fragile equilibrium.

"Meet Jonathan," Jazmine explained with a fond smile. "Official Franklin High nerd and, unintentionally, official clown."

The two girls laughed and headed for the cafeteria.

Chapter Seven

Maude wholeheartedly disagreed with the saying that you should never meet your heroes.

Hence, she analyzed every inch of Cordelia Tragent, sitting there in real life, inside the walls of the grand Morningside Theater.

Mme. Tragent, behind an imposing white Bösendorfer piano, scanned Maude over her square-rimmed brown glasses. Her shining white hair was tied in a tight bun on top of her head, and her face, marked by the years, was set; impenetrable but very beautiful, like a statue. She wore a long red skirt, like a salsa dancer, and her hands were covered in jewels of bright colors. Her stern gray glare bore right into Maude, as if trying to determine what the young girl was made of. Maude stared back, waiting impatiently for her new teacher to finish her inspection.

She fought the urge to throw herself at her idol and gush about her most memorable performances at the Metropolitan Opera, the Opéra Garnier, and of course, La Scala in Milan.

Without saying a word, Mme. Tragent waved Maude over to join the rest of the class. She walked to the other end of the stage near the five other students, conscious of Lindsey glaring at her the whole time.

"Class, I have an announcement to make. I know that you have heard rumors about a musical that I will be directing."

Mme. Tragent stopped and surveyed her students, who whispered excitedly.

"Those rumors are wrong," she said sharply.

Silence filled the theater once again.

"I'd never create a *musical*," she said, as if the word expressed an abomination of the worst kind. "I'm a French opera singer, not a French cancan dancer. I came to the United States to train young singers and teach them that opera technique is the basis of everything," she boomed. "And that it is the best way to discipline your voice and your breathing, even if you want to be a *pop star*," she said, looking directly at Lindsey, who seemed uncomfortable under her stare.

Maude enjoyed seeing Lindsey squirm. Another reason her idol was even better in the flesh than on the poster in her room back home.

"That is why it is an *opera* that I will be directing this year. There will be a single evening performance. It will take place here in the Morningside Theater. All proceeds will go to charity. If your voice is strong enough to carry you through an entire opera, you definitely won't have trouble performing concerts during your pop careers."

The students whispered excitedly again.

Mme. Tragent waved her hand and the buzz stopped.

"You may be my students, but open auditions will be held for every role in this opera. I will direct a modern version of Rossini's *Cenerentola*."

Mme. Tragent peered at her students.

"I'm sure that not one of you knows this opera, am I right?"

The prolonged silence indicated that she was correct. Well, partly correct. Maude had listened to this opera at least a hundred times at the library. Rossini was one of her favorite composers, and his exuberant, fun operas spoke to her in ways no other composer could.

"How long have you all been taking classes with me? Years, for some of you! Do you still not know what *Cenerentola* talks about? Or maybe all you care for are the music lessons but not the musical history that is behind them? That doesn't matter, does it?"

She sighed.

"The *Cenerentola* is one of Rossini's most famous operas, in two acts," Maude said. "It's a nineteenth century remake of the story of Cinderella. In his version Cinderella is a bit different from the one we know. She's more, erm, how do you say? Spirited!" Maude said, despite her nerves. The words tumbled in French in her mind, and knowing that her teacher spoke her language made it harder for her to focus on English. Mme. Tragent looked at Maude, her face unmoving. She glanced back at the rest of the class.

The students peered at Maude with unveiled curiosity, wondering where this new girl came from and how she knew so much on her first day.

Lindsey, on the other hand, looked away. She refused to give Maude any more attention than she was already receiving.

"You will all audition for the different roles. The new student included," Mme. Tragent continued.

Maude's heart fluttered with excitement. She would do everything to get the lead. Cinderella's part was challenging, but also touched close to home. She'd always felt sympathy for Rossini's unfortunate but witty character.

"Now everyone position yourselves. Let's warm up these voices." Mme. Tragent went behind the piano and began the exercises.

Maude and the rest of the class started the various exercises that consisted of repeating Mme. Tragent's meaningless sounds, *"Ah, oh, hi, oh, uuu."*

So far so good, Maude thought.

"Position!" Mme. Tragent yelled from behind her piano.

Maude looked around her. What did she mean? They weren't in ballet class.

"Ms. Laurent, I said position!"

The boy next to Maude leaned over to her and whispered, "It means you have to stand straight. Your shoulders are a bit slouched."

Maude straightened and smiled gratefully at him. He had soft brown eyes, disheveled dark hair, and a kind smile. Maude's face grew warm. He was cute and seemed nice too.

"Thomas Bradfield, Maude Laurent, would you like to be left alone, perhaps?" Mme. Tragent's voice rang through the theater and brought Maude back to reality.

Lindsey snickered while Maude's face grew hot. Thomas straightened up and resumed the exercise.

Mme. Tragent abruptly stopped playing the piano.

"Ms. Laurent, since you seem to be in the mood to use your voice, why don't you take your score and sing the notes for me?"

Maude took her score and read the notes like she had been taught in school.

"Do, mi, fa, sol, la—"

She stopped as she heard everyone laugh except Thomas. *What now?* she thought.

"You're not supposed to sing *do, mi, fa, sol, la,*" said Lindsey snidely. "Don't you know the English notes, little French girl?"

"I'm sorry, I—" Maude started, looking at Mme. Tragent.

Mme. Tragent waved her hand.

"That isn't important," she said, looking at Lindsey sternly over her dark-rimmed glasses. "As long as you sing the notes correctly you can sing them in whichever language you want. Now, resume. The rest of you, silence!"

Maude started over and finished without being interrupted.

"That will do," Mme. Tragent said.

Maude saw Lindsey glare at her but had no idea what she had done now. Thomas was looking at her, too, but he seemed impressed.

"It's a shame," Mme. Tragent said, "that you want to become a pop star. What you'll need to work on is quite the opposite from everyone else in the class, which won't make it easy. Less articulation, less resonance, and of course less vibrato. Oh, and your French accent as you sing, we'll have to fix that too. You'll have to work hard, Ms. Laurent." She paused, still looking at her. Maude would have given anything to know what she was thinking behind those impenetrable gray eyes. "I'll give you specific exercises. You'll need to work on them at home on your own. Do you understand?"

Maude nodded, while the rest of the class whispered.

Lindsey scowled and shot Maude a dirty look. Maude only shrugged, nonchalantly.

"Now, class, take your scores, and let's start over with the lyrics this time, not the notes."

For two hours Maude sang, trying to avoid Mme. Tragent's stern stare, which always seemed to be directed at her, and trying to keep the right "Position!" as well as the right breathing, which was the most difficult part.

Two hours flew by, and Maude was surprised when Mme. Tragent announced that class was over. She gathered her things, wishing that the class could continue. She still had so much to learn.

"Hey, Maude! Which way are you headed?" asked Thomas as he joined her near the exit.

"Toward Tribeca. I'm exhausted. I never knew singing could be so tiring." *Not to mention an entire week in a whole new city*, she thought.

"Hard work pays off," he pointed out as they walked to the subway, the evening rush hour in full flow. "Congratulations on your first lesson with Madame Tragent. She usually refuses to take more than five students in her class, and never gives private classes, though we'd all pay top dollar for them."

"She probably knows I'd just be stalking her all over Manhattan if she didn't have me in her class," Maude said, only half joking.

"How come you love classical music so much?"

"I just, I stumbled on old scores in my town's library in France. I started learning and I don't know, it soothed me. I found it comforting when things weren't going right in the real world. And I love the stories in opera. It's not just singing, there's a whole story and lots of drama. So you think, 'better them than me,'" Maude said, admiring the lights of the city.

"I never saw it that way. I just really thought it was a great way to have good technique."

Maude dodged a glamorous couple hurrying inside a restaurant. "Maybe you're right."

"I'm always right!" he boasted.

"And humble too?"

They both laughed.

"I have no idea how I'm going to adjust to all this. But I'm determined to improve."

"It seems to me you're off to a pretty good start."

"Not true. You heard her: 'You need more practice, Ms. Laurent. A lot of practice,'" she said, imitating Mme. Tragent's grave tones.

"Are you kidding? That's about as close to a compliment as you can get. For a first class, I'd say you did a great job. She said you needed practice, which is her way of saying that you have potential. You should've seen Mary's first day."

"Who's Marie?" Maude asked, using the French pronunciation.

"Exactly. Mary's gone. Her first day was her last day as well. Madame Tragent told her to never come back. And she'd taken singing lessons for ten years. Gosh, you're the only one who knew *La Cenerentola*. How did you know?"

Maude didn't want to admit that she identified with stories about orphans, so she just said, "I think it's a beautiful opera. Cinderella is very spirited in it. She isn't like Cinderella in the Disney version, who just waits for Prince Charming. She has a sense of humor, and the opera is very funny. Even Prince Charming is different. His character is more complete, more active. He disguises himself as a valet to see how women behave around him when they think he's just a servant."

"Would I make a good Prince Charming?" he asked, looking at her slyly.

"It depends. Can you sing as a tenor?" she asked, equally sly.

He laughed. "I obviously don't have the low range of a

baritone or a bass. I have the vocal agility of a tenor, the voice of every romantic hero in opera."

"In opera, not in real life," Maude retorted.

"You're tough." Thomas laughed.

"You have to be tough if you want to make it in the big city. Isn't that true?" Maude teased.

"Yes, that's very true, Maude Laurent," he said, stopping in front of the subway entrance.

Maude liked the way he said her name. After having been called "Ms. Laurent" sharply for the last two hours, hearing her name said in a soft tone was quite refreshing.

"Very well, Thomas Bradfield," Maude said, preparing to leave. "See you next time."

"I mean," Thomas hesitated, then said in one breath, "Maybe we could, like, go out one of these days outside of Madame Tragent's lessons."

"You mean, like a date?" Maude asked, looking at her feet, suddenly extremely shy.

"Exactly. A date. If you want."

"I'd like that." She raised her eyes from her boots and flashed him a smile.

"I think I'd need your phone number," Thomas suggested.

"Oh right!" She fished her phone from her coat pocket so fast that it tumbled from her fingers and dropped to the ground. "I don't know my number yet, sorry!" she exclaimed, picking the phone up. Thank goodness it had a solid case.

"You're funny!"

"I've only been here a week." She giggled.

He gave her his number and she rang him with her phone immediately.

"Got it, Maude Laurent. I'll text you!" he said, watching her go.

Maude continued to smile as she entered the subway station. She'd barely made it inside the train when she heard an announcement.

"Ladies and Gentlemen. Due to a technical problem on the two line, this train will be running local . . ." Maude's groan covered the end of the sentence.

Chapter Eight

"Soulville is the best place to make music," Jake explained as he guided Maude through the offices the next day.

Jake, a musical aficionado and one of Soulville's most loyal receptionists, had taken an instant liking to Terence's most recent protégé. He readily repeated how much he admired the story of Maude's extraordinary route to discovery.

"We have three mastering rooms, five studios, and four production rooms," he continued. "The acoustics are amazing! Terence made sure of that. That's because the echo chambers are unique: the sound isolation allows the sound engineers to sweeten the music tracks with a rich reverberation. You'll learn more about all that when you start recording. You'll be recording in Studio A, the best studio this house has to offer. And for now, you'll be working in MCR."

"MCR?" Maude asked, thinking this was a new English word she didn't know.

"Matt's Creation Room," he explained as they crossed the lobby. "We've got quite a few rooms here that artists use to create in, even sleep in sometimes."

Maude's eyes instantly fell on the Steinway concert grand piano.

"She's a beauty, isn't she?" Jake said, following Maude's gaze.

She could only nod.

"She's Soulville's mascot,'" he explained. "She's also cursed."

"Really?" Maude scoffed.

"Don't laugh," Jake warned her. "This piano is a custom-made Steinway nine point six crafted in 1863 by Steinway & Sons for the Morningside Theater, and everyone says it's cursed."

"What do you mean?" Maude asked, her curiosity piqued.

"I mean that nothing but the most horrific sounds come from this instrument, even when played by the best pianist."

"When was the last time you tuned it?" Maude asked warily.

"It's regularly tuned by the best piano technicians," Jake insisted. "It's cursed. Everyone agrees."

An involuntary shiver ran down Maude's spine as she looked at the rosewood Steinway.

"I'll show you the kitchen and the creation room, and the tour will be over," Jake said, ushering her along.

Matt's Creation Room was a wide, colorful space dedicated to music. The room was bathed in light streaming through wide windows, and he'd obviously decorated according to his own tastes.

The walls were splashed with bright-orange paint, and green sofas, scattered with cushions, contrasted with the serious, dark upright Yamaha piano in the center of the room. In addition several guitars, a violin, drums, and a bass guitar were scattered around. The walls were like a private hall of fame covered with posters and relics of famous singers, and one even displayed pictures of Matt and his three platinum albums: *Matt*, *Superstar*, and *Moving On*.

In the far-right corner of the room, boxes were piled

haphazardly. Maude noticed a woman's leather boot spilling out of the one at the very top.

She wondered why there were female items in the room, then decided he must be keeping his ex's things. Maude felt certain she, whoever she was, had had a good reason to break up with him.

After finishing her scales Maude stood next to the windows to practice for her audition for *La Cenerentola* the next day. She bumped into one of the boxes and winced, rubbing her knee. The column of boxes swayed dangerously but stayed put.

Maude turned to the window and began singing "Una volta c'era un re."

It was a beautiful, sorrowful aria that Cinderella sang in the first scene, about a king who looked for true love not in splendor and beauty but in innocence and goodness.

Maude had difficulty getting into the spirit of the song as she surveyed the incredible view of Times Square from the top of Soulville Tower. Nevertheless, she tried to sing mournfully in Italian. She heard Matt enter and was satisfied to think that she hadn't betrayed any emotion when he arrived, unlike their previous encounters.

"Isn't Cinderella supposed to be singing with melancholy? Why are you smiling?" he asked when she finished.

Maude turned around, almost regretfully.

"Hello to you, too, Matt. Glad you could make it." She greeted him, ignoring his comment.

"I get it, no small talk." He threw his leather bag on the closest sofa. "By the way, *tu veux qu'on parle français ou anglais*?" he asked. (Do you want us to speak English or French?)

Maude thought it'd be a relief to speak French from time to

time. But she really wanted to speak English as fluently as possible. Besides, if she spoke French, he'd think they were friends. She could tell from his laughing eyes that he was thinking about her angry outburst in the subway.

"Anglais," she replied firmly.

"English it is. Let's get down to business."

"I know you're supposed to do most of the songwriting, but, well, I've been working on a song," Maude said, taking a sheet of music out of her file.

"Great, let's hear it!" he said enthusiastically. "Composing is one of my favorite parts of the creative process."

"It isn't finished yet, but I thought we could work on it together, since you're supposed to be some sort of 'wizard with words' or something."

"I'll ignore that last bit of sarcasm and pretend you just paid me a compliment," Matt declared, unaffected.

Maude went to the piano and sang:

"Strolling in the streets of Paris late at night

"The Eiffel Tower sparkles, full of light

"I look around the city smiles at me

"There's no other place I'd rather be."

"Stop!" Matt interrupted.

"What's wrong?" Maude asked, surprised and displeased at his tone.

"Everything!" Matt exclaimed, crossing his arms over his chest.

"That's harsh."

"Not everything. The rhythm's jazzy," he admitted. "But, come on, Maude. You're singing a song about Paris? Beautiful Paris, Paris full of light. Paris, the wonderful."

"What's wrong with that?"

"Don't you see what's wrong? Paris is nothing like that!"

"Of course it is. It's one of the most beautiful cities in the world," Maude protested, crossing her arms angrily.

"For a tourist," Matt emphasized. "You've described Paris like a tourist would, Maude. Paris is only partly what you've described. Come on, you've lived in Paris. How is life in Paris? Going to school every day, taking the subway every day?"

"I've never lived in Paris. Excuse me for having the point of view of a dowdy, provincial peasant!"

"You aren't from Paris?" asked Matt. "Terence said—"

"That video of me was filmed during the only day I spent in Paris. As a *tourist*. I am from the north of France. The Pas-de-Calais département to be exact," she said, raising her head proudly, as if announcing that she was an empress.

"From the north of France? Where it rains three hundred and sixty-three days a year?" he mocked, grinning.

Maude's cheeks burned. How dare he make fun of where she came from.

"I'm assuming you're Parisian. Your arrogance is a dead giveaway."

"I am, actually. Was. I consider myself a New Yorker, not a Parisian these days. Manhattan is my home."

"I suppose that's why you're so quick to criticize Paris."

"You suppose wrong." Matt cocked his head to the side, his wavy, dirty-blond hair brushing his shoulders. "I love Paris. I'm just not as blinded by its beauty as you are."

"So not only am I a provincial peasant, but I'm also a blind one?" Maude asked in disbelief.

"I never said you were a peasant." His gray eyes shone with humor.

"You're too kind," Maude retorted, sarcastically.

"All I'm saying is that Paris is a lot more than what you say in your song. Paris isn't just a beauty queen. She's full of passion. She's the city of the French Revolution. And every other revolution, as a matter of fact. Today, Paris is also the epicenter of every important strike or revolt. Piece of advice: avoid the subway on a strike day or you'll be crammed in with hundreds of other people wishing you could be anywhere else in the world. Paris is a city full of life, like every big city. Paris can be very dirty too. There's lots of pollution. All I'm trying to say is that you should describe Paris as she really is, the different layers. Not some soapy, postcard version of it. Put more emotion in it."

"I haven't spent my life in Paris like you have. So excuse me if the only Paris I know is the one I visited on my only day there. You didn't even listen to the whole song."

"Don't need to," he said, taking her sheet nevertheless. "Let me see. 'Walking along the Seine / The wind blows softly like a whisper.' Seriously? Why do you withhold so much? You need to dig deeper into your emotions."

Maude's eyes blazed as she snatched the sheet from him.

"A little sensitivity wouldn't hurt," she stated coldly. "I wonder why I even bother taking advice from someone who was singing a song called 'Love Doctor' two years ago."

"Ouch. Now *that's* harsh." Matt winced. He seemed thoroughly ashamed of that song.

"Too harsh?" Maude mocked relentlessly. "Did I hurt your feelings? Why don't you call the love doctor so he can fix you up?"

Matt hid a smile.

"Really, word wizard. Where was all your brilliance when you were singing:

"Call the Love Doctor cuz my heart is breaking

"Losing you, babe, means losing everything

"Call the Love Doctor cuz my heart is breaking

"Without you, babe, I am nothing."

Maude sang, mimicking him. She wished she didn't know the song. But just like Lindsey Linton's simple lyrics, these ones had stuck through the years.

"That's totally unfair. I was young back then and I'd been stupid enough to sign with Glitter Records. They didn't allow me to write my own songs on that album."

"Perhaps they were right," Maude stated dryly.

"Get down from your high horse, Miss Maude," Matt coaxed in a gentler tone. "Every song needs work. And this one isn't an exception. Your songs need to reflect who you really are. Dig into your deepest, darkest feelings. Don't you know that the best songs were written about suffering?"

"So now you're going to give me a musical history lesson?"

"It's part of my job. Terence said you needed to learn about more contemporary artists since you're stuck in Beethoven's nineteenth century."

Maude remained silent, arms crossed tightly across her chest. Matt shrugged and headed to the piano. He wore a sullen expression as he started Nina Simone's version of "My Man's Gone Now."

"Blues," he said. "Whether about heartache or general good ole dissatisfaction, blues always expresses sorrow or suffering."

As he sang, the lyrics went straight to Maude's heart. She listened with her ears, her heart, her soul. She was amazed not only by Matt's technique but also his unique capacity at interpreting a song that had nothing to do with his initial pop music career. And with such feeling too. While he played, eyes closed, she admired his broad, straight shoulders, his calm but assured stance. He was a remarkably accomplished artist, and she almost regretted having been so harsh about his "Love Doctor" song. He certainly had grown as an artist since then.

He stopped playing and turned to her.

"You *do* understand what I mean!" he exclaimed, pleased to see Maude responding to the music. "I chose Nina Simone to show you something else. Just like you, Nina Simone had a classical background. When she was younger she wanted to become a concert pianist. Her skill was beyond measure, and she used it in a wide repertoire of jazz, blues, and R & B songs. And I think you can do the same. Music knows no limits, and I get why Terence insisted on signing you."

Maude remained silent, thinking about his beautiful performance. She had shivers. Still, she said, "Look, what you played was really nice and all, but I'm just not into popular music."

"I can't believe it. You're one of these classical snobs."

"I'm not a snob. It's just, I've always dreamed of becoming an opera star, and that requires sacrifice."

"But you're here. And we're supposed to create a song that's *both* classical *and* pop, so you're going to have to get over yourself."

"How about this: you bring the pop, and I bring the classical."

"No, we're both going to bring classical and pop."

"What do you know about classical?"

"Unlike you, I've never limited myself in terms of music. I listen to everything."

"I'm not limited."

"Prove it."

"Okay, I'll listen—"

"You're not going to listen. You're going to feel." Matt inched closer to her, and she felt her heart skip a beat. Probably because he made her so angry.

"What are you doing tonight?"

"I—" *Is he asking me out?* Maude thought, panicked. He couldn't. Two date proposals in a week? New York was full of surprises.

"We need to continue working on the song," Matt said firmly.

"Oh, of course," Maude said, though not without a hint of regret. Matt pulled out his phone and moved away from Maude.

"Hey, Craig, I need a fake ID by tonight. Yeah, I'll pay the rush fee. Okay, thanks."

"What? A fake ID. For whom?"

"For you. We're going out tonight."

Chapter Nine

The Wild Garden was one of the biggest nightclubs in New York, sprawling the length of an entire block in Bushwick, Brooklyn. Some people went so far as to call it the epicenter of electro music. The vast space, filling a former industrial complex, had several outdoor and indoor venues, each with a unique theme, and housed the wildest EDM events of the year.

When Maude entered the crowded main hall between Matt and Jazmine, she was immediately conscious of the many eyeballs that converged on them, mostly on Matt. He looked amazing in a white tank top underneath a designer black zigzagged overcoat that only he had the confidence to pull off. Maude reviewed her choice to wear simple jeans and a black crop top. She might be the only French girl in the world without a sense of style. At least her perfect Afro, from which wafted a sweet scent of coconut oil, was her crowning glory.

Still, she wished she possessed Jazmine's confidence. She'd strutted into the nightclub in towering heels that accentuated her slender curves.

Maude had never been anywhere even close to this. It scared and fascinated her at the same time. Her eyes were blinded by the incredible patchwork of blue and pink lighting sweeping across hordes of stylish, dancing partygoers and shining on the beautiful plants creeping up the walls. At the center of the dance floor was a female DJ swiping her turntables. She was perhaps the most conservatively dressed of all: she only wore a black cap and black T-shirt and tights. Her striking purple lipstick would alternatively become pink or blue whenever a flash of light illuminated her face. Maude was fascinated by her energy and concentration as she alternated between her turntables and waving to the crowd. Taking it all in, Maude felt a rush of excitement. The bass beat, and *boom, boom, boom* seemed to come from inside her body.

Maude barely had any time to register all this before Matt yelled, "I'll introduce you to some friends."

He led them up to the wide mezzanine where groups of people sat around tables or on leather sofas, drinking colorful cocktails while wine bottles rested in coolers.

Matt led them to the end of the mezzanine where a couple were making out next to a tattooed guy sipping a beer.

"Hey, Karl." Matt greeted his tattooed friend, slapping hands.

"Good to see you, man," Karl said, speaking to Matt but fixing his gaze on Maude. "It's been a while. How are you? Where you been? No one's seen you since you announced you were taking a break from your career."

"I'm good, I'm good." Matt looked like he was on the verge of saying more but held back. Finally he added, "I've been busy."

"This your new girl?" Karl asked, still looking at Maude.

"Oh, I'm definitely not his new girl," Maude declared.

"She's too smart for Matt," Jazmine added with a giggle.

"Thanks for that, Jaz," Matt said easily. "I'm working with her. You can both tell Maude she doesn't have anything to worry about: I never mix business and pleasure."

"Oh, this guy?" Karl said. "Definitely. He's a saint. Because some of the girls he worked with would definitely have pleasured his business, if you see what I mean."

"Unfortunately, I do," Maude said uneasily.

For the life of her, she couldn't understand why she didn't feel overwhelmed with relief at the knowledge that Matt would keep things professional. Another part of her wondered which girls he'd worked with had wanted more from their relationship. She wouldn't be one of those, for sure. Besides, she and Thomas had been texting like crazy. It wouldn't take them long to settle on a day for their first date.

"Wanna dance?" Matt asked Maude.

"I can't," she stammered. Nobody would believe that she'd never been to a party. "I mean, maybe later."

"Jaz?" Matt asked.

"O' course!" was Jazmine's enthusiastic response.

They both hurried down as a new song blasted from the sound system.

Maude sat next to Karl and wondered what she was doing there. The music was loud, and it was nothing like classical, but then she couldn't ignore the fun the people downstairs were having. She wished she knew how to dance. Then again, the moves she saw weren't extremely complicated. She'd never danced except in front of her mirror, and then only when no one was home.

"I haven't seen Matt out here in months," Karl said. "He gave us less and less news and stopped completely right after he broke up with Tiana. Never answered our group texts."

Tiana.

Maude wondered if she was the reason Matt had taken a

break from his career. Her thoughts drifted to the female clothes in his creation room. Were they Tiana's? And was she the person he was referencing when they'd met and he'd said he was on his way to see a subway musician who "meant a lot to someone I cared about"?

"But, hey, he seems happy to be working with you," Karl pointed out.

"The feeling isn't mutual," she said, still thinking about Matt's ex.

"Ah, don't be like that. Sure, he gets anal about music. But only because he wants to get the best out of his artists."

Jazmine ran back up the mezzanine stairs and waved to Maude. "You've got to come down with us. It's no fun without you. Come on!"

"I don't know how to dance," Maude stammered.

"Nobody does." Jazmine clutched Maude's arm. "I mean, I do. But this isn't a dance competition."

As Jazmine pulled her up off the sofa, Maude gave herself a mental kick and agreed.

Together they made their way downstairs, elbowing through the crowd until they found Matt, just as the music changed.

At first, Maude froze. But then an upbeat, pop and funk song came on. The rhythm burst in her ears, but still she couldn't dance.

Matt looked at her puzzled, then he leaned close to her as the words of the female singer reverberated throughout the venue.

"Won't you let me

"Lose control

"Won't you let me

"Touch your soul."

"It's not that complicated. You just have to let go!" he shouted in her ear. "Can I show you?"

Maude stiffened, then nodded, tongue-tied. He placed his hands on her hips and swayed them to the rhythm of the music. At his touch, Maude felt a fire spread through her body, and her eyes widened, her breathing becoming shallow. They were inches from each other, and she felt inexplicably drawn to him. Startled, she stumbled, and, losing her balance, wrapped her arms around his neck for support. Surprise shone in his eyes, then he smiled. She wanted to return his smile but her mind froze, so conscious was she of his proximity, of the smell of his soft cologne and his warm touch.

"You want to lose control

"Why not let go

"Let it explode."

They continued to dance, the loud beat drumming in their ears. She closed her eyes, and it was like everything and everyone else disappeared. She could feel Matt's breath on her neck, and one of his long blond curls brushed her forehead. She opened her eyes and looked up at him. His gaze was troubled for a moment, and Maude looked at his lips, wanting desperately to kiss them. Then she recalled what Karl had said about not mixing business and pleasure. What if Matt thought she was flirting with him?

She immediately let her arms fall to her sides and shouted in his ear, "I'm going to find Jazmine!"

He nodded curtly and removed his hands from her waist, as if they'd caught fire.

Maude thought she read relief in his eyes. She couldn't tell because he turned abruptly away and headed back up to the mezzanine.

Maude's heart dropped. Why had she danced with him? It had to be the music's fault. Her glare drifted over to the DJ. The power the girl had, her command of the audience. If classical had the power to soothe, did pop have the absolute power to ignite?

As these thoughts floated in Maude's head, she found Jazmine, who was dancing with two other boys, and joined them.

"You having fun?" Jazmine yelled.

"Best night ever!" Maude answered. She meant it too. She'd never had friends to go out with. Even if she had, the only nightlife in Carvin was the quiet *bar tabac* on Grand Place. Maude was growing fonder of Jazmine by the minute. Maybe Matt wasn't so bad either.

After a while Jazmine and Maude headed to the outdoor terrace, which was lit up by strings of hundreds of fairy lights. They found Matt leaning against the railing, sipping a beer.

"I don't think you hate popular music so much now," he said, smiling at Maude's approach. "Do you?"

"That was fun," Maude admitted.

"Fun is nice, but you can go further," Matt said. "All you have to do is dig deeper. Try finding some suffering in you. *Don't* sing the *Cenerentola* with a smile. Although you look like a girl who's had it all. You know, the nice girl from the north of France, who grew up in a quiet, small town with her loving mom and dad and brothers and sisters, always top of her class, quick tempered when things didn't go her way. A bit spoiled, I guess. You have to put all that—"

"Spoiled?" Maude blurted in utter disbelief, the word echoing through her mind. Of all the things he could've said about her, *spoiled* was the last word that could have appeared remotely appropriate. Was that how he saw her? She'd lost both parents

before she even had a memory of them and lived with the pain of their absence every day. The Ruchets weren't cruel, and she wasn't sure they loved her, but they had certainly never spoiled her.

"You know nothing about me, Matt," she said, her voice quivering.

Jazmine stepped in. "He doesn't know—"

"You obviously know nothing about suffering or you wouldn't idealize it the way that you do. You see it as a romantic notion that gives depth to songwriting. Like a breakup. And it does. Not because the singers actually thought of it in an artistic way, but because that's how they lived. You'll *never* understand that," she finished, trembling from head to toe.

She turned away, rushed down the stairs, and left the club.

Chapter Ten

Maude was still fuming the next morning as she stood backstage in the Morningside Theater listening to the other *La Cenerentola* auditions. She was also increasingly nervous as she watched the other students perform. She couldn't forget Matt's words as they continued to echo in her mind. Although she hated to admit it, his musical advice was sound, even though he hadn't judged her correctly.

To think he saw her as a pampered, spoiled brat! His perception of her resembled her own opinion of Lindsey, she realized.

She couldn't, *wouldn't* dig too deep into her feelings of abandonment, sadness, and loneliness. She'd left those in Carvin. Ignoring them, pretending that they weren't there, had worked for her so far. If she unleashed them they would consume her, and everyone would see who she really was: the poor, abandoned orphan they could all feel sorry for. Maude wanted to be able to hold her head high, not bow under their pity.

Maude forced a smile as she saw Thomas wink at her before walking on stage, facing Mme. Tragent and singing his solo. Thomas was incredibly at ease as Prince Charming, and was a talented tenor. Nothing would ever deter this Prince Charming, just like his interpreter. Thomas obviously took singing very seriously. Even during Mme. Tragent's class his concentration rarely wavered. He never seemed shaken by her sharp glare or the icy remarks directed toward him. Maude could tell he was determined to get to the top, and she knew he possessed the talent and will to become a famous pop star—even if he had to go through Mme. Tragent's classical lessons.

Maude clapped once when he finished singing but stopped in time to avoid embarrassing herself.

"So, how was I, Queen Maude?" he asked as he joined her backstage.

"The perfect Prince Charming!" she exclaimed.

"Am I *your* perfect Prince Charming?" he asked, looking at her with a deep, serious gaze.

Maude faltered, but before she could answer Lindsey shoved past her and headed to the stage.

"Sorry. You were in my way," she said snidely.

"Good luck," Maude said calmly. "*Break* a leg," she added, happily imagining Lindsey limping on crutches.

"Only losers need luck. *I* have talent," Lindsey replied before striding on stage and singing Cinderella's solo.

She does *have loads of talent*, Maude thought as she listened to the other girl. Her technique was excellent and her voice assured, though she couldn't reach the high notes Maude could. When she sang in the middle of her range her voice was steady and disciplined from years of hard work and singing classes with the best coaches. Still, as Maude listened, something was lacking. Lindsey was standing hands on hips, holding her head high, as if she owned the world. Her attitude clashed with Cinderella's solo, which was supposed to be a lament and hope for a better life.

Maude looked at Thomas and, judging by his frown, she could see that he was thinking the same thing.

"She isn't in character," Thomas whispered, his frown deepening.

Maude nodded. Although Cinderella was a spirited character in the opera, in this song she was supposed to be melancholic. She wasn't the least bit arrogant like Lindsey was at that moment, looking like she would just trample her evil stepsisters if they appeared on stage and demanded their clothes and breakfast.

"He was right," Maude said softly.

"Who was right?" asked Thomas curiously.

"Matt," Maude said speaking more to herself than to him. Deep in thought, she continued to watch the performance and barely noticed Thomas's frown at her mention of Matt.

Lindsey finished and proudly walked off stage, her heels clicking louder than ever and almost covering Mme. Tragent's voice as she called Maude to the stage.

"Good luck singing after me," Lindsey said coldly.

Maude didn't hear her, couldn't hear her, as she was no longer aware of anything but the song she had to sing and the realization that Matt had been right all along. She walked on stage and stood straight before a stern Mme. Tragent, whom she barely noticed either.

Lindsey could never impersonate Cinderella because she had always gotten what she wanted and had never craved anything, had never hoped for a better life.

As Maude began Cinderella's solo, hands clasped to her heart, she pictured herself back in Carvin the day after she'd learned the name of her father. She'd googled his name but had found nothing. Sitting alone in the living room, Maude had wished with all her heart that she could learn more about her Nigerian-French family. And then, remembering that she would soon leave Carvin, she had felt a new, developing sense of hope. Hope that she would one day be able to sing without having to hide in a library. Hope that she'd discover who her father and mother were, and how they'd died, even if she had to knock on every door in New York to find someone who knew them.

But since she'd arrived, something had held her back. She was having so much fun she was almost scared to discover why her parents' identity had been kept secret for so long. What if knowing changed her entire life and her sense of self? Not knowing allowed her to dream that they were heroes, angels. Maybe her father had drunk coffee in the same coffee place as her or strolled along the same streets she did. Knowledge meant there was no room left for illusion; only for dealing with the hard truth of their fallible humanity.

As she sang Maude allowed her emotions to surface without letting them consume her. She dug deep into her sorrow to share Cinderella's pain and allowed her mezzo-soprano voice to explore its lower register.

Maude ended Cinderella's solo and came back to reality with a start. She was no longer in Carvin. She looked at Mme. Tragent. The stoic teacher's face remained as impenetrable as that of a stone gargoyle on the cathedral of Notre-Dame.

Maude hastened off the stage to Thomas, who was waiting for her.

"You were great!" he exclaimed.

"Don't lie to her, Thomas," Lindsey said haughtily. "Her technique is far from perfect. You added way too much vibrato in the last lines, and you should really learn to stand straight while you sing or Madame Tragent will kick you out of class."

"Your vibrato was perfect, Maude. This is an opera, not pop music. That added fluctuation, that tremor gave a lot more depth and feeling to the song. Maybe you should try that next time, Lindsey. You know, showing *feeling*. You looked like you walked straight out of Wagner's *Valkyrie*, ready to smash everything standing in your way!"

"I guess it's easier for Maude to relate to Cinderella. She is, after all, nothing but a poor orphan herself, isn't that right, Maude?" Lindsey asked, wrapping her venom in a fake, sweet smile.

Maude smiled sweetly back and said, "You're absolutely right. What puzzles me, though, is why your parents *still* haven't given you up for adoption, Lindsey."

With that, she swept past an angry Lindsey, Thomas closely following her as they left the theater.

"I bet you and I will get the leads," Thomas said as they walked outside.

"We don't know that for sure. I'd rather not jinx it. Besides, Lindsey is right. Her vocal technique is very good. Madame Tragent might choose her for the role of Cinderella. At least I put up a good fight."

"What you may lack in technique you make up for with character. You were right, you know. Opera is also about the story. Give yourself some credit. I'm positive that you'll be the Cinderella to my Prince Charming."

Maude's playful laughter resounded like a waterfall, and Thomas gazed at her affectionately.

"The Cinderella to *your* Prince Charming? You're forgetting that Cinderella is the main character and Prince Charming is nothing but an accessory to her happiness," Maude teased.

"That's because Rossini didn't know *I*, Thomas Bradfield, would one day play the part, and that I would completely eclipse Cinderella."

"I should warn Madame Tragent not to choose you. Your, erm,"—she hesitated, but luckily the word she wanted to say was the same in both English and French—"*ego* could ruin the entire opera."

"What makes you think she would listen to her newest, greenest student?"

"Hey! She said I have what it takes to become an opera singer," Maude teased.

"Doesn't mean you're going to become Madame Tragent's personal and trusted confidant."

"True," Maude acknowledged. "I don't know if she has any friends or family. She's so stern and cold. Not everyone can have a Thomas Bradfield as a friend."

"I guess not," he answered with a pleased smile. "The good thing is we'll only have to wait a couple of days for the results. In the meantime, we can go on our date. It'll be more fun than texting."

Maude nodded and suddenly felt a lump in her throat. Even a couple of days seemed like years. As she gazed into Thomas's eyes she felt she wouldn't mind being the Cinderella to his Prince Charming in the least.

Chapter Eleven

There was never a dull moment in the Baldwin house.

Living in a large musical family was not dissimilar to traveling with a circus: silence was rare, and it was impossible to feel lonely. The Baldwins were joyful and noisy.

They all played an instrument. The deep tones of Jazmine's electric bass were the first notes that woke the whole family in the morning. Cynthia playing Bach's Concerto for Two Violins in D minor were the last notes heard at night before going to sleep. At various times of the day, especially on weekends, Victoria's *udu* drum echoed through the house, often accompanied by Terence's guitar. The two formed quite a musical pair, though they each had a fondness for different music styles. Terence Baldwin's heart and soul belonged to Motown. Since she'd arrived, Maude and Ben had spent the early part of the evenings in Terence's studio discovering the legends of Motown.

"Now, listen to the Jackson Five. The brothers had a long career together, and their repertoire was wide: rhythm and blues, soul, funk, and then disco. They represent an entire generation."

Ever since her night at the Wild Garden, Maude was in awe of everything Terence was teaching her about popular music. He opened her ears to different musical styles, and to the different roles played by the instruments that she, at first, had a hard time distinguishing.

"Listen to the electric bass in this song, Diana Ross's 'The Boss,' from 1979. That distinct rhythm is one of the characteristics of disco: the electric bass lays down the rhythm. You can tell the difference with the songs from the Supremes era in the 1960s. Those songs like 'Stop! In the Name of Love' or 'You Can't Hurry Love' were more of a soul and R & B style. Diana Ross was great at reinventing herself. That's something that you have to learn as an artist: never rely on what you think you know or what you think sounds best. Keep an open mind and open yourself up to different types of music from all around the world and across time."

Maude nodded, snapping her fingers to the rhythm of the song.

Jazmine came in with her bass guitar and followed the rhythm of "The Boss" so Maude could hear the unique role the bass played in the song. Maude and Ben danced, with Ben demonstrating his unique disco moves. They twirled and whirled, arms flying, hips swaying, hands clapping. Cynthia soon joined them. An obviously amused Terence observed the scene.

Maude, who at first had been worried about disturbing the household with her long hours of practicing either the piano or singing, soon realized her music blended into the general, delirious atmosphere of the home. The *Cenerentola*'s Italian lyrics frequently accompanied Cynthia's final notes of the evening. Maude had always loved the song "Una volta c'era un re," but ever since the audition, it held a particular place in her heart and filled her with hope that she'd get the part.

Life might not have been peaceful at the Baldwins but the family got along . . . most of the time.

That evening at the dinner table, they had one of the heated debates that they enjoyed.

"You can't seriously think that an artist has to *make money* to be considered an artist?" Jazmine asked her father as she passed a bowl of rice to her brother.

"In the eyes of society, definitely," Terence said, emptying the water jug into his glass.

"Because society should define who is or who isn't an artist?" Victoria scoffed. "Art can't just be defined by institutions like museums or record labels," she added with a sly smile directed at her husband.

"Soulville isn't an institution," Terence said, after taking a sip from his glass.

"It's not exactly a charity, is it Dad?" Jazmine argued.

"I can turn it into a charity if you want." He laughed. "But then who'd pay for all your expensive clothes?"

"That's not the point," Jazmine said hotly.

"Of course not." Cynthia chimed in. "A professional artist is someone who decides to carry the heavy burden of having to make their way through a world that doesn't believe that artists should be paid for their work."

"An artist can only be defined by what they believe they are," Victoria argued.

"Yeah, if I decide I'm a rock star, I am!" Jazmine cried, striking the table with her fist. "Tomorrow will be a definite moment on my path: we're holding auditions for our new guitarist. You coming, Cynth?"

"I can't." Cynthia looked flustered for a moment then quickly returned to the initial debate. "You can see yourself as a rock star, but no one else will see you that way. Not unless you're getting paid and not just rehearsing in the school gym. I'd say you're a rock star in the making," she added gently.

"But what about all those artists nobody knows?" Jazmine asked worried. "What about the people who don't have access to institutions, or record labels, or museums?"

"I want to give that access to as many people as I can. Why do you think I went all the way to France to find Maude?" Terence said with a twinkle in his eye.

Maude smiled. She did enjoy a good Baldwin debate, though she'd always been too shy to take part in them. Until now.

"But, Terence, in a way, I kind of came to you by the magic of social media," Maude said.

"Yeah, Dad, if Maude hadn't blown up on PixeLight you'd never have heard of her." Ben piped up.

"True, but you know as well as I do that Soulville has scouts."

"Scouts who look for artists in the places that they know," Victoria pointed out. "They don't exactly go off the beaten paths."

"They may not, but Matt does. He goes off incognito and brings me interesting artists nobody's ever heard of."

"So, if I decide to create art in my room, like with clay," Ben said, folding his hands behind his head, "I'm still considered a professional artist."

"Nobody wants to see your ugly clay men, Ben." Jazmine threw a spoonful of rice at her brother. The rice grains struck his forehead and slid down his nose.

"Hey!" He launched another spoonful at her but she dodged it swiftly.

And just like that a food fight broke out at the table. Jazmine threw rice, Cynthia and Maude bits of chicken, and Ben crushed potatoes and catapulted them at Maude, while the adults called for order amid their own laughter.

Until the doorbell rang.

Ben flew out of his chair and dashed out of the dining room.

Maude heard the door open, and then Ben spoke.

"What are you doing here?" she heard him ask, and then she started with surprise when she recognized Matt's voice. "I'm going to the movies with your sisters."

And suddenly Matt was in the dining room.

Jazmine shook off the grains of rice that hung on her clothes and hugged him.

"If we're going to the movies, I want to see something fun, not too serious or dramatic."

Maude thought serious and dramatic weren't things she'd have ascribed to Matt's personality.

"How about that new vampire movie, *Vampire Love*?" he suggested.

"You mean the one in which you were supposed to play the lead but turned it down because you didn't want to damage your new and improved reputation as a serious artist?" Terence asked.

"Exactly," Matt answered, laughing.

Maude started to leave the dining room.

"Hey, Maude, you're coming with us, aren't you?" asked Cynthia.

Maude hesitated. She hadn't been to the movies in New York and had been dying to go with her new friends, but she certainly couldn't go if Matt was going to be there.

"No, I have work to do," she replied, refusing to look at Matt, even though she was very aware that his eyes were on her.

"Come on, Maude," said Victoria gently. "You deserve a break. You've been working hard these past three weeks."

"You should come," Matt insisted softly, a hint of guilt on his face.

Maude raised a wary eyebrow. Never would she spend her evening with someone so quick to pronounce judgment on her supposed spoiled upbringing.

Maude looked directly at him and said, "No, I have better things to do tonight. Maybe some other time."

Maude left, wondering if that was disappointment she'd seen on Matt's face. As she went up the stairs, she heard Jazmine ask, "So, are we going or what?"

"Yeah, let's go," Matt answered.

"Ben, you're cleaning up," Maude heard Terence order, followed by a series of whines from the youngest Baldwin.

When Maude heard the front door slam, she sighed in relief and went to the piano in her room, not wanting to acknowledge the small, creeping feeling of regret she had at not going to the movie with the others.

Ben interrupted her thoughts when he walked into the room a few minutes later.

"It's too bad you didn't go to the movies. I would've liked to go but Dad won't let me see a vampire movie after what happened last time. I covered my eyes during the whole thing but still had nightmares for weeks. Dad shouted at the girls for taking me to see a scary movie and they didn't talk to me for days. I don't think it's fair because I was only ten back then. Now I'm eleven."

"That makes all the difference," Maude said as seriously as she could, not wanting to hurt Ben's feelings. "Say, Ben. Tell me something. How close are Jazmine, Cynthia, and Matt?" she asked, feeling uneasily that this question somehow shouldn't pique her interest as much as it did.

"Oh, Matt's a part of the family now. We've known him for years, and he even lived with us for a while. He plays video games and watches anime and K-dramas with me when he comes. Hey, do you want to come play with me?"

Maude looked at the piano and back at Ben. There was no way she would be able to concentrate on her music after the evening she'd had.

"You know what, Ben? That's a great idea! Just give me ten minutes, then I'm all yours."

She waited until Ben left the room before plopping on her bed with the laptop the Baldwins were lending her.

In the Google search bar, she typed *Ma* but didn't need to go any further as a detailed list of suggestions instantly appeared.

Matt Girlfriends, Matt Mother. Matt Funeral. Matt Love Doctor Video, Matt Songs, Matt Albums, Matt Parties, Matt World Tour.

She wanted to know about one particular thing that Karl had mentioned.

But she hesitated. She really shouldn't be doing this. Curiosity wasn't a good trait. But who would know?

Maude clicked on *Matt Girlfriends.* A list of twenty out of over eighty million results appeared in less than a second. She scrolled rapidly down the page her eyes widening as she did so. *Matt and actress Toni Terrell in love. Matt having brunch with model Stella Madison two days after breakup with Toni Terrell. Matt and Tiana Henderson spotted together at US Open. Matt and Tiana Henderson break up.*

One article explained that Matt and Tiana had gone through

a very messy breakup after an equally messy seven-month relationship. Another then detailed his list of ex-girlfriends.

Albums, songs, collaborations, fights with the paparazzi, sightings, charities and fundraisers, hair gel endorsement, Hugo Boss commercial, jet-set parties. Maude browsed quickly through several articles and realized there was little Matt hadn't done, and none of it improved her opinion of him. He definitely was a wild child.

She had to stop!

Just maybe after she clicked on the suggestion *Matt Mother*, she decided.

She was about to click on the link when an article caught her attention.

Matt and Lindsey Linton.

Wait, Matt and Lindsey?

With an eagerness Maude felt half-ashamed about, she clicked on the title, but she never got to read it because Ben chose that exact moment to pop his head in.

"Mauuuude, are you coming?" he asked impatiently.

Startled, Maude slammed her laptop shut and jumped off her bed. She hadn't realized that ten minutes had turned into twenty, and she probably didn't *want* to read another article about Matt anyway. Especially if it involved Lindsey Linton.

"Sorry, Ben! I just got caught up. Let's go play video games. But you'll have to teach me how, okay?"

"Okay, but don't learn too fast because I really like winning against beginners," he admitted as they left the room.

Chapter Twelve

"So, how was *Vampire Love*?" asked Maude the next morning at breakfast, trying to maintain an air of dispassionate curiosity.

"Oh god, so funny!" Jazmine giggled as she fetched a bottle of orange juice from the fridge. "After being ambushed by a herd of crazy fans, we got in twenty minutes after the film started. As if that wasn't awkward enough, Matt criticized Jason Taylor, the lead, from the beginning to the end of the movie. We almost got kicked out. He's so silly! He did say he was looking forward to working with you next week, though. He's really sorry about what happened at Wild Garden, you know. He had no idea about your parents. He's the last person who'd take that lightly after the loss he suffered."

Maude nodded, thinking losing a girlfriend was not even close to losing two parents. "Speaking of men, I absolutely need your advice," Jazmine said.

"Yes, you have my blessing to date Brad," Maude said in a serious tone although her lips twitched. She was relieved to change the subject.

"This has nothing to do with Brad the Joker, as you called him."

"I said 'the joke' not 'the Joker.' Give me some credit."

"At any rate, it isn't about Brad. Do you remember Jonathan?"

"Tall, skinny Jonathan?" Maude asked.

Jazmine nodded, frowning.

"He auditioned?" Maude asked, astonished.

Jazmine nodded again.

"He actually managed to keep his guitar in his hands for the entire song?"

"I know, I know, he doesn't fit our look. He's got large, Harry Potter glasses. He's scrawny and looks like you could break him faster than a twig. He drops anything that comes into contact with his two left hands. However, when he plays, you could *almost* forget he looks like a complete nerd. Almost, but not quite. That's why we're hesitating to take him on."

"Were there other guitarists you would consider?"

"That's the thing. He was *the* best. He had a Jimi Hendrix vibe, you know."

"Then take him." Maude shrugged, not seeing what the problem was.

"That's what Cynth said, along with, 'physical beauty isn't everything, Jaz.' But it's not that simple." Jazmine sighed. "Matt was the only one who got it. He understood that even though Jonathan is a great guitarist, he also has to fit with the rest of the band. Especially as he would stand out as the only guy in our group."

Maude glowered. So not only was Matt a jerk, he was also a superficial narcissist.

"Look on the bright side, at least you know you could never fall for him. So he would probably last longer than all your other guitarists put together," she observed philosophically.

"You're right, Maude!" Jazmine exclaimed, a smile creeping across her face.

Just then, they heard a dreadful noise coming out of Ben's room. It was midway between a baby's bawling and a dying cat's last pleas.

"Oh god," Jazmine said, covering her ears. "It's started."

"What's started? *Torture*," Maude added in French. "Is someone torturing Ben? And us at the same time?"

"We have a tradition."

"Does it involve killing poor, innocent kittens?" Maude cringed as more noise echoed through the house.

"Not at all. During our eleventh year we have to experiment with all sorts of instruments and on our twelfth birthday we decide which one we feel the most comfortable with, the one that we can't part with. It's a tradition that Mom invented. She loves traditions, especially when they involve music. That's why Ben is torturing us with his bagpipes. Let's just hope he improves quickly."

"When is Ben's birthday?"

"In July. And in the meantime, we're going to hear a lot of different instruments."

July, Maude thought, her heart sinking. If she failed and had to go back to Carvin she wouldn't be there to see which instrument Ben had chosen.

"Hey, are you okay?" Jazmine asked, noticing Maude's face falling, her eyebrows knitting. "Don't worry, it won't be that bad. You can put in earplugs if you want. I'm sure that's what Cynthia's doing right now during her yoga session," she teased, and started to clear the table.

Maude smiled feebly but she couldn't get rid of that awful, gnawing feeling in her chest.

Chapter Thirteen

That night, after tossing and turning in her bed, Maude concluded that sleep wouldn't come.

She'd had a great three weeks with the Baldwins. How could the mention of July, when she would be returning to Carvin, disturb her that way? *If* she was returning.

When had she started to care? At what moment had she fallen in love with this city?

The end of January was approaching, but July was still far away, she tried to reassure herself. If her singles were a success she'd get to stay as long as she wanted. But how would she create three pop hits if constant fighting disrupted her collaboration with Matt? The deadline for their first single was fast approaching, and she was working on her own without any positive results.

She and Matt had to find a way to work together.

Maude slipped out of the room, went down the stairs, careful not to make any noise, and headed for the kitchen.

She was surprised to hear someone moving about. As she got closer she realized it was Victoria, making herself warm milk.

Maude hesitated, not wanting to disturb her.

Victoria was the person in the Baldwin family Maude knew the least. She had gossiped with Jazmine, chatted and played the piano with Cynthia and her violin, played video games with Ben, and spent countless hours with Terence learning about music. Victoria was another story.

Truthfully, Maude was somewhat intimidated by her. Victoria had a special aura, something Maude had never seen in anyone else. She was a strong woman unafraid of everything, who let nothing get in her way. The Baldwin matriarch was a women's rights advocate and ran an organization that fought for those rights. She had founded the group with her best friend, a lawyer named Nathalie Fern. The members, men and women, met once a month at the Baldwins' house to discuss issues, including the women's shelter Victoria had created eight years earlier.

Maude had heard Victoria speak at one of these meetings during her first week in the city, and had been in awe of, and a little intimidated by, her strong, assured tone, her recall of detailed facts, and her power of persuasion. Cynthia and Jazmine had beamed with pride at their mother, although they couldn't perceive it through the eyes of a newcomer the way Maude did. Victoria brought joy, jokes, and laughter to the household even while facing daily challenges at the shelter and in her work. Maude was amazed by her inner strength.

She was still debating whether she wanted to interrupt Victoria's midnight snack when the older woman turned around and spotted her.

She smiled and asked, "Having trouble sleeping too? Do you want some warm milk?"

"I don't want to disturb you."

"Nonsense. Come on in. I can't make hot cocoa like Terence does, but mine isn't too bad. Don't tell him I said that or he'll brag about all the things he does better than me. As if there were so many," Victoria added with a loving smile.

"You have to admit, he *is* a great . . . chef!" Maude triumphantly used a word she knew existed in both languages. "I've never eaten so many delicious meals in my entire life."

"That's a good thing, then. I told Terence he had to spoil you and fatten you up just right."

Maude laughed at Victoria's honesty, but then, she did have an appetite.

"Maude," Victoria started, "I don't want to be nosy, and you can absolutely tell me if I'm overstepping, but may I ask what happened to your parents?"

Maude looked down at her hands uneasily. "I don't know. Nobody's ever wanted to tell me who they were."

"Not even your foster parents? Why not?"

"I have no idea," Maude said. "I've asked them but they refused to tell me, so I gave up. All I know is that my father was a French-Nigerian man called Aaron Laurent."

"French-Nigerian? Interesting. I'm Nigerian-American."

"You're Nigerian?" Maude asked, astonished.

"From the Igbo people. My full name is Victoria Chioma Okafor. My relatives and Nigerian friends all call me by my Nigerian name, Chioma. My parents emigrated here before I was born, and my siblings and I grew up here."

"I read about the Igbo, the Yoruba, and the Hausa, and that there are over two hundred tribes in Nigeria. But I have no idea which one is mine."

"You can be an honorary Igbo if you'd like."

"I'd love to," Maude squealed. "Umm, how do I do that?"

"My dear Maude." Victoria cupped Maude's chin and

squeezed it affectionately. "Only you can define who you are. Don't let anyone else do that."

"Oh gosh, do you speak Igbo? Does Jazmine?"

"I speak it, but I didn't teach my children, much to my father's despair."

"Oh, that's too bad. Why didn't you teach them?"

"I was uncomfortable teaching them a language that Terence couldn't understand, though he was all for it." Victoria paused. "There were so many things we wanted to teach our children, so I made a choice. As parents we make choices all the while fearing that our kids might resent us in the future the same way we resent our parents for some of the choices they made."

"I always heard that children *understood* their parents when they in turn became parents."

"We understand more, but we don't always agree." Victoria laughed, then sighed. "If you knew how many things I still disagree with my father over. It's a real battle to decide what we want to teach, what our children *want* to learn, and what we have time to teach. I taught my kids other things: Igbo cuisine and dress, for example. They know exactly where their grandparents and all their ancestors came from. Terence and I created our own family traditions. I let them choose their instruments at twelve. Most importantly, I gave them a thirst for learning. Whatever they want to learn, they can and will, whether they're five or fifty. If and when they're ready to learn the Igbo language, they will."

"That makes sense."

"Your parents, they also did the best they knew how to, even if it was for a short time. Do you know that you can research information on your parents by contacting the French administration?"

"Sometimes I'm afraid that their deaths were so tragic that my foster parents didn't want to tell me. I wonder if—"

"—if not knowing is somehow better than hearing a truth that is too hard to bear," Victoria finished.

Something in Victoria's voice made Maude look up at her. For a split second she saw something in Victoria's eyes. It was the look of a suffering that had been too long suppressed and silenced, and could only be comprehended by another person who had suffered a similar anguish.

Victoria was the first to break the spell as she got up and poured another cup of hot chocolate.

"So Terence has taught you all about Motown's glory days, has he?" she asked, smiling.

Maude nodded. She was still puzzled by what Victoria had inadvertently revealed but she didn't want to appear nosy, so she refrained from probing.

"He and I differ on our tastes in music. Although I'm fond of soul and rhythm and blues, I have a particular taste for Nigerian and world music. Terence and I spent most of our lives in New York, but I only met him during my year abroad in Paris. That's how small the world is."

"In Paris! That's so romantic," Maude gushed. "Imagine this: you guys probably walked past each other here without knowing you were meant to be." She thought of Matt, a French boy she'd met in New York. Had they ever crossed paths in France? Not unless he'd ever been to Carvin.

"I've heard you play the udu, and it's a beautiful instrument." Maude hesitated. "I was wondering if you could teach me more about this drum and Nigerian music. Only if you have a little time. I know you must be very busy with your job and getting funding for the shelter and everything."

"I'll always have time for you, my dear Maude." Victoria smiled one of her dazzling smiles, and Maude looked at her gratefully.

"One of my friends has a Nigerian wedding coming up in the spring. By the time we get you to that wedding, I'll have taught you everything I know about traditional Igbo music."

Chapter Fourteen

The morning the results of the *Cenerentola* auditions were due, Maude woke just as the first rays of the winter sun sparkled over the Hudson River and dappled the dust-flecked Tribeca Bridge. With daylight, her tangled emotions resurfaced. She wanted the role so badly! Performing in front of a real audience—especially as Rossini's *Cenerentola*—would be a milestone.

But she also wanted to make Terence and Victoria proud. They had already given her so much. Clothes, food, kindness, and most importantly, a sense of belonging. Maude wanted to give back in the only way she knew how: by singing.

When she and Jazmine went to the theater that morning, she was determined to take the news with the bravery of a Viking and the stoicism of a Greek philosopher.

"If you don't get the part, we'll drown our sorrows in buckets of ice cream," Jazmine reassured her.

Maude nodded limply. She couldn't bring herself to speak.

As she got closer to the theater, the girls saw Thomas surrounded by a happy crowd.

Maude beamed.

"Thomas must have gotten the male lead! Let's go congratulate him!"

“Don’t you want to find out your role first?” Jazmine asked, hurrying behind her. Suddenly, a girl from her lessons cried out: “Maude! You’re the new Cinderella!”

Maude’s heart stopped for a full second. Could it be true? She ran over to the cast list posted on a cork bulletin board at the entrance of the theater.

Sure enough, her name was there. CINDERELLA: MAUDE LAURENT.

“Congratulations, Maude.” Jazmine hugged her tightly.

When she let go, Maude stepped back and bumped into someone. She whirled around to face a disgruntled Lindsey, who’d just seen her result. Maude turned back to see which part Lindsey had been given.

“‘Clorinda,’” Jazmine read out with a satisfied smile. “The role of the evil stepsister fits you perfectly, Lindsey. I see you’re also the understudy for Cinderella. Understudy!” Jazmine mocked.

“Jaz,” Maude said gently.

Faced with Lindsey’s confusion and discomfort, Maude couldn’t help but feel a creeping sympathy for the girl even though she had been nothing but mean to Maude since she had arrived. Lindsey remained silent for a moment. She appeared to be fighting back tears and rage at the same time. Her lower lip trembled for a split second. She straightened in an attempt at dignity and turned to Maude.

“You don’t deserve this part. You’ve been in Madame Tragent’s class for barely two minutes. Your voice is weak, your technique is next to none. You can’t act, you can’t sing, you barely manage to finish your vocal exercises!”

Maude’s budding sympathy instantly dissolved.

“You’re entitled to your opinion,” she conceded graciously. She was too happy to let Lindsey’s foul mood get to her.

"Maude deserves this part and you know it, Lindsey," Thomas said as he neared the small group.

"You should be grateful Madame Tragent even gave you a part at all," Jazmine added.

"She'll ruin the whole show, you'll see," Lindsey taunted. "Good thing I'll be there to pick up the pieces. Don't say I didn't warn you!" she called as she walked away.

"Don't listen to her, Maude," Thomas said.

"Lindsey can't rattle me." Maude laughed. "I guess congratulations are in order Mr. Prince Charming."

"Congratulations to you too. I'm sure we'll be great together," he replied. Maude nodded energetically, then searched for her phone.

She couldn't wait to tell Terence and Victoria.

Chapter Fifteen

Maude had never been on an actual date.

As she sat, tucked between Cynthia's knees on the floor of her room getting her hair braided, she had no idea if the nervousness lodged in the pit of her stomach was due to that or the fact that she had never received or given a real kiss.

There *had* been one instance, but it didn't count. At least not to Maude, and she wanted to erase it from her memory. It had been with Antoine in seventh grade. She'd had a major crush on him since the sixth grade, and when he told her he thought she was pretty and had asked her out of the blue if she wanted to be his girlfriend, she'd said yes. Maude had jumped up and down in her room for half an hour that same evening.

Well, their relationship lasted about a week, but she'd gotten her first kiss. At recess, on a Friday afternoon in the school cafeteria, after he'd eaten fried fish for lunch, he'd leaned toward her and kissed her. There had been a bit of tongue, some saliva, and quite a few smooching noises. Not at all the romantic first kiss Maude had dreamed of. She had been so disappointed that she had broken up with him two days later, after having avoided him for an entire day. She wondered if it was just him or if maybe she was a bad kisser.

"There, all done," Cynthia said as she put the final touches on Maude's hair.

Jazmine and Cynthia took a step back to admire their work. They had styled her hair into a Grecian-inspired braid, making Maude feel like one of the ancient goddesses she'd seen in the Louvre's antiquity wing.

"You look great." Jazmine sighed. "This unnamed boy you never mentioned won't know what hit him."

"It's too new and I don't know him too well yet. I don't want to jinx it."

"Simple but elegant. You look perfect," Cynthia chimed in.

"You're the best." Maude thanked Cynthia.

"Thank goodness Mom and Dad went out or they would've wanted a picture and Mom would've chatted with your date," Jazmine remarked.

"This date is no big deal," Maude insisted for the hundredth time. "He's going to show me around New York."

"And he invited you to a fancy restaurant," Cynthia added playfully. The girls dissolved in giggles until they heard the doorbell ring.

"That's your cue," Jazmine said.

"Hm, maybe I should go check out this young man," Cynthia said, wagging her finger.

"I think I should too. You know, check out his background, his family, their profession. And have *the* talk," Jazmine said, shaking her head.

"Don't you two dare!" Maude warned, giggling. "Just stay locked in this room. I don't want to see you peep."

She hurried downstairs and opened the door. Thomas stood there wearing a leather jacket and jeans, with his dark hair brushed back and sleek. She thought she'd never seen him look so handsome.

"Ready for our first stop?" Thomas asked.

Maude nodded and closed the door behind her. They walked to Battery Park, talking happily along the way.

Upon arrival, Maude and Thomas made their way through the crowd to buy tickets for the ferry.

"We're all set. Follow me," he called, waving two tickets. Hundreds of people crowded onto the ferry, and Maude followed Thomas to the upper deck.

"I hope you don't get seasick," he said, leaning on the rail.

"I have no idea." Like so many things in Maude's life right now, this was a first.

"So tell me, what's it like working at Soulville?"

Maude thought she perceived a flash of envy in his eyes. As soon as it appeared, it dissolved, leaving her to wonder if she'd imagined it.

"It's amazing. I mean,"—she was about to mention how irritating Matt was but held back. Somehow it seemed inappropriate to talk about him on her first date with another boy—"it's a bit difficult, getting used to so many new things but it's still cool. You should come visit one day."

"I don't think they'd want me there."

"Why not? You're so talented, I'm sure it's just a matter of time. Maybe work on your social media. Cynthia insists it's *très important*," Maude added in French. "I'm not very good at it yet. Thank goodness she's patient."

"But the execs, they pressure you to deliver."

"Some. Like Alan. He acts like my mere presence bothers him."

"I'm going to tell you something," Thomas said, changing the subject. "This is the first time in five years that I've gone to the Statue of Liberty."

"Really? You don't do this every week?"

"Did you go to the Eiffel Tower every day?"

"I didn't live in Paris. If I had, I'd have gone up the tower every day! Even twice a day."

"Would that be before or after school?"

Maude relented. "Hm, I see your point. Didn't you grow up here?"

"Nah, my family moved here from Chicago because of me. My parents always believed I'd be a star. When I wanted to be in a commercial at five, they encouraged me to do it. My mom took me to a gazillion auditions."

"What was your first commercial then?"

"Milk. What else? At that age it wasn't going to be a car commercial."

"Maybe a bumper-car commercial."

"Then I took my first singing class, and I knew I preferred singing to acting. When I signed with a big New York agency, my family followed."

"It's great that you have all that support."

"It's a double-edged sword. I'm lucky, but at the same time, I feel pressure to succeed because I don't want their sacrifices to be in vain."

"I'm sure they'd never see it like that."

"But I would." His eyes grew somber. "Anyway, I shouldn't be saying that to someone who lost both her parents when she was little."

It seemed like he wanted to know about her parents, but

Maude couldn't bring herself to say anything more. Besides, she knew very little about him and wanted to know more. Why spoil the day talking about death?

The horn blared loudly, announcing the ferry's departure. Maude leaned against the rail to watch the boat slowly move away. She breathed in happily, and the sea air filled her lungs. She closed her eyes for a moment then opened them again and peered at the water, the waves joyfully crashing against the boat as the wind murmured in her ear, accompanying a seagull's laugh.

"Look," Thomas called, wrenching her from her train of thought.

Maude lifted her eyes to take in the beauty of the Statue of Liberty as the ferry approached Liberty Island.

The regal statue stood on a pedestal, her body draped in a simple but majestic coppered toga and with a determined look on her face. Her crown and torch glistened in the soft morning sun.

Maude had rarely felt such excitement surge through her as she climbed the narrow staircase to the top of the statue, halting only to catch her breath. Thomas seemed amused by her enthusiasm.

When she arrived at the crown, Maude stopped, stunned. Although the air was chilly, a warm glow filled her as she took in the magnificent view. The city in all its splendor spread out before her, separated by the water but still so close she could almost reach out to it.

"It's gorgeous."

"Let's take a selfie!" Thomas said.

Maude obliged and smiled while he put his arm around her and raised his other arm. He snapped the photo and asked, "Can I post it?"

Maude internally debated. She wasn't sure why she wanted to keep this wonderful moment private, then thought better of it. Cynthia did want her to be more social-media friendly.

"Okay," Maude said. She turned back to the view, hardly believing how lucky she was to be there.

She hummed the music to "Un soave non so che" from *La Cenerentola.*

Suddenly she felt the urge to sing in this beautiful setting, and she couldn't refrain from quietly singing the first words that came to her mind, the lyrics of *La Cenerentola* Act I.

"What is this fond alarm?

"Why does my heart beat so wildly?"

She felt Thomas stand close behind her. He joined in, singing almost inaudibly, but Maude could hear every word, and it sent delicious shivers down her spine as she felt his breath on her neck.

"I well could tell, but that I dare not speak."

Maude turned to face him and they continued almost whispering the words, looking at each other with longing.

"I fain would speak, but vainly strive:

"A nameless charm no art can give

"Breathes in each feature of that face

"How dear the smile that there I trace!"

She intuited the following events before they happened. Weirdly, at that moment, she couldn't explain why, but she thought of Matt. Just as quickly, he vanished from her mind. Thomas leaned over and kissed her. His big hands gently framed her face and as their lips met, Maude thought her legs would give way. She raised her hands and ran them through his hair slowly, as her heart beat like an udu drum. She felt his tongue on hers, and she could taste fresh mint. He wrapped his arms around her waist and pulled her closer, and she could feel his heart beating just as fast as hers. They let go of one another, still holding each other's gaze.

"Wow," was all she was able to say.

"The magic of the Statue of Liberty," Thomas murmured.

Maude could only agree. Her phone vibrated. Her jaw dropped when she saw she'd received a text message from Matt. Talk about timing. Did he suspect what she'd just done?

She opened the message and read it.

Huge breakthrough. Can you come in now?

"It's Matt. *Il dit*, erm, he says he had a breakthrough and he wants me to come right away." Maude bit her lower lip, uncomfortable. It was a bad idea to see Matt now. The fact that his face had crept into her mind right before her kiss with Thomas disturbed her. Bad idea, for sure. Yet she was dying to see Matt. It was just curiosity about the song, she was certain.

"No problem! You should go," Thomas said.

"*Tu peux*, erm, you can come with me if you'd like!" she stammered, flustered.

"Oh, I don't want to bother you."

"Come on, I'll show you where I work."

"Nah, it's fine, you do you," Thomas insisted. "This is, after all, just the beginning."

Chapter Sixteen

When Maude arrived in Matt's Creation Room, she experienced a tiny frisson at the sight of him, his head bent over his guitar. He wore an oversized blue printed shirt with sleeves she knew he rolled up with frustration when the inspiration didn't flow in the manner he wanted. She wondered what it'd feel like to be held in his arms the way he cradled his guitar, to be touched and caressed the way he strummed the guitar strings. He raised his head, and the movement brought Maude's daydreams to a halt.

Having just kissed Thomas, she thought she shouldn't wonder what Matt's lips felt like as he slid a guitar pick from between his teeth.

"Thanks for coming," he said, getting up from his orange sofa.

"I always put music before everything else," Maude replied stiffly.

"Look, I wanted to apologize about what happened last week. Jazmine told me about your parents. I'm so sorry I said you were spoiled."

Maude could tell he meant what he was saying, and something in her relented. What a difference an apology made!

"I guess, you couldn't know," Maude replied. "Just, maybe, you shouldn't make assumptions. Not everybody grows up with a mom and a dad, you know."

Matt avoided her gaze, and Maude assumed the cause of his discomfort resided in his mea culpa. But then she saw the sadness on his face. She puzzled over this until he turned back to her and flashed a quick smile.

"I wanted to show you something. I've been working like crazy this past week on three new songs: 'Leaving You Behind,' 'Reckless,' and my favorite one so far, 'Sunrise.' Take a look at the score."

She took the sheet of music, relieved to change the subject and think about something else. She quickly surveyed the score and her face softened as she read the lyrics. She steadied her breath and sang.

"You're so peaceful while you sleep

"I could watch you for a lifetime

"Immersed in a slumber so deep

"You don't hear the clock chime

"But suddenly daylight appears

"The rays of light dance on your skin

"Your morning smile chases away my fears

"With you, the shadows can't win."

Maude stopped and faced Matt.

"It's beautiful," she whispered.

"I was inspired when I wrote it," he said softly, his serious gray eyes resting on her. "Remember that morning you were practicing *La Cenerentola* here in the sunlight? I used that and, you know, extrapolated."

Maude bit her lower lip. *She* had inspired *him*?

"So I'm like your muse. Is that what you're saying?"

"Of course." Matt shrugged. "When I work with an artist, I'll use what I know about them to write a song. Just to make sure the song fits."

"Oh yeah. Of course," Maude mumbled.

"This song would be perfect for a mix of classical and pop. The arrangement could be you at the piano, a very classical piano solo, and the pop will be in your singing."

"I like that idea. Let's try it."

For the next few hours Maude and Matt worked on the piano, scratched the score, scribbled over it, and added new lyrics. It was a wonderful moment, full of playfulness, hard work, concentration, and with the undeniable satisfaction they were at last making some progress!

When the sun set over Times Square's messy exuberance, the two felt satisfied with the result and gave a sigh of exhausted relief.

"We finally have our first song to present to Terence," Matt said, stretching his legs across the orange sofa. "Let's order take-out to celebrate. I mean, unless you'd rather go home."

"I'm starving! Could we order Nigerian food? Victoria made this stew the other day called *egusi*, and I can't stop eating it."

"Victoria's egusi is the best."

"You've tasted it? Oh right, Ben said something about you being like family."

"Aw, that's sweet of him. I'm pretty sure he said that after I let him win our last round of video games."

"That boy is such a bad sport." Maude laughed. "I'll order." She took out her phone and saw she had a notification from her PixeLight app.

Matt came up behind her. "Could you order from the restaurant Igbo Kwenu? I'll show you, they've got great food."

Maude opened up the PixeLight app and gasped as the selfie of her and Thomas burst onto her screen.

"Erm, is that you and Thomas Bradfield?" Matt asked.

She swiftly turned away from him.

"You know Thomas?"

"I do," he said softly. "And I don't know how to say this without sounding like a jerk, but I don't think you should hang out with him." He ran his hand through his hair with a sigh of frustration.

Maude frowned, puzzled. "Why would you say such a thing?"

"Are you seeing each other?"

"It's very recent. Like today recent. We went out—"

"Today? You were with him *today*? What? Why? What do you see in that guy?"

"That's none of your business," Maude spluttered, indignant. "You don't get to say, 'I don't mix business and pleasure, but you don't get to date anyone else in the entire city.'"

"Is that why you're with him? Because of what I said?"

Maude realized that the true reason for her anger resided in the fact that Matt had not only firmly closed any possibility of anything happening between them but was also sabotaging any chance that she'd have with Thomas. He couldn't suspect that she'd had a mild, *extremely* mild, interest in him.

"Get over yourself for a *minute*!" Maude flung the last word in French. She steadied her breath. She wasn't going to slip back into French now or he'd know she was thrown off by his assertion. "I like Thomas. He's the opposite of you. I wouldn't date you if you were the last guy on earth."

Matt recoiled, and she could tell her words had stung.

"What did Thomas tell you about Soulville?" Matt asked, cuttingly.

"Only that it must be a dream to work here."

"He almost signed with Soulville, Maude."

"So what? What does that have to do with me?"

"They didn't sign him because Soulville signed *you*. Let's just say at the time, Thomas didn't take it too well."

"You're lying," she said in disbelief.

"Why would I lie?" Matt rubbed his face tiredly.

"I don't know. I just . . . I need to hear it from him."

"He hid it from you. Now he's posting about the two of you. He's using you to build his brand."

"I told him he could use that selfie," Maude countered. "I just didn't think he'd tag me. Listen, you and me, we work together. But you don't get to comment on my love life."

"I'm just saying you should be careful."

"You know what? I'm not hungry anymore," Maude said, though her growling stomach said otherwise.

And with that, she took her coat and marched out of the room.

• • •

"Your fingers are numbered from one to five, your thumb being number one," Maude explained that evening. "Hand position is essential. Don't slouch your fingers like that. Imagine you're holding a ball. Lower your wrist," Maude indicated gently.

Maude was giving an impatient Ben his first piano lesson. No matter how badly her day went, Maude always felt that spending time with the cheeky little boy was the answer to all her problems. Including her own boy problems.

They were both seated on the stool in front of her white Yamaha, and Ben was trying his hardest not to press all the keys at once.

“Say, Maude, when will I be able to play Beethoven and Chopin like you?”

“You’ll need a lot of practice. It won’t happen overnight.”

Ben sighed.

“What’s wrong?” Maude asked, concerned.

“No instrument suits me,” Ben explained.

“You haven’t tried enough instruments to give up.”

“My sisters knew which ones they wanted, almost like they were magically drawn to them. They mastered their instruments in no time.”

“That may be. However, for us mere mortals it takes time and a lot of practice. You still have months to make your choice.”

“What if I don’t find the right one?”

“I’m sure your parents won’t mind if you choose an instrument later. Your choice mustn’t keep you from loving other instruments. Take Victoria for example. She plays the udu and a lot of other types of percussion.”

“I want to feel the way you feel about piano. Your eyes light up every time you spot a piano, and you spend hours on this stool. When did you start playing?”

“When I was eleven,” Maude mused. “I guess I was following your tradition without even knowing it. I didn’t have access to many other instruments except for the recorder, which is the only thing we learned to play at school. You’re very lucky, Ben.”

Ben’s shoulders drooped. He obviously didn’t think he was lucky.

“Maybe you should broaden your search,” Maude suggested. “You’ve only tried instruments you already know. The world is a big place. You should try something completely new, without inhibitions or preconceived ideas.”

Ben's eyes lit up suddenly, and he jumped off the stool.

"Thanks, Maude!" he cried, hugging her tight.

"What about that piano lesson?" she called as he made a beeline for the door.

"No need!" he answered.

Maude sighed. She wasn't much of a teacher anyway. For a minute there, she thought she'd sounded just like a younger version of Mme. Tragent.

Chapter Seventeen

Maude waited for Thomas before the *Cenerentola* rehearsal the next day. She hadn't stopped thinking about the PixeLight post.

She'd messaged him the previous evening asking him to remove the tag, but she needed to see him when she asked about what Matt had said. If they were face to face she would be able to judge the sincerity of his words.

However, the little courage she possessed faltered when she saw him stride in with Lindsey.

"Oh, hey, Maude, I didn't see you there," Lindsey said snidely. "See you later, Thomas."

Lindsey sauntered away, and Thomas stole a kiss from Maude. Before he could prolong it into something more, she took his arms off her waist and said, "I need to talk to you." Her tone sounded firmer than her resolve. She had thought long and hard about what to say and how to say it properly in English without sounding overly emotional.

"What's wrong? You look worried. I untagged you like you asked."

"That's not the problem. Matt said something yesterday."

"Oh, I know where this is heading." Thomas sighed, digging his hands into his jean pockets.

"Why didn't you tell me you'd almost signed with Soulville?" Maude asked. "That it was because of me that you didn't?"

"Because I got over it, Maude."

"Matt said you took it pretty badly."

"Of course he did. I'm sure that guy likes you."

"He doesn't," Maude insisted. Thomas scoffed in response. "This has nothing to do with him. You should've been honest with me."

"I'll be honest now. Yes, I took it badly. *At the time*. But then I met you and I really liked you. You're amazing. And I didn't want you to think that I was a loser. Or for you to pity me. Or to feel guilty. Not when you completely deserve this."

Maude inhaled. Thomas sounded sincere, and she could tell he felt awful.

"Look, if you don't want us to date after this, I totally get it."

"That's not what I said," Maude said gently. Her doubt crumbled when she saw his sad face. He seemed truly vulnerable and upset. Unlike Matt, who never took a break from showing off.

"I forgive you. But just don't keep secrets like that again. I was going on and on about Soulville." Maude buried her face in her hands. "You should've told me to stop! I'll spare your feelings from now on."

"I want you to have everything you deserve. I'll get to the top on my own, you'll see."

"I believe in you."

Maude kissed him and together they headed to the stage to rehearse scene four of the first act.

Maude loved this act. It was the one where Cinderella and Prince Charming met though neither knew who the other was. The Prince was dressed as a valet, Cinderella in rags. It was love at first sight! The Prince was struck by Cinderella's beauty, grace, and simplicity. He wanted to know more about her, her family, her name. But she told him that she didn't know who she really was, that the baron wasn't her father, and that her family history was complicated and incomplete.

Maude and Thomas made a great couple. Thomas's agile tenor perfectly entwined with Maude's warm mezzo-soprano as they sang of love and enchantment.

When the rehearsal ended, Maude was surprised to see Matt sitting in the fifth row of the theater.

She hurried off the stage and stopped in front of him.

"What are you doing here?" she asked, trying to appear nonchalant, though she felt anything but.

"Relax, I'm not stalking you."

"If you must know, Thomas explained everything."

"I'm sure he did. I wish you all the happiness in the world." Matt's lips curled in a humorless smile.

"Great," Maude quipped. "You don't need to check up on me. I'm not selling him Soulville secrets. So you can go."

"I told you, I'm not here to see you." Before Maude could protest any further, Matt said, "Hi, Aunt Cordelia. I'm not late this time."

Confused, Maude followed Matt's eyeline.

Aunt Cordelia?

Maude was even more surprised when she turned around. Sure enough Mme. Tragent was standing there. Her face broke into something resembling a smile, perhaps a little rusty after having gone unused for a long time.

However, she appeared delighted to see her nephew as she hugged him and kissed him warmly on both cheeks.

"You two are related?" Maude asked, astounded.

"You're lucky to be working with two members of our extremely talented family, isn't she, Mathieu?"

"Mathieu? How ordinary." Maude laughed, while Matt grimaced.

"You thought his name was Matt? His full name is Mathieu Durand. I refuse to call him anything else."

"Thanks, Auntie. Really, you should just tell her all my childhood secrets while you're at it. You're the only person who still calls me that," Matt said, a little embarrassed.

"You'll have to excuse me, Mathieu. The costume designer isn't doing a single thing right. I must keep a close eye on her."

Mme. Tragent hurried away.

Mathieu Durand and Cordelia Tragent. What a family, Maude thought, amused.

"It's great to see you smile," Matt observed. "Don't worry, I'll stay out of your personal life. We work well together. I don't want to ruin that."

Maude nodded.

"Oh, look who's here," Matt said.

Maude swiveled around just as Thomas strode up to them, slinging his bag over his shoulder.

"Maude, you ready to go?" He wrapped a protective arm around her shoulders. Though he spoke to Maude, his eyes never left Matt's face.

"Sure!" Maude chirped with forced cheerfulness.

"Matt, how you doing?"

"Me? Fine. Maude and I have been really busy. What about you? No hard feelings about not signing with Soulville?" Matt taunted him.

Maude closed her eyes. Was civility an extinct notion?

"Before you go any further," Thomas interrupted, "I just want to make it clear that I'm not using Maude. In fact, I'll keep her out of my social media from now on. No one needs to know we're dating. Except you, I guess."

"That's absolutely none of my business anymore."

Maude smiled, hoping to diffuse the animosity. "Have a great time with your aunt, Matt."

Matt only nodded, glaring at Thomas. Maude could feel his eyes boring a hole in her back until they left the theater.

Chapter Eighteen

“The udu is a very popular instrument among the Igbo people,” Victoria said, picking up a pear-shaped drum that resembled, well, an ordinary clay water pitcher.

“I started researching the udu and read it’s now used all over the world. Like in reggae and other Western musical styles,” Maude commented.

“It’s true.” Victoria nodded. It was clear that she loved to pass on her knowledge and was pleased to see Maude so enthusiastic about learning to play.

“Now, about sound. People often wrongly think that beating a drum just means slapping your hands on it as hard as you can. That isn’t true. Technique is just as crucial as it is for any other instrument, like the piano for example.”

“Who taught you to play the udu?” Maude asked.

“My mom, when I was a little girl.” Victoria caressed the base of the instrument. “She explained that the udu is first and foremost a household item. It looks like a water jug, doesn’t it? That’s what it initially is. But the instrument has an additional hole right here.”

Victoria put her palm over the hole in the middle of the udu, then struck it, eliciting a low bass sound.

Maude watched as Victoria struck the udu's hole and its body alternately with her palm and four fingers, excluding the thumb.

"The udu is held in place by the legs, while you sit down. A bit like when you have your hair braided by Cynthia!"

Maude did a double thumbs-up. She liked Victoria so much she wondered what it would have been like to grow up with a woman like her in her life.

"You hold the top of the instrument with your left hand. Let me demonstrate."

Maude watched Victoria strike with palm and fingers on the hole, the center, and the bottom of the drum. She altered her hand position on different parts of the drum in a fast and complex rhythmic pattern. The rapid smacking at times reminded Maude of footsteps beating an unpaved road, and other times they imitated the sound of raindrops on a window. Victoria's love for her country reverberated in the instrument she played with calm concentration and a loving smile.

"Why did your family move to America?" Maude ventured to ask once Victoria had stopped. "You seem to love Nigeria so much, I can't understand why your family would want to leave."

Victoria's gaze drifted.

"Have you ever heard of the Biafran War?" she asked. "It's also called the Nigerian Civil War."

Maude shook her head. History was one of her favorite subjects: the French Revolution, Louis XIV. But aside from French history, she didn't know much. She was certain she'd never heard of that war.

"It was a terrible conflict that took place in Nigeria in 1967. My parents fled the war and came here before I was born," Victoria explained, her voice sounding distant.

Maude regretted having forced her into painful memories, and couldn't bear the thought of war. She shuddered involuntarily and looked at Victoria, wondering if her veiled sadness stemmed from the Biafran War.

"The war has been over for decades," Victoria continued. "But my life is here now. I grew up in Brooklyn, but in a Nigerian home. There are so many cultures jumbled up inside me and my siblings sometimes I wonder if we're not a tribe all on our own. When I go to Nigeria I feel at home because there's a link there to my parents. But the home that I choose to live in is here with my family. That's my new tribe."

Maude smiled. How many cultures lived inside her? She was dying to know.

"Now take your udu," Victoria said. "It won't play itself, you know!" she said in an attempt at lightheartedness.

Maude looked at Victoria adoringly and picked up her udu with a renewed sense of admiration. There wasn't a thing this woman couldn't overcome.

Chapter Nineteen

In Soulville's boardroom tensions were running high.

Terence, Alan, Matt, Maude, and Cynthia sat around an oval table. Behind them, through the large windows, snow fell over the skyscrapers. What wouldn't Maude give to be building a snowman instead of listening to Alan rant about "Sunrise"?

"We think that 'Sunrise' would make a great pop debut single for Maude," Alan said.

"No, you and Travis think that. Maude's initial version is a nice mix of classical and pop," countered Terence.

And as if Maude wasn't even in the room, Alan replied, "There's just too much piano on top of her singing, which is extremely melodic. We don't want an opera aria here."

Maude sat next to Matt and felt a huge lump of disappointment in her throat.

"We could take the piano solo out," Matt insisted. "But if we put her in a completely pop category nobody will recognize her as the girl from the video."

"Look, I'm really starting to like pop," Maude intervened. "But when I came, you said I could keep part of what made me classical." She couldn't help but feel a certain pride at having enunciated her thoughts in such clear English despite the intimidating setting.

Cynthia spoke up. "We've got some great publicity offers either way."

"Terence made a promise that he can't keep," Alan said. He had brushed part of his hair to the side to cover a bald spot, and the wrinkles around his mouth deepened with distaste. "Travis and I have both put our foot down."

"I'm CEO," Terence pointed out.

"But you're also co-chairman and you've got to answer to the board."

Terence put his hands under his chin thoughtfully.

"I'd like to speak with Maude alone please."

Matt gave Maude a thumbs-up sign as he left to encourage her.

The room cleared, and Terence turned to Maude. "I'd like *your* opinion on your piece and how you've been feeling about your stay in New York now that it's been over a month since you arrived."

"To be honest, at first I wasn't sure how much I'd like New York," Maude began. "But I like it very much. I love living with your family, and I've learned so much."

"That's great. But how do you feel—really feel—about popular music?"

"Well, I still love classical, but I think maybe I should learn more about pop. Motown is great, and electro, and Jazmine's rock." Maude smiled. "But I'm just not as comfortable as I feel I should be. I'm still working on singing it with Madame Tragent."

"Maude, I believe that you're just at the beginning. You're

making amazing progress, but if you hide behind your love for classical, you'll never discover your full potential."

"Maybe I'm just not meant to be more open minded. Maybe I'm just meant to be an amazing opera singer, and I should focus on that?" Maude wasn't sure what to feel. She stared at the snow as it fluttered past the boardroom windows.

"In the Baldwin family we believe that the more open minded you are, the greater you'll be. Just like you've opened your heart to Igbo music—"

"But that's because I've learned my father was Nigerian."

"How do you know your father didn't love popular music as well?"

Maude leaned back in her chair and raised her eyes to the ceiling. "*Bien vu*," she conceded, slipping into French.

"It doesn't matter if he did or didn't. Though I'm sure he was a smart man who must have loved Motown, just like me."

"Terence!" Maude giggled. "No one can love Motown like you do."

"You have a unique opportunity to be with a record label who will allow you to grow. Who wants you to grow. You've got three singles to release. Give yourself room to explore. By the time your six months are over you'll have grown in so many ways you'll hardly remember why you were so closed off to pop."

Terence's voice was so soft and caring that Maude could only nod.

"*Oui*, you're right. But if I have to tell Alan Lewis that he's correct, you owe me."

"Name your price. I'll take care of Alan."

"You have to teach me to prepare an Igbo dish."

"Only if you eat it with your hand."

"What if I do half and half? Half with spoon, half with hand. Then can you teach me to make an Igbo dish?"

"Which one?" Terence relented.

"*Akpu* with *ogbono* soup. Victoria says yours is better than hers!"

"When has Vic ever lied?" Terence said with a twinkle in his eye.

Chapter Twenty

"You're so peaceful while you sleep

"I could watch you for a lifetime

"Immersed in a slumber so deep

"You don't hear the clock chime."

It was Maude's first recording session, and she was to play the piano arrangement for their first track, "Sunrise." She was alone in the live room, but through the large glass window she could see Terence, Matt, and Sam, the sound engineer, listening. She'd spent hours practicing this melody and knew it by heart. She could play it with her eyes closed. She barely tensed when she saw Alan enter the control room to oversee the recording, although he knew next to nothing about recording an album. He watched her for a few minutes before leaving with a smirk on his face. She knew he was only there to make a statement: he wanted Maude to understand that he was keeping an eye on his investment.

"Time to take a break. After the break you'll play the bridge again, but a little slower," Terence said into the microphone.

Maude headed to Matt's Creation Room. Luckily, he wasn't there. Things were still a little tense between them.

As she walked over to her favorite spot by the window, she bumped her foot on one of his boxes.

Maude decided it was time to move it. The box was heavy and sealed tight, but when she picked it up, the cardboard ripped underneath, and everything inside fell out.

"No!" Maude cried in anguish.

She peered at the contents, which consisted of women's clothing, boots, and shoes. Whoever they belonged to had quite an unconventional taste. *Artsy*, Maude thought. Green leather boots and purple taffeta shirts.

They must belong to his ex, she thought with a pang. He had kept all these items lovingly.

She sealed the bottom and hurried to put the items back inside. In went shoes, dresses, and books. Just as she was about to stuff in the last few items, the door swung open.

Matt stood there. His face went from shock to anger in a split second. She'd never seen him this furious.

"What are you doing with my stuff?" He marched to the box and hurled the remaining things inside.

"I was just moving the box and—"

"I told you not to touch it!"

"I keep bumping into it. Everything just fell."

"Why couldn't you just leave my stuff alone?"

"I'm sorry. Seriously. I really didn't touch your girlfriend's stuff on purpose. I just—" Maude shoved the last boot into the box, got up, and hurried to the door.

"That wasn't my ex-girlfriend's stuff." Matt's voice stopped her. "That was my mom's."

Maude turned around slowly. She took a step in his direction.

"You mean that your mom . . ."

"She passed away seven months ago."

"That's why you took a break." Maude realized her error. That was why the suggestion *Matt Mother* had appeared in her search. Oh, why hadn't she clicked on that one instead of cyberstalking his exes?

"A break, a sabbatical. Call it whatever you want," Matt said.

"Oh, Matt, I . . ."

She couldn't express just how sorry she was, so she did the only thing she felt appropriate in the situation. She rushed to him and hugged him. He stiffened in surprise, then relaxed and wrapped his arms around her. Squeezing him tighter, she felt oddly comforted herself, and like she didn't want to let him go.

He released her with a sad smile.

"Those were her favorite things. My father wanted to throw them out or give them away. But I couldn't. So it's all here. Including her notebooks. I'm trying to read them to understand what she was like before I was born. Before she met my father. It's just a lot of musical stuff. I have so many questions. And I don't know, she's no longer here to answer them. My father and I aren't speaking. It just seems futile." Matt sank to the floor.

"I get that completely, believe me." Maude kneeled next to him. "The Baldwins don't know this, but the main reason I came to New York was because I learned my father had lived here. I came even though I don't know a thing about him except that he was called Aaron Laurent. I have no idea where to look for him. I have so many questions! I feel like if I discover everything about Nigerian culture and New York, I might understand who he was." They looked at each other and smiled sad smiles.

"You know, if your father was here sixteen years ago—" Matt started.

"Almost seventeen."

"Yeah, seventeen, then he might have hung out in this really cool place I know in Brooklyn called the Landmark. The owner is Nigerian. He's Yoruba."

"Oh. I have no idea who my people are, so I'm definitely open."

"There are lots of Nigerians there, just about everyone who enjoys good music. It's been around for decades. We could go together if you'd like? I mean, if Thomas . . ."

"Thomas doesn't care who I hang out with. And it wouldn't matter if he did," she said gently.

The sun shone brightly through the window as they looked at each other, their faces inches apart.

Just then, there was a knock on the door and they both jumped. Sam's head popped in.

"Maude? Break's over. You ready?" he asked.

"Coming!"

Sam left, closing the door behind him.

She got back to her feet and helped Matt up.

"You'll keep all this to yourself?" Matt asked anxiously. "The Baldwins will worry if they learn I'm hoarding. I really need to go through all her stuff. But I'm not ready yet."

"Definitely. No one will know. My lips are sealed," Maude said, locking her lips with an invisible key, throwing it away, and then imitating it floating in the Hudson River.

"Thank you, but you might want to unlock those lips. You have to go sing."

Maude laughed, and together they went back to the recording studio.

Chapter Twenty-one

Maude and Thomas trudged through the snow in Central Park. Despite being surrounded by beautiful scenery, Maude was worried her feet would turn into two blocks of ice if they walked much farther. Carvin winters were rough, but this was something else entirely. However, Carvin didn't have the same, picturesque beauty that Central Park did.

"Why does Red Eagle Energy Drink want me to make a live PixeLight video from Central Park?" Maude wailed. "In winter? This isn't a good idea."

"It's their winter edition drink," Thomas said. "It's the perfect moment to do it. Plus, we get to do it in a cool spot."

"I still don't know where you're taking me."

"Don't you like surprises?"

"I'm just curious. This alley is breathtaking," Maude said, admiring the view as a shiver of delight ran down her spine.

"It's called the Mall," Thomas informed her. "Pretty practical, huh?"

"What an awful name for such a lovely place!" Maude remarked, shaking her head in disapproval.

The name was lifeless and unimaginative in comparison to

the reality. The bare elms, dressed in a white robe of ice crystals, formed an enchanting tunnel resembling a pathway to an elfin world. Whispering secrets, the snow-draped branches entwined amorously in a wide, cathedral-like canopy. The coarse, dark bark wrinkled with centuries-old wisdom eyed the few pedestrians in solemn silence.

"I'll just give this pathway another name," Maude decided. "Whispering Walkway will be its new name because if you listen closely enough, the trees' rustling sounds like a murmur."

"I now baptize this path the Whispering Walkway!" Thomas declared in a serious tone. "A path fit for a queen."

Maude glanced at Thomas, expecting to find an amused glint in his eye. Surprised when she found none, she kissed him.

"What's that for?" he asked.

"For making work so much fun."

Thomas returned her kiss until they were in danger of forgetting that they were on a mission. Eventually, they continued their path through the snow in happy silence.

"You've got to be kidding me!" Maude exclaimed when they reached their destination.

Before her was the biggest ice-skating rink she had ever seen. The Wollman Rink wasn't very crowded, but nevertheless, Maude eyed it suspiciously.

"We should go back home."

"Are you scared?" he teased.

Maude remained resolutely silent, a worried look on her face.

"You don't know how to ice skate, is that the problem?" he asked with a look of genuine concern.

Maude shook her head.

"You're in luck!" he exclaimed. "Not only are you with the best boyfriend in the city, but you're also with an excellent ice-skating instructor. I *never* fall. Come on!"

Reluctantly, Maude followed him to get their skates, wondering uncomfortably how she would ever manage to stay on her feet without looking like a complete fool.

No one has ever gone ice skating for the first time without falling flat at least a dozen times, and Maude, although willing herself to remain in a vertical position, was no exception. She cried out, surprised, each time she returned to the horizontal position of failure. She admired Thomas's ease, skating as if he were the sole contestant in his very own Winter Olympics. Hearing his hearty laughter every time she fell flat on her butt did not help her improve.

"Laugh all you want," Maude said hotly, rubbing her knees after her hundredth fall. And she hadn't even left the edge of the rink yet!

"I can't help it! You're so cute when you fall," he said playfully. "I should let you fall just for the fun of it."

Maude rolled her eyes. He really was full of it.

"Come on, Maude," he coaxed, stifling his smile. "Just take my hand and slide away."

"I'm fine here, thanks," Maude replied, clinging for dear life to the wall that surrounded the rink.

"I never thought you were a coward," he dared her.

He hadn't explicitly used the word *chicken*, but he might as well have. Maude's eyes flashed as she straightened immediately, raising her head with all the dignity she could muster. She eyed his outstretched hand.

"If you let me fall . . ." she warned.

"I won't," he promised.

Their hands locked. Maude's heart thumped loudly in her chest as Thomas pulled her slowly away from the edge. It wasn't too bad. It was even kind of fun. Before she knew it, she was circling the rink again and again, thanks to Thomas's firm grasp helping her stay upright.

"Okay, good," he said after some time. "I'm going to let go of your hand, but you have to stand *straight and fearless*, okay? Just follow my lead."

Maude nodded and followed his instructions. Straight and fearless, she repeated to herself. In no time she was an independent skater, moving with a certain grace and remaining on her feet. *He's not a bad instructor*, she thought happily. *Excellent* was perhaps a tad hyperbolic, but he was *okay*.

He was an excellent show-off, though.

While she circled the rink, he demonstrated his skills, skating forward and backward quickly, even going as far as throwing in a few jumps.

It was her turn to give him a lesson, she decided.

Thomas was skating backward, his back to her, so he couldn't see her waiting for him at the other end of the rink. His speed was increasing gradually but his position remained steady as he hummed a soft tune over and over. He extended his arms in front of him and then let them limply drop to his sides as he drew closer to Maude.

That was when Maude sprang behind him screaming, "AARRGHHH!" at the top of her lungs. Thomas jumped in surprise, tangled his feet, and fell helplessly to the ice like a toddler learning to walk, just in time for Maude to snap a shot with her cell phone.

Maude roared with laughter while he tried, obviously still

dazed by his fall, to regain his dignity. He smiled at her amusement as she viewed her perfectly timed picture. In it, Thomas, with a look of complete surprise, was comically grasping thin air with one arm while trying to slow his inevitable fall with the other, his legs flailing wildly.

"I think," she started, trying to catch her breath, "this is a cautionary tale, a perfect illustration of the universal truth that pride does indeed come before the fall."

"You've fallen more often in one day than I have in a lifetime," Thomas said, rubbing his elbows.

"I'm a pro now," Maude replied mischievously, while offering her hand to pull him back up. "If I were you, I'd watch my back from now on."

"I believe I will," he said, getting to his feet.

"Before you fell, I heard you humming a melody," Maude said. "Is it a new song?"

"I've been working on it for a couple of days. I'd like to send it to Glitter Records."

"That's a great idea! What's the song called?"

"It's called 'Falling for You.' But I can't seem to finish it."

"Why don't you sing it to me. Maybe I can help?"

He hesitated and skated away from Maude.

"No way, you're not getting rid of me that easily!" Maude insisted, skating, somewhat unsteadily, behind him.

He sped up but she followed him determinedly, increasing her pace to match his. Finally, he stopped and relented with a sigh.

"Okay, you win. It's a song about a person who's falling in love but is afraid to admit it. The chorus goes like this:

"I look at you, could it be true

"I must be falling for you

"Can't push this feeling away.

"And I can't find the last sentence," Thomas confessed, a little frustrated.

Maude looked at him, started skating again, and sang softly almost wistfully, *"It grows and grows stronger each day?"*

"That's great!" he said, following her. "I knew you'd find something."

Thomas paused and, looking sideways at Maude, continued:

"Should I tell you how I feel?

"Would it scare you

"If I made a confession

"Love is a crazy commotion."

Maude giggled.

"Love is a crazy commotion? You can do better than that," she said, shaking her head. "What about:

"Should I tell you how I feel?

"Would it scare you if I confess?

"Nothing has ever felt so real

"Never knew love could make such a mess."

"Not bad at all, Miss Laurent."

Holding on to the side of the rink, "Miss Laurent" was feeling a bit more adventurous than when she'd first entered the rink, and tried to lift her left leg. She only succeeded in swaying dangerously before Thomas was by her side, steadying her.

"Here, hold my arm and then lift your leg," he instructed.

She did so and extended her leg gracefully behind her.

"That's fine. Now do that while moving, and I'll truly be impressed," Thomas said.

"That's not going to happen anytime soon," she replied

playfully, letting go of his arm and pushing off to join the other skaters. He watched her from afar as she circled the rink, again mulling over the song.

"Shouldn't he admit his feelings?" Maude called to him.

"What?" Thomas asked.

"The song," she reminded him. "If he's feeling so confused, I guess the best thing to do is admit them to the object of his affection," Maude suggested innocently.

"What if he's afraid of rejection?" Thomas asked.

"I can't take this any longer

"I'll admit my love to no other."

Maude sang while attempting to skate backward.

"Maybe you're right, maybe knowing is better," he mused.

"The answer may be yes or no

"At least I'll finally know."

Thomas completed the verse.

"Cool! Now can we do the Red Eagle live video? Can you film with my phone?"

She handed him her cell phone and he gave her a thumbs-up. They practiced for another hour until Maude felt ready.

She took the Red Eagle can from her bag and opened it with a *phish*.

"Ready when you are," Thomas said.

"Okay! Let's go live!"

Thomas gave her a thumbs-up and pressed Play.

"Hi, Maudels!" Maude chirped, holding up her can. "I'm spending the day at the ice rink. In the winter, I love to drink Red Eagle Winter edition. It's full of vitamins and really keeps me going all day long."

Maude, feeling bold, skated to Thomas. But at that moment,

her feet tangled together and she fell on the ice, spilling Red Eagle all over her face. She stuttered in surprise while Thomas flew to her side.

"Ow, ow. *Arrête la caméra!*" Maude shrieked frantically in French.

"Oh yeah!" Thomas stopped the live stream, but the harm was already done.

"Thomas, tell me I didn't just fall flat on my face in front of the entire world?"

"Just the ten thousand people watching the live."

Maude fell back against the ice.

She'd need more than an energy drink to get back up.

Chapter Twenty-two

The good news was that Maude had reignited her online stardom: the live video went viral. The bad news was that Maude was mortified.

If it had been up to her, she would never have left the house again. Unfortunately, the Baldwins were not the sort of family to allow one of their own to wallow for long. They had dragged her and Matt to the Silver Spoon, a fancy restaurant on the Upper East Side.

"I want everything on the menu!" Ben exclaimed, waving it under Maude's nose.

Maude jumped in surprise, looking up from her phone. #Snowfall was still trending.

"Don't even think about it, Ben," Jazmine said firmly. "Remember what happened last time you had too much to eat."

Cynthia and Matt laughed while Ben scowled.

"What are you talking about?" Maude asked.

"No sordid details at the table," Victoria warned sternly, though her eyes danced with mild amusement.

"Victoria's right," Terence put in. "This is Maude's special evening. We don't want to ruin it for her with graphic details of Ben's digestive process."

"Maude's first pre-event ritual dinner." Jazmine beamed proudly.

"Pre-event ritual dinner?" Maude asked. She had no idea what they meant. "I thought this was to keep me from thinking about hashtag snowfall," she said, sticking out her lower lip.

"Come on, Maude," Cynthia said. "I don't think hashtag snowfall is such a bad thing. Red Eagle is getting a ton of publicity."

"But they dropped me from future campaigns."

"They'll come around. This wouldn't be the first time. Let's just see how it all plays out. You can't panic every time you encounter a little failure."

Cynthia's self-confidence slightly lifted Maude's spirits. Kind of like a Red Eagle could have if she'd ingested it instead of spraying it all over her face.

"This is a celebratory dinner for two reasons. To congratulate the pair of you on the release of 'Sunrise' tomorrow. And because next week is Maude's big night, right, dear *Cenerentola*?" Cynthia explained.

"So, how are you feeling?" Jazmine asked.

"I'm feeling amazingly calm about it," Maude said. "I never thought I'd feel so calm before something this huge."

"Our morning yoga session probably helped," Cynthia stated, quite pleased with herself.

"Or it might be because all I can think about is hashtag snowfall," Maude said glumly.

"I have a little something to do with the reason she's so calm," Matt pointed out. "We've been working really well, and we even came up with two new songs, though I'm not quite sure I want to submit them to you just yet."

"Two new songs? Excellent," Terence said. "I knew you would make a great team."

Maude looked up and met Matt's serious gaze. Surprised, she quickly averted her eyes, quite aware that her cheeks were growing uncommonly warm. Maude was thankful Thomas wasn't at the dinner. He was busy working on the songs he planned to present to Glitter Records.

Her eyes flitted around the table until she realized that Jazmine had witnessed their silent exchange and was frowning slightly. Maude fidgeted nervously with her fork.

"Where's our waiter, I'm starving!" Ben cried, offering Maude a welcome distraction from her cutlery.

Like a genie being summoned out of its magical lamp, the waiter appeared in, or rather, stumbled into, the room. Hesitant, he turned the pages of his order pad quickly while muttering under his breath. He was a tall, caramel-skinned, dark-haired skinny boy wearing round-rimmed glasses and a waiter's outfit that made him look more adult than he actually was.

When he arrived at the Baldwins' table, he tripped over his own feet but caught himself just in time.

Jazmine looked up at him and gasped.

"Jonathan?" she squeaked in a small voice. "What are you doing here?"

Jonathan looked up from his pad and dropped his pen.

"Jazmine!" he exclaimed. "What are you doing here?" he echoed.

"She's here to see you, of course," Matt teased.

Jazmine shot Matt a nasty look as she said to Jonathan, "I didn't know you worked here."

"This is my first night. Hey, Maude," he added, turning to an amused Maude.

Before Maude could answer, Ben said, "Hey, Jonathan. Do

you think you'll handle our plates better than the way you handled that pen?"

"Ben." Victoria scolded him. "Apologize to this young man."

"Oh, I'm not offended. Your plates are in good hands. I think," Jonathan answered, clearly doubtful.

Maude, having heard of Jonathan's incredible dexterity with a guitar, wondered how he could be so clumsy with everything else. Every time she'd walked past him in the hall she'd witnessed him dropping something, from pencils to his glasses to several stacks of books.

Despite his clumsiness, Jonathan was liked at school. Incredibly intelligent, he never hesitated to help those who needed it, and even tutored a few football players in dire need of divine intervention. Nevertheless, he didn't seem interested in making lasting relationships or gaining popularity. But when he held a guitar, he was completely transformed and mesmerizing according to Jazmine.

Too bad he couldn't keep anything else in his hands for more than a second. *Our plates will most certainly end up crashing to the floor*, Maude thought.

The entire family all seemed to be thinking the same thing, except for Jazmine, who was staring at Jonathan with soft eyes.

"Can I take your order?" Jonathan asked as if he had rehearsed this sentence a million times.

Jazmine snapped back to reality and stammered helplessly "I'll take the salad with—"

"A salad!" Ben cried in disbelief. "Since when do you eat salad? I thought you said you wanted moussaka?"

"Right, I want moussaka," Jazmine said more firmly. While everyone else ordered, it was Maude's turn to observe Jazmine, whose entire expression had changed. She knew Jazmine well enough by now to know that she was one of the most assured people Maude had ever met. She always knew what to say at the right time and was never fazed.

It dawned on Maude that perhaps the other girl's feelings toward the guitarist had deepened. During dinner, Jazmine grew increasingly quiet while the rest of the family chatted. Matt and Maude were talking with Terence about the album while Ben, Victoria, and Cynthia were making bets on how many plates Jonathan, who was trying to be everywhere at once, would break during the course of the evening.

When a soft jazzy song filled the restaurant, Terence stood up and asked Victoria to dance. She accepted and the two headed to the dance floor.

Matt looked at Maude, cleared his throat and said, "Would you like to—"

"We should dance, Matt, don't you think?" Jazmine interrupted.

Matt looked puzzled but agreed.

Maude's eyes followed them regretfully. She wouldn't have turned Matt down if he'd asked her. Strangely, it didn't look like Jazmine was dancing with Matt at all. In fact, she was pointing an angry finger at him, and he was red in the face. Jazmine glanced over at her, long enough that Maude wondered if the conversation was about her. But Jazmine waved at her with an embarrassed smile as if to dissipate any worry. She exchanged a few more words with Matt, then stomped off the dance floor and onto the restaurant's terrace.

Matt looked like he'd been slapped. Maude got up to join him, but as soon as he saw her heading in his direction, he turned to leave.

"Is everything okay?" Maude grabbed his arm.

"Yeah, look, I've got to go."

"I thought this was our evening."

Matt began to speak, then stopped, uncomfortable. After a pause, he said, "It's really your evening."

"Wait, are you coming to my performance next week?"

She went outside to talk to Jazmine. At first she couldn't see her, but finally she noticed the other girl sitting at a table close to a curtain of glittering fairy lights that illuminated the terrace. Jonathan was with her. Not wanting to intrude, Maude was about to leave when she heard her name.

"Maude is a part of the family now, you know. I can't help but feel protective of her."

Upon hearing these words, Maude's internal glow became as joyful as the terrace's lightwork.

"Typical Jazmine," Jonathan said. "You know, not everything always goes your way."

"Typical Jazmine? How can you say that? You barely even know me."

"I've seen enough of you to know what you're capable of," Jonathan replied seriously.

Jazmine nodded. "You do see right through me, but you also challenge me."

"You've finally realized I'm more than a dorky geek."

"It's been a while. Your klutziness is charming. Behind your large glasses you seem to be laughing at a private joke that you refuse to share with anybody else. But I want in on your little secret."

"Okay, but you asked. See, this place is full of bugs," Jonathan joked. "But I was extra-careful with your plates. I personally took out all the bugs I found. Did you notice?"

"I did, Jon. I was just telling my family how Silver Spoon had improved since the last time we came. Usually there are rats running all over the place. This time, nothing."

"That's all me."

"I guess hiring a professional plate smasher has its perks."

"Yeah, too bad I'm quitting after tonight even if they don't fire me. Won't they be sorry to see me go."

"I'd be sorry too," Jazmine replied, all playfulness gone from her voice.

She looked into his eyes and leaned slowly toward him. Jonathan leaned toward her too.

And then he pulled her close and kissed her softly, tenderly at first, then with more intensity, as if being near her was the most natural thing in the world and he never wanted to let her go.

Maude turned away and closed the terrace door softly. She was happy for Jazmine.

Four words replayed over and over in her head as she headed back to the table, having completely forgotten why she'd sought out Jazmine in the first place. *Part of the family*.

Was she really? It was nice to know Jazmine felt that way about her. What about the other Baldwins?

"Do you know where Jazmine is?" Victoria asked. "We're leaving soon."

"She's out on the terrace," Maude answered, deep in thought.

"I'll go get her."

"Oh no!" Maude cried out, realizing Victoria might discover her daughter making out with Jonathan. "I mean, I'll go get her. You should rest after all that dancing."

Maude pushed Victoria into the nearest chair and hurried

back across the room. Just as she was about to open the door to the terrace, it swung open and Jonathan appeared.

"Hey," was all he said to Maude as he walked past her.

Maude rushed outside and found Jazmine sitting alone at an empty table, her hand on her lips.

"We're leaving," Maude said.

When Jazmine didn't reply, Maude sat opposite her.

"So, are you and Jonathan . . . ?"

"He kissed me! Then he walked away? Am I *that* repulsive?" Jazmine asked, baffled.

"Come on, you can have any guy at Franklin High."

"But I want Jonathan."

"You *really* like him?"

"I do. And I know he likes me too. We just shared the most amazing kiss. But he says I'd smash his heart to little pieces."

"Maybe he doesn't really believe that you like him. What about all that stuff you said about staying free?"

"That was before I spent time with him," Jazmine moaned as she got up. "Let's go home. Ugh, Maude, you're the witness to my very first rejection," she said, wrinkling her nose. "And it stinks. Lily and Stacey would laugh if they saw me right now. Rejected by the school's official nerd."

Maude wrapped a comforting arm around her. They sighed in unison as they went through the heavy door that closed behind them with a loud bang.

Chapter Twenty-three

"You look awful, Maude," Kyra, the makeup artist said, admiring her personal work of art. Maude was sitting in the Morningside Theater's dressing room in front of a wide mirror. Her dark natural hair was disheveled and her makeup gave her a frightening, unkempt look. She was dressed in gray, ashen rags that limply covered her body. She smiled at her reflection while Kyra crept out of the room. It had been quite a week.

The first time she had heard "Sunrise" in public she had been sipping a tall hot chocolate at a trendy new café in Soho with Cynthia and Jazmine. They were seated on a comfortable sofa talking animatedly about the movie they'd just seen.

That was when it happened. She'd always thought she'd be calm, cool, when she heard her song for the first time, having promised herself not to act too crazy. She instantly forgot all her good resolutions. Jumping up like she'd been stung by a bee, she spilled her hot chocolate all over her raspberry muffin and her jeans, but nothing mattered. Cynthia and Jazmine had sprung up in perfect unison as well. Right there, in front of at least thirty people, the three girls squealed and jumped and hugged, oblivious to the mess they'd made.

The waiter behind the counter looked at them and shook his head when he saw the chaos on their table.

"That's my song!" Maude yelled almost wildly.

Jazmine and Cynthia yelled back, "That's her song! She's Maude Laurent! Her voice is all over New York!"

Then they all did a crazy little dance that made the other customers laugh. The waiter softened a little and walked toward his messy customers.

"If you're famous, I want an autograph," he said, handing Maude a napkin.

Maude took the napkin. She had worked hard on getting her autograph right and in her best cursive penmanship. Put on the spot, all she could come up with was a completely stale and unimaginative "Maude Laurent."

"Keep that. Your five-cent napkin just became an important relic," Cynthia remarked, breathless from all the dancing.

Now Maude's single was being played online and on the radio, and tonight she hoped her success as *Cenerentola* would make everyone forget about #Snowfall. Cynthia was prepared to film the thunderous applause she received at the end of the performance. So much was riding on this performance. Maude's hands trembled. Hopefully, her voice wouldn't. At last! Her musical career was beginning, and not just her pop career. The opera world held its doors wide open, only waiting for her to enter. She could follow Soulville's path as well as the one her heart truly yearned for.

The audience had arrived, and the Baldwins had front-row seats. Maude felt tension rising in her throat. A shiver ran down her spine.

A knock at the door interrupted her thoughts. Maude

hurried to open it. Terence entered, her phone in his hand. She'd left it with him to keep away any kind of distraction. "How are you doing? I hope you aren't feeling too nervous. You still have twenty minutes to calm down, go get some fresh air if you want."

Maude shook her head. "I'm fine, thanks. I did want to ask you: How are the first week's numbers for 'Sunrise'?"

Terence took a deep breath and with a tight smile, said, "Maude, I want you to focus on tonight. Don't think about numbers right now. This is your evening. Besides, I've got someone on the phone here for you," he said, smiling gently. "She wants to congratulate you before you go on stage." He stretched out his arm to her, but Maude looked at her phone, puzzled. She didn't know anyone who would want to congratulate her.

"Is it Victoria? Because we already spoke this evening and—"

"It isn't Vic. Take the phone, you'll see."

He put the phone in her hand and closed the door behind him.

Maude put the phone to her ear but almost dropped it when she heard the voice on the other end.

"So tonight is your big night, huh?" Mrs. Ruchet asked.

"Mrs. Ruchet!" Maude exclaimed. "Hi! How did you know about tonight?" Maude was lost for words. She hadn't heard from the Ruchets once since she'd arrived in New York. That they'd thought of her on her big night was a pleasant surprise, one that warmed her heart. It was nice to be missed.

"Your producer, Mr. Batwing told us. He left us a message saying how important this was and that it would be nice if we supported you, and I thought why not," Mrs. Ruchet said. "How is your new single doing? Is it bringing in money?"

Maude gathered her wits. That's why Mrs. Ruchet was

calling. About money. Not because she missed Maude. She didn't want Mrs. Ruchet to ruin her evening. The sooner she ended this conversation the better.

"I have to go. I have to get ready," she lied. "I really can't chat," she added hurriedly.

"Oh, so I see," Mrs. Ruchet answered curtly. "You're snubbing the people who raised you."

"No, I just have to get ready. I—"

"It doesn't matter. You know why? Because you know the clock is ticking, Cinderella."

Maude's heart stopped.

"The clock will strike twelve and you'll have to come back to Carvin. If those singles aren't hits you'll be right back where you started. Right here. So I suggest you stop making a fool of yourself on social media and get your act together."

"What if told you that I'm busy looking for my father?" Maude's words were met with cold silence.

"Don't you dare go looking for information on your father," Mrs. Ruchet said.

"Oh, you mean, Aaron?" Maude taunted her.

Mrs. Ruchet burst out laughing.

"He never went by Aaron in New York."

"Tell me his name," Maude said bitterly, choking back tears.

"He went by his Nigerian name. Good luck learning anything about him now."

She heard Mrs. Ruchet laugh. Unable to stand it any longer, Maude hung up, her vision blurred by a flow of hot tears.

At that moment, Jazmine and Cynthia entered the dressing room, excited to see Maude one last time before she made her debut.

They stopped abruptly when they noticed the look on her face.

"Maude, what's wrong?" Cynthia hurried toward her.

Maude couldn't answer and just shook her head as she tried to prevent the tears from flowing.

"Who called you?" Jazmine asked, noticing Maude's phone in her balled-up fist.

"I can't go on stage," Maude trembled. "I can't go on like this. Tell Madame Tragent to prepare Lindsey."

Cynthia and Jazmine shared a worried glance.

"Maude, it's normal to have a little stage fright. This is your first time. You'll be wonderful." Cynthia spoke soothingly.

Maude shook her head.

"Where's Matt?" she asked, trying miserably to wipe her tears.

She needed to see him right away. Seeing his easy-going, laid-back smile would calm her and somehow reassure her.

Jazmine looked uncomfortable.

"He isn't here . . . yet."

"He didn't come?" Maude asked.

"He's going to make it, Maude," Jazmine reassured hurriedly. "I'll call him right now. I'm sure he's on his way."

She ran out of the dressing room with Maude's phone and slammed the door behind her.

She reentered a few minutes later to find Cynthia wiping Maude's face with a tissue. "Matt's on his way, he's just running a little late. Don't worry, he'll be here."

"I don't care if he comes," Maude stated as she got up from her seat and left the room quietly.

As she closed the door she overheard Cynthia whisper, "I convinced her to go on stage. I don't know if I should have. Should we call Dad?"

"I don't think so. It's too late now. She has to go on stage. Lindsey would be too happy to take her place. Let's go take our seats."

They hurried past Maude just in time to hear Mme. Tragent say, "Kyra did a great job on the makeup. You look awful!"

Suddenly, Maude was alone on stage, a broom in her hand, waiting for the curtain to rise. She heard the orchestra play the opening theme, but try as she might, she couldn't help but hear Mrs. Ruchet's voice echo in her ear.

She was a failure. Her fall on the ice was still trending and everyone in Carvin must have seen it. Probably even Stephane was laughing. She was the girl who had dreamed too big, who had dared to change her life. And what would she get for it?

She hadn't even discovered a single thing about her father, and now she'd discovered that his first name was different from the one she'd been looking for. How would she ever find out anything about him?

And to think her new single wasn't as good as she'd hoped? Terence hadn't said a word, but she knew what his silence meant.

She couldn't imagine going back to Carvin as a failure. She hadn't wanted to come to New York in the first place. But, oh, how she loved it now!

Maude hadn't wanted to think of what would happen when her six-month stay was up. Could she really go back to her dreary life? She looked down at her rags and smiled bitterly, pushing back the tears that threatened to overflow once more. In the opera, Cinderella managed to escape her condition. Maude knew she wouldn't be so lucky. She'd remain an unidentified orphan for the rest of her life. *I hate this story*, she thought angrily. It was just a huge deception. This whole opera was a farce!

The curtain went up, and Maude faced the crowd.

The room was packed. Women wore exquisite evening dresses, the men accompanying them wore their best suits, small girls were fidgeting impatiently in velvet dresses like fairy queens. Every seat, every balcony was filled with people waiting to hear the renowned Cordelia Tragent's version of *La Cenerentola*.

Maude's mind went blank.

She barely noticed the Baldwins in the front row, looking at one another, wondering if she would sing. She glanced at the orchestra pit where the musicians, puzzled, had started the opening theme again, hoping that Maude would start singing. They didn't realize that her heart was pounding a lot louder than their music, and that it was the only rhythm she could hear. What she did notice though, was a tall, slim, disheveled young man in a light-brown trench coat who had just arrived, breathlessly but quite discreetly. Matt obviously hadn't had time to change.

Maude came back to earth with a start and a painful, frightening realization. She couldn't do this. She couldn't sing. She couldn't breathe. She couldn't play pretend. Maude did the only thing she could think of doing.

She ran off the stage.

Chapter Twenty-four

Maude spent the following day in her pajamas moping while Cynthia and Jazmine tried unsuccessfully to cheer her up. They watched countless Nollywood movies on Netflix, including several romantic comedies involving fun, eventful wedding parties.

How are these actresses so perfect? Maude wondered. They could act, sometimes in two languages, dance, and seemed to be all around fearless. Meanwhile she was overcome with stage fright. Every time she thought about her previous evening, she winced. She could blame it all on Mrs. Ruchet, but that was only partially true. Nervousness had racked her all that evening; Mrs. Ruchet confirming her biggest fear was just the last straw.

"We could go shopping or something?" Cynthia tentatively asked after they had watched the fourth romantic comedy involving an Igbo-Yoruba wedding in a row.

Shopping usually got Jazmine out of a moping state, but Maude wasn't Jazmine. She shook her head.

"I'm never seeing the light of day again. Or answering my phone," she added as she looked at the twentieth notification of a missed call from Thomas. It pained her that Matt hadn't even bothered to send her a text.

"This calls for another carton of vanilla and cookie dough ice cream," Jazmine suggested.

"No, no, no!" Cynthia cried. "Maude Laurent, you're getting up off this couch and out of this house this instant."

"Are you ordering me as my publicist?" Maude adjusted her position, determined to stay right where she was.

"As your friend and, you know, honorary big sister. Seniority is everything here."

"But I want to watch Nollywood movies."

"You can watch Nollywood movies *or* you can go to a Nigerian hot spot right here in New York."

Maude's eyebrows shot up. "Here?" she squeaked.

"Oh, we haven't been to the Landmark in a while!" Jazmine jumped up from the couch.

"Matt mentioned the Landmark," Maude said. They were supposed to go together. That was before he'd shown up late at her performance and hadn't checked in to see how she was dealing with public humiliation.

"Now that you've got two Baldwin big sisters on your case, you don't have a choice," Cynthia pointed out.

"Ben would've caved at this point." Jazmine crossed her arms.

"Fine." Maude held out her hands, and the sisters hauled her up.

• • •

Central Harlem was ready for the weekend. The girls' Uber flew along 125th Street, allowing Maude to marvel at the lively, artistic neighborhood. As tattoo parlors and hair salons closed, their storefronts revealed bright graffiti celebrating the joy and resilience of African American culture. The legendary Apollo Theater's red lettering sparkled. Huge restaurant and clothing chains overlooked hustling street vendors selling food and sweatshirts. Whiffs of soul food wafted through the evening air, and through the open window Maude watched a child greedily bite into a red velvet cupcake. Her mood lifted. The music of the streets was not dissimilar to that of an opera; Maude likened hip-hop to the percussive section of an orchestra, the police sirens to the wailing of violins, and the singsong "You too babe!" as a joyful woman took leave of a vendor to the last notes of a diva's solo before exiting the stage.

The Uber dropped the girls close to Adam Clayton Powell Jr. Boulevard.

Striding in and out of the Landmark were people with gorgeous braids, Bantu knots, twists, Afros, dreadlocks, threaded updos, and other amazing hairstyles Maude had never even seen before.

The Landmark wasn't just a Nigerian restaurant nor was it just a bar or a club. It was its own artistic universe. When she stepped inside, Maude couldn't believe the energy. Blue and yellow drinks passed from the bartender's hands to the patrons while the DJ blasted all the latest Afrobeats and Afro House beats, pulling the crowds onto the dance floor.

"You see," Cynthia said pulling Maude into the crowd, "Mom's udu's nice, but Nigerians don't only make traditional music."

For the next hour the three girls swayed to electronic music from all parts of Nigeria. Arms, legs, butts, and braids swished, and the music was like nothing Maude had ever heard. Electronic sounds mixed with percussions, drums, and beats from everywhere, lyrics in Yoruba, pidgin English, and Igbo. The dancing wasn't just dancing, it was like the individual bodies had a mind of their own, like nothing could stop them. Maude couldn't believe it.

All her worries left as the beat seized her. So her single had tanked? She'd run away from an entire crowd for her first performance. Who cared?

Music was so much more than opera. And much more than rigid categories.

The DJ moved on from Nigerian musicians to other African electro artists. There were electro songs in Swahili, Luganda, Zulu, and the dances featured broken rhythms, grinding, break dancing, and dance battles. But the most expressive language of all was that of joy.

As Maude shook it out, her problems lessened.

Out of breath, Cynthia and Maude grabbed a basket of puff-puff and two mango cocktails, and headed outside to the heated terrace where other customers were enjoying the fresh air or relaxing. Taking a seat at a table near the door so they could still hear the thumping beats, Maude stuffed one of the round, savory deep-fried beignets into her mouth and offered Cynthia one.

"So you feeling better now?" Cynthia asked, sipping her mango cocktail.

"Maybe I should have done *this* before the performance, I'd have been less stressed out. I feel alive again, I feel like I can take on the world. Cynth, you have to tell me. Did I further hurt my chances at Soulville by running away last night?"

"Maude, you care too much. You have to remember what music is all about. Have fun with it again. I seem to recall a girl in Carvin who couldn't care less about pop music."

"But now I care! I want to stay and work with Soulville."

"You can want it, but you don't need it."

"I do."

"But that might be the problem, if you feel that you *need* it, that feeling will only increase your stress levels. Instead, you should just enjoy the ride. Regardless of how any of this ends up, look at all you'd go home with. *If* you go home."

"But I'd be so embarrassed if everyone in Carvin knew I failed."

"How would it be a failure? It can't be a failure if you've tried something completely new that no one else over there ever tried. Failure would have been not trying at all. Look at all you've gained: new musical interests, new friends, new boyfriend. How are you and Thomas, by the way? You answered his calls?"

"I can't talk to him," Maude blurted. "I don't know, Cynthia. I just feel like there's something wrong. I've had a hard time telling him about Soulville ever since I learned he wanted to record there too."

"I'm sure he's genuinely happy for you."

"He is. He is," Maude repeated. "Now that Glitter is showing an interest, yes, he's genuinely happy for me. But I don't know how he'll feel if they turn him down too. I hope they don't. I just feel like I can't talk to him like I talk to—" Maude stopped short. She'd been about to say Matt's name but decided against it. It wasn't Thomas's fault that both his parents were alive. But it wasn't just that. Her musical connection with Matt was much stronger than her connection with Thomas, even though he loved opera, just like her.

"Relationships are complicated," Cynthia said. She put a puff-puff in her mouth and chewed gingerly, then swallowed.

The door opened and Jazmine appeared with a man who looked to be well over his sixties.

"Told you Cynthia was here, Femi," Jazmine said.

Cynthia greeted the man warmly.

"Let me introduce you to one of Soulville's rising stars, Maude Laurent. Maude, this is the owner of Landmark, serving Nigerians and other Africans from the diaspora for over thirty-five years."

Maude's eyes opened wide. "Thirty-five years? By any chance have you ever met a Nigerian-French man named Aaron Laurent? I mean, his first name was Aaron, but he went by his Nigerian name."

"It was?"

"I don't know."

"Ain't never seen no Aaron Laurent around here, sorry, kiddo."

"That's okay." Maude's hopes sagged along with her shoulders. It seemed Mrs. Ruchet was right. Nobody knew Aaron by his first name. She felt certain deep down her father would have loved a place like this.

"Cynthia, there's an artist you need to meet," Femi said.

"You know I can't sign all your artists." Cynthia laughed.

The girls headed back inside and danced the night away.

When they got back home, Maude was sleepy but felt inspired and determined to make good music again.

The next day, the girls watched a new Nollywood movie with mounds of ice cream, wanting to prolong their previous evening. This time Maude was in much higher spirits.

Late in the afternoon, the doorbell rang.

Cynthia went to answer it and when she came back into the living room, the cold and stately Mme. Tragent followed her. Maude gasped and tried, uselessly, to hide the empty ice-cream cartons under the sofa. Mme. Tragent raised a stern eyebrow, and Maude left the containers to greet her teacher.

"May I speak to you alone, Ms. Laurent?" Her question was more an order than an actual question, but Maude nodded, nevertheless.

As they went into the dining room, Maude wished she was wearing anything other than her ridiculous pajamas.

Her teacher, on the other hand, was elegantly dressed with not a single strand of hair out of place. Maude tried unsuccessfully to smooth her rebellious curls down, but just succeeded in making them stick out farther.

"Ms. Laurent, you disappointed me greatly two nights ago," her teacher started.

"I—" Maude started to protest. Mme. Tragent silenced her with a wave of her hand.

"Terence insisted I take you into my class, and I trusted him. You showed remarkable raw talent. And for someone who had never trained her voice properly, you made a great impression during auditions for the lead. Your technique wasn't perfect, but I still chose you over Lindsey. But when it mattered, you disgraced yourself and me. And now you have me saying something I never thought I'd d say: Thank god Ms. Linton was there. I want an explanation, and I want it now."

"I'm sorry, Madame Tragent," Maude protested. "I can't explain what happened. I had a serious case of stage fright."

Mme. Tragent scoffed.

"There are some very simple rules you should follow, including not having your phone before a performance. You let your personal life interfere with your professional life. You let your emotions get the better of you!"

Maude's eyes blazed and angry tears threatened.

"Your nephew once advised me to do so," she argued, her face getting warmer with shame and indignation. "He told me to dig deeper into my emotions."

"Don't twist my nephew's words. If he told you to use your emotions, your pain and joy, to give depth to your performance, he certainly didn't mean to tell you to let them get out of hand, like they did that night! I taught her everything she knows. And I never taught her that," Mme. Tragent snapped angrily.

Who was Mme. Tragent talking about? "You mean you never taught *him* that?"

"No, I meant *her*, Ms. Laurent. I meant Isabella Durand née Tragent, Matt's mother. My baby sister," she said.

"Your sister was Matt's mother?" She'd assumed Matt's father was the connection between Matt and his aunt.

"She was. And she was a lot like you. Very gifted. But too emotional. And in the end, she surrendered to her husband's pressure and gave it all up. She wanted to be a good *wife*." Mme. Tragent threw out the last word as if it was an insult.

"I need to know right now, Maude Laurent, are you committed to singing?" The woman's eyes pierced Maude like daggers.

Maude took a deep breath and calmly replied, "With all my heart."

"Then be at the theater Sunday morning at six o'clock sharp for your first private lesson," Mme. Tragent declared before standing up and walking to the door. Maude almost fell off her chair.

"But you never give private lessons!" she exclaimed.

"Is that complaining I hear, Ms. Laurent?"

"No, of course not!"

"Good. Six o'clock sharp. Don't be late."

Mme. Tragent strode across the living room and looked haughtily at the sofa where Jazmine and Cynthia were sitting.

"Jazmine Baldwin, shoulders!" she ordered sternly.

Then she continued on her way and showed herself out.

"She's giving me private lessons," Maude said dreamily.

"Madame Tragent!" Cynthia exclaimed in wonder. "She never gives private lessons. None of my friends at Juilliard managed to convince her."

"I can't wait for Lindsey to find out!" Jazmine cried excitedly. "Promise me you won't tell her without me, Maude."

The girls laughed and proceeded to celebrate Maude's success with more vanilla and cookie dough ice cream.

When Maude went up to her room that evening, she sent a text message to Matt.

Ready to compose our next hit?

Chapter Twenty-five

"Matt! You're back!" cried an eight-year-old girl with a bouncy ponytail as she sprang into his arms. Matt and Maude had just entered Las Fajitas, a Mexican restaurant in Fort Greene, Brooklyn. Maude admired the surroundings. The place was cozy but full of life at the same time. The décor was beautiful: sombreros hung on the walls and a cactus stood next to each red-clothed table.

The place was packed, and some of the customers danced to the vivacious music played by a live band of guitars, drums, and maracas.

The restaurant had a main lounge and a rooftop, and it was so famous that the owners only opened from spring to autumn and closed during the winter.

"Of course, I'm back," Matt said, hugging the girl warmly. "How are you, Anita? Where are Rosa and Eduardo?"

"They're coming. I'm fine. Lost my two front teeth. See?"

Anita proudly exhibited the gap in her mouth as if she was presenting a trophy.

"Lovely," he said, smiling. "I bet the tooth fairy brought you a surprise, didn't she?"

"She did! I'm rich now, Matt. I can buy you a convertible if you want. Who's this?" she asked, pointing to Maude.

"Good question, Anita. Who is this lovely girl you brought to our restaurant?" asked an imposing, dark-haired woman in an apron emerging from the kitchen. She was followed by a thin, dark-haired man.

"Rosa, Eduardo!" Matt cried before being pulled into a tight bear hug.

"We haven't seen you in ages! You've neglected us. And you've become so thin, Matt. What have you been eating?"

"I came last month, Rosa. That hardly qualifies as neglect. Besides, I've been very busy working on Maude's releases. Maude, meet Eduardo and Rosa Delgado. Rosa's the best cook in New York."

"In New York? In the world you mean. Pleased to meet you, Maude. Matt never brings any of his friends here. I always thought he was ashamed of us."

"Never, Rosa," Matt assured her. "I was more ashamed of my friends. Maude is presentable, though. Is there a table left?"

"Ah, Matt, you know there's always room for you," Eduardo said, squeezing through the crowded room.

"Here, you two sit back and enjoy. I'll cook whatever you want. You both look too thin. Take anything you want, it's on the house,'" Rosa said, leaving before Matt could protest.

Eduardo leaned over to Matt and said, "You know the only thing she wants is for you to sing on that stage. So you do that when you've finished eating," he said, winking at Maude as he left.

"They seem like really nice people," Maude said.

"They're the best. And the food is delicious."

"I don't really know what to have. I've never eaten Mexican food before."

"The *machaca* is great. You should try it."

"I'll trust you."

"All right, I'll go tell them."

Matt hurried to the back of the restaurant while Maude watched the musicians carefully put their instruments down to take a break.

When Matt came back, he was carrying two large fruity drinks with tiny, red umbrellas perched on the rims.

"While we wait," he said, placing a drink in front of her.

"This place is amazing," Maude said sipping her drink.

"I've been coming here for years. Anita was barely walking the first time I ever set foot in here."

"Was it before or after you became famous?" Maude asked slyly.

"Before. It doesn't matter. I'll always be their Matt."

Maude looked at him thoughtfully before asking, "I'm curious. What's it like working with Soulville after working with Glitter and releasing three Grammy Award–winning albums with them?"

"I was sick of Glitter. I didn't want to work with them anymore," he admitted simply. "I refused to be their puppet any longer."

Maude thought of Thomas, and wondered if Glitter was the right fit for him, seeing how Matt vehemently detested them.

"Can I give my honest opinion?" Maude asked. "I thought your debut album, *Matt*, was nice. You really put a lot of thought into it. Your sophomore album, *Superstar*, was dreadful. Your hit singles 'Living the Life' and 'To the Top' totally lacked depth. As for 'Love Doctor,' you know what I think about that one."

Matt laughed at her blunt honesty.

"I completely agree with you. When Glitter discovered me they were willing to promote me as the singer-songwriter I was.

I fully participated in the creation of *Matt*. The album was a huge success, even bigger than they had anticipated, and they absolutely wanted to capitalize on that success. I'd worked almost a year on *Matt*. *Superstar* was finished in a month, and I hadn't written a single lyric on it. I hated that album. They wanted me to release a new single almost every week! For *Matt* I released three singles, but for *Superstar* I released a total of seven. I thought the album was bad, but it was an even bigger success," he said sourly.

"Too bad you didn't know Terence Baldwin back then, huh?"

"Actually, I did. He wanted to sign me at the same time Glitter offered me a contract. My mom loved Soulville's and Terence's mindset."

"Why didn't you sign with him?" Maude queried, wondering why anyone would choose Glitter over Soulville. "Glitter wanted me but I said no. They're so aggressively pop. It's like you either become an icon or you're a failure!"

"Tell me about it," Matt said dejectedly. "When we left Paris and came to New York because of my dad's promotion, Mom saw it as a great opportunity for me to start a music career after my appearance on *Kids Talent*."

"You went on *Kids Talent*?" Maude exclaimed. "I'm so jealous!" She'd seen sequences of *Kids Talent* when she was twelve. She'd dreamed of going on the show to sing an opera song, but she'd never had the courage to send a video.

"French edition. I was a very cute kid with a mean break-dance routine."

"Did you eat that whole bag of candy they give to each participant?"

"I licked the bag clean." Matt appeared particularly proud of this exploit, and Maude nodded admiringly.

"My father wanted me to sign with Glitter Records," Matt continued. "I didn't want to but he said he didn't want me to waste time. He wasn't very supportive of my whole music career but still managed to coerce both my mom and me into signing with Glitter. I was only fourteen back then and I didn't want to rock the boat. Especially since my mom had just been diagnosed with breast cancer."

"It must have been so hard for her to see you at Glitter if you felt so unhappy about it."

"I didn't show a thing. I did my best to show her I was happy with my new career. I don't know if she bought it, though. My mom always had a way of knowing my deepest feelings."

"What makes you think she knew?"

"She basically told me before she passed last year. She made me promise that I wouldn't stay at Glitter if I wasn't happy."

"Definitely sounds like she knew," Maude said gently. "But that was just a few months ago. How come you and the Baldwins are so close?"

"Oh, I may have started working for Soulville recently, but Terence and I have been musical soul mates for years." Matt laughed. "After we met, when I was fourteen, we became friends. He let me have my creation room and I was at his house so often I became friends with everyone else in the family." His eyes grew somber. "When my mom passed away nine months ago, my father and I had a huge fight. I left. I didn't want to live alone so I moved in with the Baldwins and stayed with them for six months. They're the closest thing I have to family, apart from my aunt."

"Wow, I had no idea, Matt. Did you have to leave because of me?"

"Nah, my aunt insisted I live with her. I think she did that more to spite my father. She has no idea what to do with me. I'll be eighteen soon so I'll get a place of my own."

"You haven't mended things with your father?"

Matt looked at Maude, his eyes troubled for just a split second. Then he smiled feebly and said, "That won't be happening anytime soon. He accused me of some pretty terrible things. He said it was my fault she was so sad at the end. He said I wasn't there often enough and that I was an ungrateful son."

"*Mon Dieu*. Matt, I'm so sorry."

"It's fine, Maude. You're not the one who said those things," he replied sadly. "It's rich coming from a man who put his work above everything else. He's such a hypocrite, with his stupid bourgeois rules. He studied at l'EDHEC, a huge French business school."

"I've heard of it."

"He dreamed that I'd go to HEC."

"The number one business school." Maude sighed. "Not really compatible with a pop career, is it?"

"Not compatible with who I am. It's like he doesn't know me at all. Like he doesn't even want to know."

"Would he have preferred it if you became a classical musician?"

"Ha! I'm not so sure. My mom was an opera singer, and he made her give it up when I was born. She was incredible."

"That's where you get your love for music."

"That's right. She taught me everything I know. She loved classical but listened to all types of musicians, she taught me to never scorn a music style. Do you remember the day we met?"

Maude nodded. How could she forget their first meeting?

"I was going to listen to one of her favorite subway musicians. His music is garbage."

"You sure you like that artist?"

"The instruments he uses are all recycled bottles, cans, and items he finds, well, in the garbage. My dad never broadened his views. He never understood why I love rhythm and blues, soul, funk, rock, EDM, Afrobeats. My mom did."

He had loved and mourned, while she had never known those she mourned. Two tragedies. They both felt the void left by the absence of a mother's love. *Is it better to miss a mother's warm embrace or to never have known it?* Maude wondered, feeling closer to him than she'd ever felt before.

"I'm sure she'd be very proud," she said gently.

"I don't know." He shook his head. "She might've been proud of the first album, but I know she wasn't crazy about the second. When I realized that, I wanted to leave Glitter Records, but I was tied in for another album. I told them I wanted out. They tried to calm me down by telling me I could work on some of the songs for the third album, *Moving On*, and by letting me try my hand as a composer for other artists."

"That's when you worked with Lindsey," Maude put in a little sourly. "Her song really played a huge role in both our careers, yours and mine."

"Exactly. And when 'Burning Bridges' became a hit, launching Lindsey's singing career, they wanted me to sign a new contract allowing me all creativity for my future albums. By then my mom had just passed away. My pain made me smarter. I announced I was taking a break from my singing career and went straight to Soulville as a composer and producer-in-training. And I haven't regretted it."

"The song you wrote for Diane Cameron, 'Craving,' is really awesome," Maude gushed.

"A-ha! Finally! A genuine compliment from the great Maude Laurent!" Matt exclaimed in triumph.

Maude barely suppressed a smile.

"Do you think you'll ever release an album as a singer again?" she asked.

"It's definitely an option, but right now I'm happy where I am. With you," he answered, his eyes resting on her. "I mean, working with you and everything," he added quickly.

Maude's face grew hot under his stare, and she grabbed her drink, almost spilling it over the tablecloth.

"Enough about me," he said quickly. "How is your search going? Found any new info about your father?"

Maude sighed. "I went to Landmark with Cynthia and Jaz last week, and I completely embarrassed myself asking the owner if he knew my father."

"Do you have any info on your mom?"

"None. That's why it's so important I find out about my father first. Then I can look for her."

"Can I ask you something?"

"Of course."

"What's the thing you'd like to know most about your parents? Apart from how they passed away?"

"I want to know if I look like them."

"Makes sense. I wonder one thing."

"You have questions about my parents? Why?"

"I wonder who you got your temper from."

Maude gasped with a smile. "It's not my fault you constantly get on my nerves."

"Regardless, I'm sure they were good looking. They gave you that for sure."

Maude smiled, pleased beyond words, but with no idea how to reply to his compliment. She was flustered.

Luckily, at that moment, the waiter brought their food, and Maude turned her whole attention to her plate. She grabbed a spoonful of her dish and shoved it in her mouth. Then, two things happened simultaneously. Her mouth was suddenly on fire, and she saw, through misty eyes, Matt take a photo of her with his cell phone all the while laughing hysterically. She was too confused to understand what was happening around her. Her throat went dry and her eyes watered as she desperately gasped for breath.

"Water!" she croaked, choking over her food.

Matt, still laughing, poured her a big glass of water. She grabbed it, spilled half of it on the table, and drank it greedily like a camel in the desert. She then successively poured herself three glasses of water before being able to utter a word.

"For future reference," Matt said between snorts of laughter, "drinking water doesn't help."

"You're dead," she croaked to a hysterical Matt.

"Hey, at least you didn't insult me in French!"

"You think this is funny? I'd like to see you try now. You owe me that."

"No way. I already tried it once, and I'm never doing that again. I don't have a death wish."

"Victoria always cuts back on the pepper in her Nigerian dishes specifically for me. And you're making me eat a mouthful of this volcanic sauce?" she asked wiping her eyes.

"The picture looks great. Take a look."

Filling the small screen, Maude's face was frozen in a look of sheer horror, her eyes bulging, her hands at her throat, her lips curled upside down. Maude laughed. She looked completely ridiculous.

"That's how you'll look when I'm done with you," she threatened, handing him back his phone.

"We can share my plate. There's enough to feed an army."

Maude nodded, and they shared Matt's platter of food: tacos, nachos, tamales, and quesadillas. There really was enough to feed an army. Maude and Matt, who had been starving, finished the entire platter all the while chatting happily, only stopping to dip their nachos in guacamole. They were like two long-lost souls who had found each other and couldn't stop talking, making up for lost time.

Maude had rarely enjoyed anyone's company so much, and was amazed to think she had actually hated Matt after their incident in the subway. They argued playfully about everything from other singers and composers to their very own songs and their tastes. From pop and rock to Afrobeats, K-Pop, Afro House, EDM, hip-hop, soul, and R & B. Every artist Maude knew by heart or that she had just discovered was dissected and analyzed. Every random subject was an excuse to argue and debate.

"You really think New York is better than Paris?" she asked.

"Don't you?"

"I love New York but you don't understand what Paris represented for me. It was absolute freedom. I was free from Carvin, my routines and chores, even if it was only for a day."

"You've been free in New York for over three months," he pointed out.

"That's true. Mr. Baldwin coming into my life was a turning point. Paris is the reason for that. It's where everything began, it's where I found the courage to sing in front of a real crowd, where the viral video began. Paris will always be the city for me no matter how much I adore New York. You lived in Paris a good part of your life, that's why you take it for granted."

"Okay, I see my mission isn't over yet. We should get going if I'm going to show you the other musical venues you need to see," he said, getting up.

The band had started playing again, and couples were dancing.

"Where do you think you're going?" asked Rosa appearing out of nowhere, her daughter by her side. "You do know you aren't leaving here without getting on that stage, Matt? A little improvisation won't do you any harm, and you know it. Maude can sing with you, seeing as she's a singer as well."

"What do you think, Maude, are you up for it?" Matt asked.

"I've never improvised before," Maude confessed, looking tentatively at the stage.

"Now is a good time to start," Rosa urged.

"Oh, please, Matt, sing for us," Anita pleaded.

"Only if Maude comes with me."

"I never walk away from a challenge," Maude replied. *There's a first time for everything*, she thought with wry humor. Her first instinct should have been to run, seeing as she had never improvised, and the last time she was on stage had been a disaster! But the tiny voice in her head told her she'd rather be tortured in a Middle Ages dungeon than let Matt sense an ounce of fear from her.

She listened to the band composed of drums, guitar, and maracas. The rhythm was getting louder and quicker as Maude approached the stage, and her heart began beating as fast as the drums.

She could do this. She could improvise. At least she hoped

she could. If Matt could do it, so could she. *And better than him, too*, she thought with a flash of fiery pride.

Matt took the first microphone and said, "Hello, everyone. I was talking to my friend Maude here, and she was telling me that Paris is the best city in the world. And I explained that New York was the greatest city. But she's quite stubborn and she keeps insisting!"

Matt was a definite crowd pleaser. Not a hint of shyness, not a trace of bashfulness emanated from him. His confidence had won over millions of people around the world, and as she looked at him, Maude understood why. Beyond his penetrating stare and his devastating smile lay something deeper. Maude had sensed it in the creation room and witnessed it here in even greater proportions: he wholeheartedly and undeniably loved music. Just like she did, Matt *lived* for music.

"So, I'm going to need your help convincing her, okay?" he yelled.

The crowd yelled back in agreement.

"All right, here goes."

"You're new in New York

"So look at the view

"Stop standing around

"While the city flies past you

"New York never sleeps

"Party all night long

"Get up on your feet

"Dance from night till dawn."

The crowd cheered as Maude climbed on stage and grabbed the second microphone. She sang:

"Rats all over the place

"Subways breaking down

"Coffee spilled in my face

"The list goes on and on."

The crowd encouraged Maude loudly again, and she looked at Matt defiantly before taking on the chorus:

"New York's the place to see

"Paris the place to be

"Paris beats New York any day

"Just give up and walk away."

Matt continued:

"Strikes every day

"Protests once a month

"That's Paris for you

"Girl, you know it's true.

"New York's the city of the free

"Led by the Statue of Liberty

"Concrete maze, blissful haze

"A lively mess, a melting pot

"Tied together in a tight knot."

Maude danced to the beat of the drums, her feet thumping, her mind whirling and hands clapping. Then she stopped and answered, raising her head a little higher:

"New York City sounds okay

"Paris takes my breath away

"Music is in the air

"Rhythm is everywhere

"Dancing in Moulin Rouge

"Beats New Year's in Times Square."

Matt sang:

"Paris is the place to see

"New York is the place to be

"Paris versus New York City."

Maude sang:

"New York's the place to see

"Paris is the place to be

"I'd choose Paris over New York any day

"So just give up and walk away."

Maude paused and sang slowly:

"Let's agree to disagree

"My heart belongs to Paris

"You love New York City

"Come to Paris some time

"I'm sure I'll change your mind."

Matt walked to Maude and ended the song softly:

"Paris versus New York City

"Where you are is where I'll be

"Forget Paris versus New York City

"You're all that matters to me."

Then they sang together softly:

"Forget Paris versus New York City

"You're all that matters to me."

Matt and Maude stopped singing, their eyes locked, as if nothing else in the world mattered. Maude's heart raced as the sound of the drums slowly died, her eyes searching his as his last words echoed in her ear. *You're all that matters to me.*

Suddenly a loud cheer erupted from the crowd, who started singing the chorus of the song. Feet thumped; hands clapped. Soon, Maude and Matt left the stage to loud applause.

"I guess that wasn't too bad for a first time," Matt yelled over the noise.

"It was better than not too bad. Don't you hear the crowd?" Maude yelled back.

"One thing is for sure," Matt said. "We've finished your song about Paris. We'll work on the instruments, but this song is as good as done, Maude."

"You mean to tell me that we're going to present this song to Terence?" Her new single! They had finally finished writing her song about Paris, and it was a hundred times better than she had anticipated.

"Yes, that's exactly what I'm saying. There's a good rhythm, a playful banter between the female and the male character. This will be a hit."

"Playful banter, characters," Maude repeated, feeling a lot less elated. "Right, it was just playful banter."

Matt was about to say something but was interrupted by the Delgado family.

Anita jumped into Matt's arms.

"You two were great," she said throwing him a loud kiss.

"Next time you two come I hope I won't have to drag you on stage," Rosa said, shaking her finger at Matt.

"I promise, Rosa," he said kissing her cheek. "We have to go now. I still have to show Maude what she's been missing in France all these years."

"All right, Mateo. Take good care of Maude, she's a keeper," she said, turning to Maude. She wrapped her arms around the young girl and held her tight and whispered, "He needs someone like you in his life."

Maude nodded, unsure of how to respond.

"Let's go, Maude." Matt's voice called her back to reality.

She followed him out of the restaurant reluctantly. "Do we have to go? This place is great!"

"I know! What did Rosa tell you back there?"

"Nothing. Just to find the best revenge for the trick you played on me with the spicy machaca."

"No way! I hope you won't follow her advice."

"I think I will, Rosa Delgado is full of wisdom."

It was only once she got home that Maude noticed she had five missed calls from Thomas. She immediately called him back.

"Hi," Thomas answered.

"I'm sorry I didn't get your calls. I was out all day with Matt—"

"You're spending a lot of time outside Soulville with him."

"It's for work. His mission is to make me discover new forms of music. And it worked!"

"He can't make you discover music through Musicfy?"

"Come on, it's not the same. Live music and Musicfy. There's no comparison."

"I guess. So what was the song?"

"I—" Maude hesitated.

"You don't want to tell me. Wow, it feels like you're keeping a lot of things from me lately."

"That's not true."

"You never told me who called you before our performance last week."

Not wanting to delve into Mrs. Ruchet's conversation, Maude just said, "The song isn't a secret. It's just that it's so amazing, I don't know if it'll sound great over the phone."

"You know what? Just don't sing it, that's fine," Thomas said irritably. "Don't mind me. I have terrible taste in music, apparently, because Glitter turned down all my songs."

"Oh, Thomas. Why didn't you tell me?"

"I called you a million times."

"I'm sorry."

"Look, it's fine, I'll talk to you later. Bye."

He hung up and Maude was left staring at her phone, miserable.

She felt like the worst girlfriend. She'd been so caught up in songwriting that she'd been unavailable when he needed her most. She wasn't supportive. But she could do better.

She brought the phone to her lips and recorded her new song, "Paris versus New York," as a voice message. She pressed resolutely on the arrow to send it to Thomas.

Then she wrote him a text message.

Hope this cheers you up

Sorry for not being there

But I'm available now. Meet up at Times Square?

Three dots popped up on his side as he typed his answer. The three dots remained wavering for another minute, a clear sign of his hesitation.

Finally, he answered:

Song is fine. Needs work

Maude, disappointed by his lackluster response, threw her phone on her bed. She'd expected a bit more enthusiasm.

Her phone buzzed again. She'd received another message from Thomas.

Would rather hear you sing your new song IRL

Okay for Times Square, I'll leave now

Maude smiled, then sighed. Of course he'd like the song more if she sang it to him. She'd cheer him up and make him forget about his bad day.

She grabbed her phone, stashed it in her bag, and walked out the door. Deep down, as she thought about the amazing day she'd had, she wondered uneasily if Thomas didn't have reason to doubt the nature of her relationship with Matt.

Chapter Twenty-six

At 6 a.m. sharp Maude arrived at the theater. It was her first time there since her missed performance, but she was so happy to have another chance with Mme. Tragent, she could swallow her pride and do whatever it would take.

"Close your eyes and relax," Mme. Tragent said as she circled Maude.

Maude closed her eyes but was unable to relax under Mme. Tragent's stern stare.

"Did I say close your eyes and tighten your fists?" Mme. Tragent asked. "Loosen your shoulders, Ms. Laurent. Now turn your head in slow circles. Round and round clockwise. That's good."

Having slept with difficulty the previous night, Maude was afraid she'd doze off if she relaxed completely.

"Relaxing before singing is essential, Ms. Laurent. Stress won't help your technique and it certainly won't help your singing or my ears. My ears cannot tolerate mediocre singing."

Maude flinched. How could she have fallen from singing Cinderella's part to being accused of mediocre singing?

"I never said you were a mediocre singer, Ms. Laurent," Mme. Tragent said, as if reading her student's mind.

Maude's eyes shot open in surprise.

"Eyes shut, Ms. Laurent!" she ordered sharply. "Your face is an open book. The least observant person can read your emotions. I am far from being your average reader. You must learn to control your emotions. Your audience isn't interested in your personal life. They don't want to see you battling your inner demons on stage."

"I understand." Maude nodded her agreement.

"Did I ask you to speak, Ms. Laurent?" Mme. Tragent asked coldly.

Maude almost answered no, but stopped just in time.

"How can you relax if you're speaking?"

How could she relax when her teacher was mentally torturing her? Maybe giving her private lessons wasn't a privilege. Perhaps it was just Mme. Tragent's way of exacting vengeance.

"Is my voice a distraction, Ms. Laurent? Do you think I am torturing you for my own pleasure?"

Maude shut her eyes tighter and tried to steady her breath.

"Open book," Mme. Tragent observed disdainfully. "How's my nephew?"

Maude felt blood rising to her cheeks but she remained silent.

"Silence. Finally. The sound I wanted to hear."

She circled Maude like a hawk.

"You obviously have feelings for my nephew," she continued. Maude's eyes opened wide and she was about to protest, but again held back just in time. "Eyes closed," Mme. Tragent repeated impatiently without bothering to look at Maude.

"When will you learn to hide your emotions, Ms. Laurent?"

Maude tried to wear a mask of indifference but couldn't quite succeed. "My nephew is a player, Ms. Laurent. Any tabloid will tell you that."

Maude's breath quickened and she struggled to maintain a blank expression.

"I don't think he's ever been in love, and it's unlikely he will ever be. Don't ever make the mistake of thinking you can change a man. You'll only waste your time."

Maude steadied her breath and erased any trace of emotion from her face.

"Good," Mme. Tragent acknowledged satisfactorily. "Open your eyes, Ms. Laurent."

"As a singer you'll sometimes have to perform in the worst conditions. Sick, hungry, cold. Conditions won't be ideal. The people you love won't always be supportive. It may happen that they'll be the cause of your distraction. A bad breakup right before you perform, bad news, a dying brother, a pregnant sister going into labor minutes before you go on stage. Whatever the reason, life has a way of butting in. That's why it's important for you to learn to put that aside before you go on stage. Before ruining another one of my shows," Mme. Tragent admonished sternly.

Maude smiled, already imagining herself as a lead in an upcoming opera.

"Not that I would dare put you in another one of my operas," Mme. Tragent added. "Have you ever been to the opera?"

Maude remained resolutely silent.

"You may answer my question," Mme. Tragent said.

"I've watched a million of them online."

"That's not the same as a live performance."

"I've never been to one," Maude mumbled.

"That might explain part of the problem. Well, I'll take you to your first opera."

"Me and my favorite soprano at the opera. It's a dream come true!"

"Not just you and me." Mme. Tragent huffed. "I've got five other students, remember? You've received enough special treatment as it is. And flattery won't get you anywhere. Now, about your technique. Since you're becoming a pop singer, you need to use less vibrato. Straighten your shoulders for the following vocal exercises."

Chapter Twenty-seven

Dressed in a flowy yellow, medallion designer dress with a small train, her hair tied in an impeccable bun high on her head, Maude stood in front of the beautiful Metropolitan Opera House. From her vantage point near the fountain, the lights gave everything an incredibly romantic glow. Maude gazed in awe at the five arches of the façade, wanting to stamp each moment in her mind. Her first visit to the opera. She thought it was essential to pause outside to take this moment in. There would be life *ante* and life *post* first opera, and savoring the lead-up was just as crucial as the rest of the experience.

She crossed the threshold.

Despite the crowd drifting through the lobby, she quickly found the group of Mme. Tragent's students standing near one of the enormous murals by the artist Marc Chagall. Thomas was elegantly dressed in a black tuxedo. Lindsey was there, too, in a dazzling carmine dress. The latter huffed her disapproval at Maude's approach, but Maude ignored her and kissed Thomas hello.

"You look amazing," he said, with the look of someone who could not believe his luck.

"Right back at you," Maude replied, thinking they did in fact make a good-looking couple.

“I’m not really used to wearing a tux, but I could get used to it. Gives me a James Bond vibe.”

Mme. Tragent looked lovely, having let her brilliant white hair down in waves around her face.

“We’re all here,” Maude said.

“Not exactly, there’s one more person missing. Ah, there he is.” When Mme. Tragent’s mouth twisted into a pleasant smile, Maude intuited who had arrived even before she saw him. Only one individual could make Cordelia Tragent light up that way.

Matt strode into the opera house wearing a tight-fitting night-blue suit instead of the usual tuxedo. His hair was pulled back in a sleek, low bun. The thud Maude’s heart gave seemed as loud as a gong. She focused instead on one stray black bead on her clutch bag. Interesting little bead indeed. But not interesting enough to sustain her attention once Matt spoke.

“I’m here, let the party begin,” was his laid-back greeting.

Lindsey cried, “Matt!” and scurried over to his side to hug him. He stepped away, not quickly enough in Maude’s opinion, and not obviously displeased with the attention.

“What are you doing here?” Thomas asked, with a baleful frown.

“Hello to you, too, Thomas,” Matt replied cheerfully, making light of Thomas’s annoyance. “My aunt wanted to spend some quality time with her favorite nephew. Hard to refuse.”

“Now, now.” Mme. Tragent intervened. She straightened her nephew’s tie. “Who can tell me what *La sonnambula*, or *The Sleepwalker* in English, is about? Apart from Maude,” Mme. Tragent added immediately.

“Easy, there’s a love triangle,” Matt began, craning his neck to ease the pressure of his aunt’s meddling fingers. “Amina, a poor orphan, and Elvino, a rich villager, are to be married, until a mysterious stranger arrives."

"I'm not asking *you*, Matt," Mme. Tragent interrupted sharply. "I'm asking my students."

Thomas stepped forward. "Elvino's jealous because Count Rodolfo doesn't hide his attraction to Amina. Zero boundaries, that count."

"Maybe Elvino's right to be jealous," Matt interjected, with a wicked grin.

"Amina is faithful to Elvino and loves only him."

"Are you sure? You're *really* sure about that?" Matt scoffed.

"The opera says it, Matt. Not me," Thomas countered. "The only problem is that Amina is a sleepwalker. She sleepwalks right into Count Rodolfo's room in the inn where the whole village finds her. And Elvino, thinking she's been unfaithful, breaks off the engagement."

"You guys both forgot the Lisa character," Lindsey put in. "She likes the count but she's been in love with Elvino since, like, forever. She can't wait to console him when he breaks up with that stupid sleepwalker. He even agrees to marry her. Being patient pays off," Lindsey said, eyeing Thomas.

"She's not a stupid sleepwalker," Maude said, wrapping a protective arm around Thomas. "She's got an illness. And Elvino, once he realizes that Amina is a sleepwalker, gets back together with her and they're happily married at the end."

"Very good, Thomas and Lindsey," Mme. Tragent congratulated them in a rare moment of kindness. "Maude should learn that when I say, 'Not Maude,' it means 'Not Maude.' But you both understand the opera extremely well."

"Not really, Aunty," Matt interjected, raising a finger as if he was in a classroom. "My opinion's always been that Amina unconsciously actually loves Rodolfo, the handsome stranger. She just won't admit it. That's why she ends up sleepwalking into his room. What do you think, Maude?" Matt turned to Maude, and all eyes turned to her.

She dug around in her mind for an appropriate answer to a thinly veiled debate about the status of her relationship. Luckily, at that moment, the bell rang, indicating that they should head to their seats.

Maude sighed with relief, lifted her skirt, and followed Mme. Tragent.

The group was seated in the balcony of the stunning gold and burgundy auditorium. Matt and Lindsey sat in the seats next to Thomas and Maude. Mme. Tragent sat on the left of her nephew. From where she sat, sandwiched between Thomas on her left and Lindsey on her right, Maude admired the golden damask curtain and the chandeliers shining like the brightest stars of the Milky Way. The burgundy seats made her feel like a queen as she listened to the musicians tuning their instruments in the orchestra pit.

Maude frowned slightly when she saw Lindsey slip her arm under Matt's. He caught her gaze and cocked his head to the side, unapologetic. Maude immediately averted her eyes and snuggled closer to Thomas.

Soon the performance began with the choir's entry. Lisa soon followed, lamenting the approaching nuptials.

As soon as Amina, sung by a young South African soprano named Beauty Mbatha, entered, all eyes were on her. Her joy and radiance illuminated the entire stage.

Once the soprano began to sing, Maude's heart surrendered

to the beauty of her voice. Her high notes, higher than any notes Maude could ever achieve as a mezzo-soprano, were like warm raindrops from heaven, and her delight in the role was expressed in her whole demeanor. Maude squeezed Thomas's hand with rapture.

Oh, if she were to sing in an opera one day! If only she hadn't ruined her chances with her first opportunity to perform.

Concentrating on the opera again, Maude watched as the fiancés, an orphan and a wealthy villager, lived a life of bliss until a stranger arrived and stirred the man's jealousy.

When the charming Count Rodolfo sang in his low, bass range, that of a tempter, Maude thought her uneasiness would brim over inside her.

Witnessing Amina playfully interact with the stranger, Maude thought perhaps Matt's interpretation held merit.

Amina didn't seem wholly indifferent to the count's attentions. Even Maude had to admit that the count's bass notes were full of charm and hard to resist.

What about her own relationship? Perhaps only Maude was unfaithful, and Amina appeared to be so simply because Maude wished to justify her own hesitations. Even as she sleepwalked, the heroine still dreamed of her lover, but it had become plainer than ever that Maude preferred Matt to Thomas. Matt's playful demeanor tiptoed persistently in her mind. She glanced at him in the dark, and winced when she saw that Lindsey had rested her head on his shoulder. Maude pushed down her anger, certain the sentiment stemmed more from the fact that Lindsey disrespected the opera than because Matt didn't seem to mind.

The first act ended in a whirlwind of arias and dramatic orchestration as Elvino canceled the wedding due to Amina's supposed infidelity.

The lights went back on signaling intermission.

"I got a call from Glitter," Thomas said, checking his muted phone. "I'm going to call them back. Meet you at the bar?"

"I'll be the one at the end of the line singing Amina's arias," Maude said. She left the balcony and Matt followed her.

"Still unsure about Amina's hidden feelings for Count Rodolfo?" he asked as they arrived at the opera lounge bar. Maude pretended not to hear him as she surveyed the platters of colorful sandwiches, drinks, and amuse-bouches. He repeated the question.

"Stop joking, Matt," Maude said. "Why are you really here?" She chose a tiny square salmon sandwich and a sparkling apple juice.

"Like I said, quality time with my aunt."

"Because living with her doesn't allow you to spend enough quality time with her."

"You got me." He raised his arms like a robber surrounded by a police squad. "I knew it was your first time at the opera and I wanted to be a part of that. And offer you your first tiny, over-priced sandwich." He paid her bill in full. Maude laughed and took a bite.

"I appreciate that. But you don't have to be so mean to Thomas."

"You mean, Elvino."

"I'm not Amina," Maude retorted. "I know what I want. And you're not Count Rodolfo."

"Says who? He's a real gentleman. He doesn't take advantage of Amina in her sleep, and he defends her virtue to her idiot fiancé, who seriously doesn't deserve Amina."

"So just because Count Rodolfo spares a sleeping Amina

she should choose him instead of her true love? Talk about low standards."

"All I'm saying is that she's too busy holding on to Elvino even though she realizes that he's not good enough for her. She sings it in the second act."

"Not good enough for her? You can't be the judge of that."

"He doesn't get her. That's why he breaks up with her when there's the first sign of trouble."

"Thomas and I get along great."

"Not like we do."

"You don't mix business and pleasure."

Silence met her retort. His gray eyes rested on her face with a softness she'd never encountered before. It was as if his gaze looked into the depths of her heart, her mind, her whole being. They were both prey to a prevailing question: *What if?* The answer in her eyes was only a repetition of the same question. Her heart jolted, and the clinking ice cubes in her glass indicated a soft tremor had seized her left hand. Her glass suddenly felt like a boulder.

"All I'm saying," Matt finally said, "is that in real life Amina would have left Elvino for Count Rodolfo."

Maude turned away, disappointed and puzzled.

"I'm going to go now," Matt added.

"What?" Maude croaked, dismayed.

"I came for another reason. Today would have been my mom's forty-second birthday, and anything was better than staying home alone. Thanks for the company."

"You should stay until the end of the opera."

"I don't think that's a good idea. Count Rodolfo doesn't get the girl. He's got no business hanging around Amina anyway. I heard there's a surprise ending in this production. You'll tell me about it?"

"Maybe Count Rodolfo gets the girl at the end."

"I doubt it." His eyes filled with a sudden sadness. "Ultimately, the count only wants Amina to be happy. Good night, Maude."

Matt walked away. Maude couldn't shake the feeling that he was about to say more, that perhaps he had feelings for her. Was it only the fact that they worked together that kept him from declaring them? And how *did* she feel about her relationship with Thomas?

She had to talk to Matt she decided as she whisked away and down the stairs, tripping over the train of her dress, losing a shoe and stuffing her foot back inside. She arrived breathless in the lobby only to see Lindsey link her arm with Matt's. Together they sauntered out of the opera house.

No longer hungry, she threw the rest of her sandwich in the nearest bin. The bell rang and she ran back to her seat, where she met Thomas.

"You didn't come to the bar?" Maude asked.

"The call dragged on a bit, but I've got great news. I sent a new song to Glitter and they want me to release it with them!"

"That's great!" Maude wrapped her arms around him happily. She felt like a weight had been lifted off her. She hadn't realized just how much his failure had affected their relationship.

They sat in the dark and the second act began. As the act developed, Maude could only see it through the lens of Matt's analysis. When Amina sang that Elvino didn't deserve her love and when she wished him happiness, Maude felt that perhaps Elvino and Amina *didn't* belong together.

Quickly the truth triumphed. Elvino and Amina were back

together. With a flurry of joyful violin bows dancing in the orchestra pit the village rejoiced. Until the last seconds. Completely contrary to the original ending, Elvino jilted Amina at the altar and married Lisa!

Amina ended up alone.

The whole audience gave a collective gasp before erupting in thunderous applause as the final curtain fell.

What an ending, Maude thought dismayed. Amina was alone.

That's when she knew: it didn't matter whether Matt wanted her or not. She couldn't stay with Thomas.

Vive l'opéra! she thought, bemused, and joined the audience in its standing ovation.

Chapter Twenty-eight

The following days were intense. Spring had come at last. Maude and Matt recorded her new single and she did several successful brand campaigns, including one for a teen pimple cream, and could not have been prouder. She also filmed the video for her upcoming "Paris versus New York City" single.

Thomas was busy working with Glitter, and they saw less and less of each other, leaving her no time to tell him that she'd decided to break up with him. And to be honest, she didn't know how to do it, which was why they decided to celebrate their four-month anniversary and Maude still hadn't said a word. They went to dinner at Ambrosia.

Once there, Maude felt an acute sense of disappointment.

The restaurant was nice, but she couldn't breathe. The low square dining tables were covered with elegant, pale-pink silk tablecloths. At the far right of the room, a stern-looking pianist was playing softly on a grand piano. The waiters were standing upright in their somber black and white uniforms, their bowties stuck perfectly under their pointy chins. *They'd never drop their plates*, Maude thought, smiling at the memory of Jonathan's short but tragic career as a waiter.

"What are you smiling about?" Thomas asked, glancing up from his menu.

"Oh, I was just thinking of a friend of mine who also happens to be the worst waiter to ever set foot in a restaurant."

She looked around. Couples were whispering over lit candles and glasses of wine. Her mind wandered back to Las Fajitas, where everything was lively and wonderfully noisy, and she sighed.

"I don't really know what to choose. Any suggestions?"

"The shrimp is a very nice starter. You could try that."

"Hm," Maude mused. "Are you telling me it's good when actually it's spicy and you just want to take my picture while my mouth is in flames?"

Thomas looked at her blankly.

"No, I just meant it's good. Ambrosia doesn't serve any spicy dishes," he added matter-of-factly. "Thank goodness for that."

Maude's face fell, but Thomas didn't see it as he was busy waving the waiter over.

Maude almost wished the shrimp were spicy, but, as Thomas had said, they were delicious but plain. At about halfway through their course, Maude saw a tall, blond young man enter the restaurant alone. She held her breath as she looked at him. She could see only half of his face but felt sure it was Matt. Her pulse quickened as the young man talked to the waiter, who then directed him to his table. He walked past Maude and Thomas.

It wasn't Matt.

She felt an immense wave of disappointment.

At that moment she knew she could no longer hide the truth from Thomas. She no longer wanted to be with him. She had to end things. Now.

"Thomas, I think we should talk," Maude started.

At that moment her phone vibrated. It was a text message from Jazmine:

Go on Musicfy, now! Hurry. It's a disaster!

"I just received the weirdest text from Jazmine. I've got to go outside for a couple of minutes. Do you mind?"

She hurried outside without waiting for an answer, just as she received another text message from Jazmine.

Jazmine wants to share this song with you

Maude clicked on the link provided and put the phone to her ear, but almost dropped it when she heard the song:

"New York's the place to see

"Paris is the place to be

"Paris beats New York any day

"Just give up and walk away."

Her song, "Paris versus New York," was on Musicfy. But how was that even possible? It wasn't her voice!

Suddenly Maude let out a small cry as she recognized the singer. It was Lindsey, singing HER lyrics!

Maude's head spun and she thought her legs would give way underneath her. This couldn't be happening. She had to be dreaming! How could Lindsey have known this song? The music continued and the male part began. Once again, the voice sounded oddly familiar. However, it wasn't Matt's voice. As she saw Thomas walking toward her, her eyes widened in disbelief.

Thomas's voice was singing Matt's part!

"Oh my god," she choked, stepping away from Thomas as he reached for her. "Don't touch me."

"What's wrong?" he asked.

"What's wrong? What's wrong!" she shrieked. "You stole my song, Thomas!"

He started to say something but she interrupted him.

"Don't lie to me! It's online right now! Oh my god, is that

why you wanted us to have dinner tonight? Because you knew it would be released today? Is this some sick joke?"

"No, Maude, listen," he said, reaching for her again, but failing. "This isn't a joke. I didn't know they'd release it tonight. It was supposed to be released in a couple of weeks. I— "

"That's your excuse?!" she cried in disbelief. "You didn't know the song you stole from me was going to be released tonight! Are you kidding me? You stole my song, Thomas! From me, your girlfriend. How could you?"

"My girlfriend, you sure about that?"

"What do you mean?"

"I mean you've been eyeing Matt ever since the night at the opera and maybe even before that."

Maude's face grew warm with embarrassment, and immediately anger threatened to overflow. French words rushed to her lips but she bit them back and forced herself to continue in English. "Even if that was true, how does that give you the right to steal from me, you freaking, *two-faced jerk*!"

"Maude, please, calm down. Let me explain!"

"What the hell is there for you to explain? You *betrayed* me, Thomas. You lied to my face. I sang that song to you in confidence. And you used it and recorded it! With LINDSEY LINTON!" Maude rushed back into the restaurant to grab her bag and coat. Thomas followed her, calling her name.

"Maude, listen. *You* got to sign a contract with Soulville Records. And I was happy for you. When I met you, I fell for you. But how do you think that made me feel, huh? You kept tiptoeing around me, afraid to hurt my feelings."

"I was right, wasn't I? You couldn't handle my success."

“That’s not it. But, Maude, my parents are counting on me. All their hopes rest on me. I know you can’t understand that.”

“What?” Maude whirled around, not even caring that the other customers were looking at them. “So now it’s my fault I can’t understand because I’m an orphan!”

“That’s not what I meant,” Thomas said in anguish.

“Since you’re such a parental expert, what would your parents say if they knew just how big of a liar and a thief their little boy is, huh?”

“I don’t want to lose you, Maude. But you know I’m ambitious. That’s one of the things you liked about me. You would never have stayed with me if I hadn’t become a star. Isn’t that what you like about Matt?”

“Matt and I get along because I can talk freely with him. I can be myself. To think, I watched every word I said to you, I was so afraid of hurting your feelings. Deep down I knew I couldn’t trust you. Because the only thing I did tell you, you used against me. You said that the song was bad.”

“It needed work. But when I brought it to Glitter through Lindsey, they knew it’d be a hit. They offered me a contract. I’m with Glitter Records now.”

Maude turned away disgustedly, shaking her head. She grabbed her bag and left the table but Thomas caught her arm and held on tight.

“Please, don’t go,” he pleaded.

She looked at his hand, feeling his fingers tighten around her arm.

“You repulse me,” she said coldly. “Take your hand off my arm right now or you’ll regret it,” she warned him, her eyes dark with pain.

Thomas slowly unlatched his fingers. She snatched her coat from her chair and left the restaurant, head held high.

When she arrived home that evening she was greeted by Jazmine's grim face. "It's all over the internet. I'm so sorry, Maude," Jazmine whispered.

Maude didn't utter a word. She walked past Jazmine and locked herself in her room. Thomas had betrayed her. Her song, the song she had worked on for weeks, had been stolen from her. Her hit song had been stolen. It was the song that was supposed to revive her career after her first failure. This one was special.

And to hear Lindsey sing her part!

Maude held back her tears. She refused to cry over this, even though they were tears of anger.

Thomas didn't deserve tears.

Thomas may have betrayed me, she thought angrily, *but I certainly won't let him break me or my career.*

She walked to her piano and sat down angrily. Slowly, the lyrics formed in her head, and a melody echoed relentlessly through her brain. That night Maude didn't sleep. She didn't hear the door slam when Terence and Victoria came home, didn't hear Terence argue on the phone with Alan. She worked the entire night on her song, perfecting it, molding it with her rage, betrayal, and cold determination.

It was only when the first rays of the pale spring sun made their way through the sky that she fell asleep, exhausted but satisfied.

Chapter Twenty-nine

"She gave our song to the enemy!" Alan Lewis bellowed, banging his fist on the oval table of the conference room. Maude shrank deeper into her seat, wishing she could disappear. She might as well have been invisible. Alan spoke as if she wasn't there!

"How long are you going to stand by her while she makes mistake after mistake?" he asked, his face red with anger.

"How long will you keep looking for excuses to get rid of her, Alan?" Terence asked, his voice composed but his face determined.

"I'm not looking for excuses. She's handing them to me on a silver platter!" Alan spluttered.

"Maude's still young and inexperienced. She shared information with her boyfriend."

"You should have watched her closer instead of giving her all the freedom to *create* and *compose* and *write* and *sing* and waste my money!"

"I take full responsibility, Alan. As for the freedom to create, that's what every artist needs. And no matter what you think, Alan, the song Maude and Matt composed was a great song. That freedom to create you so sternly frown upon gave birth to an immense hit."

"I know it's a hit!" shrieked Alan hysterically. "It's all over Musicfy playlists. Thomas Bradfield is going to be famous. We never should have let him go."

Terence Baldwin spoke calmly.

"I think this proves we were right to let him go. I could never work with an artist capable of such base conduct. Thomas may be famous today, but that will only be because Maude and Matt wrote a song worth listening to, not Thomas. Matt would never have composed a song like that if he had collaborated with Thomas."

"You don't know that, Baldwin. I don't think we should keep her. This girl is too much trouble. We can terminate her contract now and cut our losses. Travis agrees with me."

Terence's eyes flashed. He didn't see Maude jump out of her seat.

"Soulville's keeping Maude Laurent, Alan. We're going to start working on her third single right away. I refuse to—"

Maude didn't hear the end of the sentence as she left the room and headed for the lobby. Nobody ever used the allegedly cursed concert grand piano.

But she would play it. She sat on the bench and began her melody. The piano's keys were hard, and the sound was rough.

By the time Alan and Terence arrived to see what was going on, they weren't the only ones to have gathered around the ancient piano. The singers working in the neighboring rooms, including Matt, had assembled in the lobby. Terence and Alan approached and saw Maude playing.

Then her voice rang out full of emotion:

"I trusted you, I fell for you

"Your eyes were kind, your heart felt true

"How did you dare, oh how could you

"Take my heart and break it in two."

Her voice quivered with heart-wrenching emotion as she sang the chorus:

"Betrayed but not broken

"A door shuts, another opens

"I'll be strong, I will move on

"Your memory won't last till dawn

"Betrayed, but I refuse to be broken

"In time you will be forgotten."

Her hands ran across the piano as she played her solo without singing. Usually when she played, it was effortless. On this piano, however, she felt the energy running through her arms and exploding at the tips of her fingers when they made contact with the hard, clunky ivory. It was as if Maude was fighting against the resistant keys, trying to dominate, to master them, and the result was breathtaking.

She started singing again, her pain visibly spread across her face.

"Your lies echo in my head

"Can't sleep, I toss around in bed

"My heart is full of regret

"What should I have seen?

"What didn't I get?

"I should've known better

"I should've realized sooner

"Although I was burned

"I can stand up and say lesson learned."

She bent her shoulders and slowed the pace of her song.

"Our memories, forever marred

"I see you for who you are."

She picked up the tempo and her notes rang loudly, reverberating against the walls of the room as she played the final part of her song:

"Know that you will always be

"The two-faced liar who betrayed me

"Know that you will always be

"The two-faced liar who never cared for me."

The final solo bars were Maude's triumph as the hard keys submitted to her power and strength. She demonstrated her brilliance as the piano accompanied her beautiful complaint and enhanced her pain and suffering. Like the phoenix rising from its ashes, Maude had given the ancient rosewood piano a new life.

Terence looked at his partner smugly. Alan was dumbfounded. Maude knew he didn't understand much about the creating process, but he knew gold when he saw it, and this was it.

"Release this single before Lindsey Linton does or Maude's out."

"This one will be pop *and* classical," Terence said firmly. Alan's silence was an assent.

Terence smiled at Maude.

Lindsey Linton and Thomas Bradfield were no match for her.

Chapter Thirty

Maude's heart brimmed over with excitement at the prospect of attending her first Igbo high society wedding at a premier country club in New Rochelle with the Baldwins and Matt.

Finally she would live her Nollywood dream!

For her grand debut she wore a gorgeous custom-made crimson skirt, a vibrant yellow puffed-sleeved blouse, and a red coral bead necklace, all like those traditionally worn at Igbo weddings. She carried a beaded clutch, and low-heeled slippers perfect for dancing all night completed her outfit. Maude had never felt so stylish in her entire life, and her hand fan gave her a refined air that she didn't know she possessed.

Victoria's naturally regal demeanor was heightened by the beautiful pink head tie that she wore like a crown and a purple wrap tied around her waist like a long skirt that narrowed at her ankles.

This time, when Maude's heart skipped at Matt's appearance in his handsome two-piece suit, she didn't feel guilty. After all, she was a single girl.

The Baldwins, Maude, and Matt arrived at a waterfront mansion.

The outdoor section where the guests sat was decorated with lively streamers, the chairs were brightened by ribbons, and the beautiful natural backdrop of the countryside deceived Maude into thinking she was no longer in New York, though she hadn't left the state.

Over three hundred guests had gathered in colorful attire to celebrate the couple.

As Terence greeted their friends, Maude looked around and followed Victoria to their seats on the bride's side.

"Here, you should have this." Victoria handed Maude a handful of neatly stacked one-dollar bills.

"Do I need to pay entry?"

"You'll see." Victoria smiled. "Just follow our lead."

"You've done this several times?" Maude asked Matt nervously as they took their seats.

"At least once a year since I've known the Baldwins. The music is crazy good."

"Do you ever do anything that doesn't revolve around music?" Maude teased.

"Is anything in this life not filled with music?"

"Let me see," Maude mused, tapping her chin with her forefinger. "Eating!"

"Even the sound of someone chewing is music."

"Ew, not music I want to hear."

"I'll pay attention when you eat jollof rice at the party."

"No, don't!" Maude pushed him playfully.

"Too late! I'm pretty sure I can make a song out of the rhythm of your chewing."

"How about you stop obsessing over me and focus on the wedding?"

"My only obsession is music," he said, though his lingering gaze suggested quite the opposite.

The crowd quieted and turned their eyes to the mansion's door. From it emerged the beautiful bride dressed in a white head tie, a matching dress accentuating her lovely curves, and a white coral bead necklace. Surrounded by a group of dancers, she danced rhythmically to the drums' beats, including the udu, waving a white feather fan. Her dancing was slow, deliberate, so that all eyes would follow her. And they did. Maude thought she was the happiest bride she'd ever seen.

The first procession was followed by the groom's procession. Elegantly dressed in a white *isiagu*, a long-sleeved top with vivid patterns, and silk trousers, he danced with a more upbeat rhythm.

As his procession ended, he took a seat, surrounded by his best men.

The bride's procession came out a second, then a third time, each time with a beautiful traditional outfit, the third being the handsomest of all. Her intricate updo was strewn with rows of red coral beads. Her dress was a flowing forest green with a contemporary cut and a long train sweeping the ground.

This time, she held a cup.

"What's that?" Maude asked Victoria.

"That's palm wine. It's a tradition. She must give it to her groom. Other men in the audience will call to lead her astray. But she must find her groom. It's proof that she has chosen him."

Maude watched fascinated as the bride hesitated and moved from one man to another before she reached her groom, who waited for her, his eyes brimming with love and pride.

The official ceremony soon followed, marked by blessings and a ritual that consisted of sharing a kola nut. The bride grimaced slightly at the bitterness of the nut.

"This is what I call a wedding," Jazmine said. "I'll def do my wedding like this."

The couple went inside the mansion, and when they reappeared, it was as husband and wife.

The guests surrounded them and sprayed dollar bills on the happy couple.

"That's what this is for!" Maude cried. She fished in her clutch and threw her bills. Ben looked at his bills with regret, hesitating over whether to throw them or not.

"Ben," Victoria said sternly. "I told you, you'll get to keep a few bills, not all."

"It's just, I really want to buy the latest *One Piece* volumes and add them to my manga collection. This is the exact price."

"Do you want to get grounded?" Victoria asked.

Ben turned to the couple and threw a fistful of bills in the air.

"I need to go to the Anime Con next week," Ben said to Maude sheepishly. She laughed and continued to send her bills one by one in the air, as did Jazmine. Cynthia filmed Maude with her phone for posterity.

Then came the food and dance. Maude's dancing skills had improved, but she still felt shy dancing, so she headed to the buffet. Using a large plate and an additional bowl, she helped herself to portions of jollof rice, egusi, pounded yam, and pepper soup with catfish.

Maude looked at the pounded yam with relish. It looked like mashed potatoes but was heavier. She hesitated about using a spoon, then dived in with her hand, splitting a bit of yam from the rest of the compact mass and then adding egusi with goat meat. Once in her mouth, the meat, spices, and flavors all melted on her tongue. What a joy to eat with her hand! It felt like the most natural thing in the world.

After finishing her egusi, she dipped her hand in a bowl of clean water, rinsed it, and glanced at the jollof rice. By then she was full, but she couldn't stop. The food was just too delicious!

As she swallowed a forkful of the long-grain rice, tasting the tomatoes, vegetables, and spices, it dawned upon Maude that something wasn't right. All around her partygoers and family members ate and laughed.

She should have been eating with her own parents, her own family. In her mind, she painted an imaginary picture of herself sitting at a dinner table with her parents, or what she imagined her parents looked like. She added herself in the middle and an imaginary little brother and thought that was what the perfect version of her family would look like. She should have tasted these foods with her parents; not alone at a wedding with perfect strangers, where she was reminded that she knew nothing about her relatives. A feeling of sadness washed over her, and as she chewed her food, the picture became more and more precise, involving scenes of laughter and jokes, herself getting grounded and storming away from the dinner table, celebrating her birthday, food fights with her little brother, who oddly looked like Ben.

Maude munched on to her heart's desire, deep in thought.

Munch, munch, munch.

"Sounds like music to me," Matt said, appearing at her table.

Maude's dreamlike bubble burst. She recalled Matt's earlier comment about music and laughed so hard she almost choked. She hid her lips with her fan to avoid him seeing what was in her mouth on top of hearing her.

She swallowed and lowered her fan.

"You've got a bit of yam on your cheek." Matt indicated the food with a wave of his hand. She brushed it away, or thought she had.

"No wait. It's still there. Here." His fingers brushed her face. She noticed the smoothness and warmth of his hand, and felt the blood rise rapidly to her cheeks. His eyes rested on her; his hand remained on her cheek. His gaze resembled the one the groom had given his bride and Maude felt her heart race. Why hadn't Thomas's touch ever felt like this?

"Maude!" Ben ran to her. The spell was broken. Matt's hand left her face and he turned to his own plate.

"Am I interrupting?" Ben asked, his eyes moving excitedly between Maude and Matt.

"Not at all!" Maude said, stuffing rice in her mouth to hide her discomfort.

"Mom wants to talk to you."

Maude swallowed her mouthful. "Talk to you later?" Maude asked, avoiding Matt's gaze.

Without waiting for an answer she rose and followed Ben to his mom's table. Victoria, deep in conversation with an elderly man, looked up only when Maude approached. The man had a white beard and was dressed in a rich isiagu, and wore a red cap on his head.

"Maude, I'd like to introduce you to Chetachi. He knows every Nigerian family who lived in New York. Maybe he can help you find your father. I'll leave you two together."

"Thank you, Victoria!"

Victoria swished away and joined the dancing.

"So, young lady," Chetachi said in a grave tone. "Who are you?"

"Quite a simple question for anyone but me," Maude answered shyly. "My father's name was Aaron Laurent. But he went by another first name, a Nigerian name, from I don't know which tribe. And he lived in New York before I was born, sixteen years ago. He died I'm guessing before or at my birth. I don't know."

"Aaron?" The man's eyes flashed with a quick recognition, but just as soon as it appeared, the flash was gone.

Maude's eyes ignited with hope.

"Do you know him?"

"I've never heard of an Aaron Laurent. That can't be his name."

"No, you know him, don't you?" Maude insisted. "I can see it."

Chetachi's face shut down, and Maude thought he wouldn't say another word.

"His last name was not Laurent," Chetachi finally said. "No Nigerian I've known was ever called that. You won't find him looking for him with that French last name."

"But he was French-Nigerian."

The man's sudden laughter startled Maude.

"I've never known a French Nigerian man in New York."

"Really?"

Maude recalled the conversation between the Ruchets. She'd assumed her father was French-Nigerian.

"I've been assuming he was French since my last name's Laurent."

"That's not exactly a Nigerian or a British-sounding name."

"But my foster family, they said I was part Nigerian. And if I have my father's name . . ."

"That isn't your father's last name, child."

Maude's jaw dropped as the truth dawned on her.

"Laurent is my mother's name? But why?"

"It seems to me your father didn't legally recognize you."

Maude felt her throat thicken. Her father hadn't cared for her? "What did you know about my father?"

"Nothing," the man said simply. "But I'll give you some advice: forget your father. Don't look for him. Look for your mother's full name." His lips twitched like they were holding something back. Maude thought he was on the verge of saying more, but all he said was, "She should be easier to find within the French system."

Maude could tell he knew something, and it frustrated her that he refused to give her a proper answer. She also knew he wouldn't say another word.

"Thank you, sir," she said politely, though she wanted to scream. "I think I'll go now."

Maude left, feeling heartbroken. She rushed inside the mansion and into one of the rooms, but she wasn't alone for long.

"Maude, are you all right?" Matt asked, entering soon after she did. "I saw you speaking to that man."

"Apparently my father wasn't French, and he didn't legally recognize me," Maude spat. "He didn't care for me at all."

"I'm sure that's not true. You need to keep looking for him."

"How? I don't have his first name or his last. I don't understand. Laurent is my mother's name, and she was French. My father was Nigerian. Where did they meet? And why wouldn't my father care at all?"

"Maybe he did," Matt said. "Why would your foster parents be worried about you finding your father if he was just a man who never cared about you?"

"That's true," Maude said, mulling the idea over. "That's true! He probably did care! Oh, Matt, thank you!"

She threw her arms around him and hugged him.

Realizing just how impulsive she'd been, she moved away from him.

"Come on, we should enjoy the wedding! Don't worry about that now," Matt said.

Maude nodded. "I'll join you in a second," she said.

She took out her phone and went to the browser and typed in the Google search bar: *Finding your birth parents + France.*

All this time she'd thought she needed to find her father when perhaps her mother had been right under her nose, a mother who had legally given her daughter her name. Matriarchy; what was the world without it? There was no way anyone could hide her parents' identity any longer.

Having found the administrative office she needed to contact, Maude rejoined the party and danced until dawn.

Chapter Thirty-one

"Alan, as usual, is all riled up," Terence declared at the dinner table a few days later. "Ever since Thomas stole your song and made the Billboard Hot 100, Alan has been talking about suing Glitter Records."

"Lawyers, huh," Victoria said with slight but unmissable contempt. "That's never a good idea."

"That's what I told him. He's set on it, however. I keep telling him it's a waste of time. Even if we won, it would still be months of bad press for Soulville and for Maude."

"You're right. She can't launch her single in the middle of a trial," Jazmine agreed.

"Thomas should still pay for what he did, though," Cynthia remarked. "Maybe a trial could be a good way to start. He had no right to steal her music from her."

"I agree with you, Cynth," Maude said. "However, I plan on beating him fairly. I'll knock his single off the Billboard Hot 100."

She was more than determined to beat Thomas and Lindsey by releasing a greater hit. She knew "Betrayed but Not Broken" was solid, and this time no one would steal it from her. She just wished Alan would stop watching her every move like a hawk.

"He's at number thirteen. I'm sure he could have been in the top three if he'd used our musical arrangement instead of that dreadful, ear-piercing beat he used," Terence said, wincing.

"Right, Dad, because stealing her lyrics wasn't enough, he really should've taken her musical arrangement too!" Jazmine exclaimed sarcastically.

The whole table laughed.

"He'll be another one-hit wonder, I'm sure," Victoria said sympathetically. "I honestly don't think suing is the right way. We've always managed to keep lawsuits out of Soulville's business, and I think it should remain that way. You know how much I hate lawyers."

"Come on, Mom, lawyers aren't all bad," Cynthia argued. "Nathalie Fern, founding member of your women's rights association, is a lawyer, and she's great."

"She's probably the only one I know of. Believe me when I tell you most of them can't be trusted."

"I agree," Terence chimed in. "Remember that ex-boyfriend of yours, Vic? Ted Willow. He became a lawyer and the worst scoundrel too. But then, I never trusted him, even back then."

Victoria nodded in agreement while her children gasped in surprise.

"Ex-boyfriend?!" they yelped in unison.

Victoria laughed.

"Oh please, kids," she said waving her hand nonchalantly. "You do know your parents had a life before you, don't you?" she mocked them.

"I didn't," Ben replied mournfully.

"Mom probably had more of a life than Dad, because he didn't care about much except music back then," Jazmine teased.

"As if that's changed." Cynthia giggled.

They all laughed. Maude could almost picture Terence as a sixteen-year-old band geek.

"Ahem." Terence cleared his throat. "I think we're moving further and further from the initial topic."

"Yeah, lawyers stink!" Ben exclaimed, pinching his nostrils.

"That isn't true," Cynthia said softly. "And I firmly intend to become one," she added half defiantly, half bashfully.

Dead silence filled the dining room. Victoria's fork hung limply in midair, and Jazmine, who was drinking, almost choked. Maude looked around the room, wondering what was happening.

"What?" croaked Victoria.

"I want to become a lawyer," Cynthia repeated, her voice firmer.

"You're at Juilliard, *the world leading* performing arts college, and you want to be a *lawyer*?" Terence asked, as if he'd misheard.

"I want to become a lawyer," Cynthia repeated. "I've been meaning to announce this good news to you for a while, but I—"

"Good news!" Victoria spluttered. "I'd go for *surprising*. Good, definitely not," she said, narrowing her eyes.

"Victoria," Terence said gently.

Cynthia looked taken aback as Victoria rose from her chair.

"I— Any other Nigerian parent would be thrilled to have their daughter study law," Cynthia stuttered miserably.

"I thought I'd raised my daughters to explore interesting, brave, *new* possibilities, not go into conventional, stuffy careers in which conflict is encouraged just to make more money!" Victoria hissed fiercely.

Then she stormed out of the dining room.

Terence seemed as surprised as his wife and stood up as well.

"Dad," Cynthia pleaded.

"You might have announced this piece of news in a proper manner, Cynthia," he declared before leaving the table.

"That went well, Cynth," Jazmine said after her parents had left. "Since when do you want to become a lawyer anyway? This is the first I've heard of it."

"Mom is totally blowing this out of proportion!" Cynthia exclaimed. "I've been working with Nathalie every Friday and Saturday afternoon since January, and I really love it." Cynthia's eyes brightened as she spoke about her internship.

"And Mom doesn't know? Maybe just give them a little time." Jazmine sighed. "They obviously can't imagine that a Baldwin child could make a career out of anything other than music."

"Especially something as boring as law," Ben added.

Cynthia narrowed her eyes at her brother, who hid behind his napkin.

"Let's face it, our parents have always had a thing against lawyers. I don't think they would have minded your change of calling so much had it been anything but law," Jazmine acknowledged, wrinkling her nose.

"I'm guessing they thought you wanted to work in the music industry since you entered Juilliard and work at Soulville," Maude put in. "They'll need time to adjust."

"I could never be a lawyer," Jazmine said, thinking aloud. "No briefcase would be big enough to carry my bass guitar. And I absolutely cannot part with it," she said.

"You guys have to help me speak to Mom."

"When she's like this?" Jazmine said. "No way. I'd rather be anywhere else. You're on your own, sis." She then shoveled large bites of food into her mouth and hurriedly left the table.

"Jazmine! You haven't finished your plate! Ben?"

Ben didn't even bother to find an excuse. He just took his plate to finish his dinner upstairs.

Cynthia rolled her eyes as she watched her siblings vanish one by one.

"Maude, are you leaving too?" Cynthia asked.

"Sorry, Cynth, I've got loads of work to do this evening," Maude answered, gulping down her water before scurrying out of the dining room.

Maude made a quick stop in the living room to see if she'd received any mail. A stack of unopened letters was piled on the coffee table. She rummaged quickly through them. Gas bill, water bill, a magazine subscription for Victoria Okafor-Baldwin, Jazmine's April issue of *Vogue*, and a *New York Times* special edition.

Nothing for her.

She hurried up to her room and turned on her laptop. She checked her emails for the hundredth time that week and nearly shrieked when she saw she'd received a new message from the French administration, the Conseil national pour l'accès aux origines personnelles (CNAOP). She read it.

Ms. Laurent,

The CNAOP has received your request for information as to the identity of your parents. Unfortunately, we are unable to give you their identity for the following reason: your mother is listed as unknown.

However, we can confirm that the birth of Maude Laurent was registered at the Bichat-Claude Bernard Hospital in Paris on September 7.

According to the law n°93-22 of January 8, 1993, a

mother can give birth under the name X when she wishes to keep her anonymity. This applies to the father's name also. This law was meant to protect mothers who are in danger, which means your mother's name is not traceable. However, under this same legislation, mothers have been encouraged to leave letters, objects, and information in case their child were to look for them. This is not an obligation. But it is our mission to give these things to the abandoned child if he or she seeks to retrieve them.

In your case, your mother left a box in your name. It has not been opened. For you to retrieve it, you must come to Paris with your ID card . . .

Her mother didn't want to be found?

Her head spinning, Maude reread the email several times.

Her mother hadn't wanted her to know who she was. And yet she had left Maude a box. Maude reread the email yet again. She had been born in Paris! The Ruchets had always led her to believe she'd been born in the north of France. No wonder she'd always felt an inexplicable attraction to that city. Her heart beat a little faster as she read, "This law was meant to protect mothers in danger." Had her mother been in danger at the time of her birth? And from whom? Was she not with Maude's father at the time? Was he the danger?

Maude shut her laptop firmly. She was filled with cautious excitement but couldn't let this email drive her crazy. She'd find a way to go to Paris when she returned to France, but right now there wasn't much else she could do.

She'd never been closer to finding out more about her parents.

Chapter Thirty-two

"That was tolerable," Mme. Tragent remarked cynically.

Maude had just finished singing "Tra la la…Coupe-moi, brûle-moi" from Georges Bizet's *Carmen*.

"Just remember, your character is playful, witty, and full of charm. She knows it and so does everyone else in the opera. Don't hesitate. Your laugh isn't as charming as it should be."

Maude held back an impatient sigh. She'd tried at least thirteen different laughs but none suited her demanding teacher.

Mme. Tragent moved away from her piano, closer to Maude, and looked at her thoughtfully. "When singing opera you have to be wholeheartedly in character. Every detail counts. That laugh of yours was too jittery. It scorched my poor ears," she said, walking away.

"That's because I've been forcing twenty different kinds of laughs!" Maude protested.

Mme. Tragent turned abruptly to Maude, facing her with flashing eyes. Maude recoiled, then decided against it, straightening defiantly and letting out a light, graceful, witty laugh.

Mme. Tragent hid an amused smile.

"That's better," she granted.

Maude heaved a sigh of relief. Even laughing demanded a

herculean effort with Mme. Tragent. Nevertheless, she enjoyed singing *Carmen*.

"I know you enjoy every minute you spend here," Mme. Tragent observed with her uncanny knack of reading people's thoughts. "No matter how harsh I am, you still comply."

"I want to improve," Maude replied truthfully.

"You have improved, Ms. Laurent. You can now sing pop whenever you want. And you can sing opera. Whenever you want."

Maude peered at her stern teacher curiously. Mme. Tragent complimenting her students was a rarity Maude had only heard of but had never actually witnessed.

"You have what it takes to become a remarkable operatic singer if you wish. With more classical training, of course. Have you ever considered pursuing a classical career?"

"Before coming to New York I wanted to pursue a classical career," Maude admitted.

"And now?"

"I can't say the idea of becoming an operatic singer isn't thrilling. However, classical music is exclusive. It's impossible for an operatic singer to sing anything else. I've discovered pop, jazz, rock, rhythm and blues, and soul. I would never want to give those up."

"Who says you would have to? Take Barbara Hendricks, for example. She's a world-renowned soprano operatic singer and yet—"

"And yet she also sings jazz professionally," Maude finished, nodding. "I see what you mean. Nevertheless, she's one of the happy few."

"You must make your own path. Shape your own career

whichever road you choose," Mme. Tragent advised. "I heard extracts of your upcoming single."

Maude winced, waiting for her teacher's sharp criticism.

"It wasn't as awful as I thought it would be," Mme. Tragent continued. "You and Matt did a good job using different musical influences. Mixing elements of pop and classical is a feat. It makes for an interesting song."

She paused, observing Maude with her penetrating stare.

"You're lucky to be working with Terence. I hope you realize that. He gave you the freedom to experiment and to create music reflecting who you really are. Matt wasn't so lucky with Glitter Records. Classical music is a part of you and blends well with every modern musical style as long as it is done correctly. Don't erase that part of you just to fit into a category, a label."

"I wouldn't dream of it," Maude replied solemnly.

Mme. Tragent looked anxiously at Maude.

"I hope you'll always have so much freedom, but I'd be wary of Alan if I were you. He's a shark who would've been better off at Glitter than at Soulville."

Maude smiled ruefully.

"Just don't let anyone else steal your songs and you'll be fine," Mme. Tragent added dryly. "Now, enough daydreaming. Start over from the beginning!"

Chapter Thirty-three

After weeks of intense studio work and the filming of a video, Soulville was just days away from the release of Maude's new single "Betrayed but Not Broken."

Soulville was hosting a party for the event, and everybody was caught up in the buzzing excitement. But Maude had other important things to think about.

She needed to go to Paris to retrieve the box her mother had left her, but she hadn't the faintest clue how to do it. Her social and work calendars were packed.

In three days her single would come out, and a week after that she was to attend Franklin High's annual summer dance. It was exhilarating and frightening at the same time. While these events were worth looking forward to, they were also a reminder that her stay was inevitably and inescapably coming to an end, unless her single reached the top three on the Billboard Hot 100 or Musicfy's Top 100.

"All right, Maude, that was great," Matt said from the other side of the room. "Let's take five. Apparently Terence and Alan want to speak to us."

"About what?" Maude asked, as she joined him in the sound room.

"About your release party," Alan answered as he and Terence entered the room.

"I'm totally ready to perform. I've been practicing again and again for—"

"You won't be performing," Alan stated bluntly.

"What?" Maude interjected.

"*We* have decided," Alan started. He turned to Terence, who wore an expression of deep disapproval but who remained silent. "We've decided that you aren't ready to perform."

"I'm ready," Maude insisted. "If this is about what happened with *La Cenerentola*—"

"It has everything to do with that evening."

"A release party is meant to promote the artist," Matt intervened. "What's the use of throwing a release party if no one even gets to hear her sing?"

"There will be reporters, producers, people from the music business. It's too much pressure on Maude for now. Once the single is a hit she'll sing at other events. For now, the stakes are too high."

"I made one huge mistake, I know that," Maude pleaded. "I'm never making that mistake again. I can sing Friday night, Alan."

"How do I know you're not going to have a serious case of stage fright again, huh?"

"I've worked on it, Alan! Madame Tragent gave me some really great tips: eating light before the performance, no cell phone, getting plenty of sleep . . ." Maude's voice trailed off once she realized Alan couldn't care less about what she said.

"So, what now? You're going to keep her cooped up for the rest of her career?" Matt sneered. "She's a singer, Alan. Singing in public is part of her job and she needs to do it every chance she gets. She's ready for this."

“No,” Alan said firmly. “Instead, you two are going to be promoting this single to every reporter in the room. You’ll be interviewed together, you’ll smile for the cameras and say ‘cheese’ for the entire evening.”

“Together?” Maude asked.

“You heard me. We’re going to be selling you two just as if your single had been ‘Paris versus New York City.’ You’ll tell them how well you work together, that you’re the best of friends, that it was the greatest experience you ever had. You’re going to make this work,” Alan finished.

He looked them each squarely in the eye before walking out. Maude turned to Terence pleadingly.

“I tried, Maude,” Terence said, as if reading her thoughts. “He won’t budge, and Travis agrees with him. I’m outnumbered. Just remember that this will still be your evening. Your music will be played. We’re finally releasing that pop and classical song you wanted. Your single will speak for itself,” he added softly.

“I hope he’s right,” Maude whispered as she watched Terence leave.

Chapter Thirty-four

Soulville Tower had been turned inside out for the event. It was like an open house where the guests flowed from room to room with glasses of champagne in one or both hands. Alan had used his connections to gather the most influential people in the music industry to promote Maude's first single, and her music filled every room.

Everyone quietened as Maude made her entrance, gliding softly across the stage in an elegant coral one-shoulder dress with a ruched bodice and flowing skirt. Her shoulder was draped with a row of flowers, the floral applique looking as soft as her brown skin. Her hair was elegantly coiffed, but nothing stood out more than the wide smile that lit up her face, her eyes, and her entire being.

"Hello, everyone," she started smoothly. "I want to thank you all for coming this evening for the release of 'Betrayed but Not Broken.' I would also like to thank Soulville Records for making this dream come true. I couldn't have done it without the most talented singer-songwriter I've met. Matt, thank you."

Matt, understanding his cue, came up on stage beside her like they had planned, and diligently proceeded to smile at the cameras.

"We'll answer all your questions," Maude said. "Meanwhile, I hope you'll enjoy this wonderful evening!"

Maude and Matt left the stage and were immediately led away by *Beats* reporter Lexie Staz, who ushered them into a studio. She was tall and wore a silver dress and black Louboutins. She hid behind large Ray-Ban glasses and wore a childish grin. But Maude had heard that behind her glasses and her naïve look she was a woman with remarkable instincts. She fed on information and reveled in discovering hidden details, masked expressions, and secrets of any kind.

"So, I want to know everything about your collaboration," she started, with a dazzling smile.

"Ask away," Maude answered.

"How was it? Did you always see eye to eye or were there times where you wanted to rip out each other's throats?"

Maude and Matt looked at each other and laughed.

"I can't say we got off on the best foot," Maude answered between giggles. "The first time we met Matt spilled coffee on my brand-new coat."

"I didn't do it on purpose," Matt put in playfully.

"As we worked together, we got to know each other better. Matt has taught me so much about music, about writing and singing, and gradually, we really clicked. When I arrived from France all I knew was classical music, and he really helped me discover all sorts of different styles and rhythms."

"Like you said, you're French and so is Matt. Which language do you speak when you're together?"

"English, of course!" Maude exclaimed, thinking of the only time she had spoken in French to Matt.

"Except when she's angry with me," Matt added slyly, as if reading Maude's thoughts.

"That happened once!" Maude exclaimed in mock indignation.

Lexie Staz laughed at Maude's indignation then pursed her lips musingly.

"And you're away from your family and friends in France? Don't you miss them?"

A dark shadow clouded Maude's face for a split second as she thought of the mother she knew little about. She quickly smiled again before answering.

"Terence Baldwin and his family have been great. They've treated me like I was one of their own, and I'll never forget it."

"About the creation process, now. What are your influences?"

"Like I said, before coming to New York, I only knew classical music. Matt and the Baldwins broadened my views, and we wanted to put a large range of influences in each song we wrote. In 'Betrayed but Not Broken,' the song has a pop element but the piano solos are quite classical. I was inspired by Beethoven's *Tempest* to portray a poignant emotional distress."

Lexie's eyes bore holes through Maude. "Were you in a state of emotional distress when you wrote this song? Is this song aimed at someone in particular?"

Maude hesitated, disconcerted.

"The first thing I taught Maude," Matt put in, "is that the best music comes from suffering. Speaking about pain is something every good musician should be able to do. And Maude did it incredibly well in 'Betrayed but Not Broken,' in which she talks about the painful realization that betrayal can cause. Everyone can relate to that."

Maude looked at Matt and sent him a silent thank-you.

"And what about you, Matt? How did you like working with Maude?"

"I loved every second of it," Matt said softly. He turned away from Maude and cleared his throat. "She's one of the most talented singers I've ever worked with, and I look forward to working with her again."

Maude could tell Lexie Staz had also clocked Matt's affectionate smile, but she was taken aback by the reporter's next probing question.

"Your love life has taken quite a toll. Since you've started working with Maude you haven't been in the tabloids. Can you say that Maude has had a calming effect on you?"

Matt laughed while Maude looked away. She felt uncomfortable speaking to a prying journalist about her work with Matt, especially concerning a supposed "calming effect" that she had never even observed.

"I was out of the tabloids before working on Maude's album and you know it, Lexie. This collaboration, however, has been a great experience, if that's what you mean."

"So you mean to tell me that you and Maude haven't considered becoming more than friends, even after spending so much time together in the studio?"

"I'm not Maude's type," Matt said, smooth as always.

Lexie raised a curious eyebrow at Maude, whose face was burning up.

"So, no special guy in your life, Maude?"

"No. Not anymore, I mean. I honestly haven't had the time. Working, discovering a new city, that didn't leave me any time for dating or getting to know guys."

"Except for Matt."

"Yes, but he's more like a brother to me now, so I'm still waiting for Mr. Right," Maude said, almost flinching at the expression *Mr. Right*.

"Sometimes Mr. Right is *right* under your nose." Lexie smiled mischievously. "Okay, that's a wrap!" she said, turning her Dictaphone off.

Then she scurried off like a small insect that had gotten everything it needed. Maude turned to Matt.

"How was I?"

"It was fine. You shouldn't take her too seriously. Never speak too personally, or she'll eat you alive."

"Thank goodness you answered that question on suffering and betrayal."

"That's typical Lexie Staz. And the next reporter who questions you on love or a boyfriend, just say a simple no. Don't give too many details."

"Or I'll just say that I'm not your type if they ask me if we're an item," Maude said.

"That would be an outright lie," Matt replied suavely, before pushing the studio door open and heading over to a crowd of reporters.

Maude followed him with a wide, pleased grin. She never would've imagined that she was Matt's type since she was nothing like the glamorous celebrities he usually dated.

"Hey, that's Chad!" Maude pointed to a tall, chubby young man with a red cap.

"Who?" Matt asked, following her gaze. "Ah, Chad the Expat."

Noticing he'd been spotted, the influencer dashed to Maude and Matt and greeted each with a hug.

"Glad you could make it," Maude said, smiling from ear to ear. "I didn't know if you would."

"Last I heard, you were in India," Matt said.

"I'm dead tired. I flew from New Delhi to New York yesterday."

Chad rubbed his eyes and the dark circles under them. "Wouldn't have missed this for the world."

"This evening wouldn't have been complete without inviting the person who started it all," Maude said.

"You did all the hard work. All I did was give you a platform."

"I'll be eternally grateful for that."

"Grateful enough to write a song called 'Chad'?"

"Maybe not." Maude laughed. "Though I've wanted to write a song about a crazy stalker for a while. I could call *that* one 'Chad.'"

"I'll pass!" Chad joked.

Maude heard her and Matt's names being called.

"That's Alan," Matt said. "We should report for duty or he'll remind us that time is money."

Maude hugged Chad good-bye and left with Matt.

They were inseparable for the following hours, smiling and answering every question with grace, wit, and charm. Maude was completely at ease and was enjoying herself so much that she barely saw time fly. Until her phone buzzed. The caller ID appeared in full view and before she could hide it from Matt, he read the name.

"You're still talking to Thomas?" he asked, sounding hurt.

"No." She wondered why he was calling her now. "But I should answer. Give me a second."

Maude moved away from Matt.

"Why are you calling me?" she asked once she'd answered the phone.

"Maude! I wanted to say congratulations on your new release."

"You've got some nerve. I thought there was an emergency."

"There is! Maude, I want to make you an offer."

"I'm not interested."

"Seriously, it's a good one."

"Bye, Thomas."

Maude hung up and returned to Matt's side.

But later in the evening she felt a knot in her stomach as she saw Matt talking to a newcomer she knew all too well.

"Hi, Maude." Lindsey greeted her sweetly as Maude approached the pair.

"I didn't know you were on the guest list."

"Alan invited her," Matt replied.

"I'm so glad I came to this little gathering. Did I miss your performance?"

"I'm not performing tonight, Lindsey, and you know it as well as I do," Maude managed to say through gritted teeth.

"What? No performance! That's perfectly ridiculous!" Lindsey laughed. "Unless . . ." She paused then continued. "Unless Alan is afraid that you'll run off the stage again."

Lindsey's piercing laugh drilled Maude's ears.

"Don't worry, Maude, I'm here now. You can perform, and if you want to run off stage, I'll take up where you left off," she finished snidely before walking away.

To Maude's surprise, Matt followed Lindsey determinedly and caught up with her as she took a glass of sparkling water from a waiter. Biting her lip, Maude watched them speak animatedly, until Matt looked Maude's way with a pained expression. Maude wondered what Lindsey had said, but Matt walked swiftly away, pinning a broad grin on his face as he approached Maude and a reporter.

Maude instantly felt something was wrong. Although a smile was still plastered on his face, Matt's countenance grew increasingly cold as the evening waned.

She sighed, feeling like every time they took one step forward they immediately took two steps back.

Chapter Thirty-five

"Know that you will always be

"The two-faced liar who never cared for me."

Maude, facing the mirror, combed her Afro as the last notes of her song died out. She had been in the process of preparing for the 1970s-themed summer dance when her song started playing. It was probably the tenth time she'd heard it on the radio since her single had been released, but she never got tired of the warm feeling she felt whenever her voice streamed out of Musicfy.

She hadn't disappointed Mr. Baldwin or Matt or herself. And that was what she loved about it. She was proud of what she had accomplished, and hopefully she'd get to stay in New York and work on her debut album.

Maude's thoughts were interrupted by a light knock at the door.

"Come in!"

"Are you ready? Jazmine will be ready any minute now. But first I'd like to talk to you," Terence began as he took a seat on the corner of her bed.

"I'm done. What's wrong? You look very serious," Maude said, wondering how anyone could feel concerned when she was so utterly, blissfully happy.

"I don't know how to say this, Maude."

"Oh. I think I can guess," Maude said, eyes downcast. "The numbers aren't great."

"The numbers are great. You've made it onto the Billboard Hot 100 *and* Musicfy's Top 100."

"But not in the top three, right?"

"You're at forty-nine on Billboard and thirty-eight on Musicfy. It's nothing to be ashamed of, Maude. Much better than 'Sunrise'! But it's not enough for us to give you a contract for a full album." Terence rubbed his tired face with his hands. "If we'd released 'Paris versus New York City' as a second single, 'Betrayed but Not Broken' would have been in the top three. I just know it."

"I'm sorry, Terence."

"You're sorry? Why would you be sorry? I'm the one who's sorry."

"It's my fault Thomas stole my second single, my fault this new single's results are average."

"They're not! The single's been streaming like crazy."

"I made you waste all this money," Maude continued. "I wish I could give it all back."

"Maude, Maude, Maude." He hugged her. "You were not a waste. You're one of the best artists Soulville has ever had."

"You really think so?"

"If it was only up to me, I'd give you the contract. But the board won't hear of it. Still, we've got one bit of good news. Since you're going back to France, Cynthia thought maybe you'd like to play for an audience there. We don't want the *Cenerentola* performance to be the only experience you have as a performer. Cynthia booked you a spot on a show called *Terre à Terre*. Do you know it?"

"Everyone in my class watches it." Maude smiled sadly. "I'm glad I'll get to play in front of an audience."

Her heart pounded loudly in her chest at the thought that suddenly dawned on her.

"Oh, but that means we're going to Paris!" she cried.

She would be able to retrieve her mother's box!

"Yes," Terence confirmed. "We're going to Paris. The entire Baldwin family will be there to support you. Matt's coming, too, he has some business to attend to. And then we'll go to Carvin to say good-bye. We'll miss you so much," he added. Maude looked up at him, tears welling in her big brown eyes. Terence's face was fraught. "I wish there was more I could do."

Maude brushed back her tears.

"You've already done so much! And don't worry, I'll be fine. For now, I'll just have fun. When are we leaving?"

"In a week," he answered softly. "Enjoy yourself tonight."

He kissed her gently on the forehead and walked quietly out of the room. Despite the sadness Maude felt, the display of affection on Terence's part made her heart glow. There had never been any affection in her previous home; the one she'd be going back to. She tucked this scene into her treasure chest of loving memories to retrieve once she was alone in Carvin.

• • •

"Do you think I look anything like Diana Ross?" Jazmine asked in the taxi on the way to Franklin High.

She checked her Afro in the rearview mirror.

"You might be mistaken for her very distant cousin," Maude mused. "Open your eyes a little wider and you'll look just like her. Anyway, you won't be playing only Diana Ross's songs this evening, will you?"

"Of course not! We've got a huge list of disco hits from Chic to the Jacksons and Barry White. You'll see."

"I hope you aren't too nervous about your band playing in front of the entire school. Not to stress you out or anything, but if the summer dance sucks, it's on you. That's a lot of pressure," Maude joked.

Jazmine was the most confident person Maude had ever met, and she couldn't imagine her feeling the least ounce of pressure about a high-school dance.

"I'm not worried about our band. There'll be a DJ, too, you know. It's just—" She hesitated.

"What's wrong?" Maude asked, concerned.

"Jonathan's been acting strange the last couple of weeks. I know he doesn't want us to be more than just friends, but still, he's been growing distant."

"What do you mean?"

"I don't really know. It's just a vibe I've been getting." Jazmine turned to Maude anxiously. "I've never liked a guy this much, Maude. It kills me to feel we're growing apart."

"Why don't you talk to him about it?"

"I don't really know how to bring it up."

"I know what you mean. Matt's been avoiding me since the release party, and I don't really know how to get our friendship back on track."

"You should definitely talk to him at the dance tonight."

"Tonight?" Maude asked, surprised. "He's coming to the dance?"

"Yes, with Lindsey." Jazmine wrinkled her nose. Then she looked at Maude and realized that Maude hadn't known.

"He didn't tell you," she said, biting her lower lip. "God, Matt can be so—"

"It's fine." Maude reassured her quickly, although her face said otherwise. "It doesn't matter. I'm glad you told me. That must've been what they were talking about at the release party."

"I don't even know why he's going with the girl who stole your song."

"It was his song too. Apparently, he's forgiven her." Maude shrugged, trying but failing to appear nonchalant.

"Have you forgiven Thomas?"

Maude shook her head. "I haven't spoken to him since he called me at the release party."

"Why would Matt forgive Lindsey and come to the dance with her? He knows how much I hate her!" Jazmine exclaimed, as if that was a justification.

Maude couldn't help but laugh at Jazmine's indignant pout.

"I don't think he chooses his girlfriends to suit your tastes," Maude pointed out. "Let's forget Lindsey. Tonight's going to be a fun evening, no conflicts! I'll clear things up with Matt and we can be friends again." She hesitated at the word *friends*.

She wondered if they had ever actually been friends. They were a good team and wrote great music together. Were they *friends*? Not when her heart beat the way it did when he was near her.

"If you ever become friends with Lindsey, you're dead to me," Jazmine warned as the taxi pulled up in front of the school.

"That will *never* happen." Maude laughed as they exited the cab.

When they entered the school, they discovered that the gym had been completely transformed. The blaring lyrics of the Bee Gees's hit “Stayin’ Alive,” a blinding disco ball, and neon balloons greeted them. Metallic confetti fell into their hair. Bell-bottoms and platform shoes were sweeping the dance floor while wiggling dancers were trying but not quite succeeding in copying the fancy moves they had seen in 1970s-themed movies. Jazmine left to go set up the stage with her bandmates, while Maude hit the dance floor.

She’d barely started dancing when she heard frantic, high-pitched squeals and shrieks of delight, and people rushed around her to the doors.

Matt and Lindsey’s entrance was a noticeable event, and two-thirds of Franklin High’s female population rushed to Matt. Not having any paper on hand, they didn’t hesitate to ask for autographs on various body parts.

Maude went to get herself a drink; her throat was very dry suddenly. Seeing them together was harder than she thought it would be, and she didn’t want the dazzling couple to notice her.

Unfortunately, Maude’s wish wasn’t granted, and Lindsey made a beeline for her.

“Maude! So happy to see you!” Lindsey yelled over the music.

“I’m sure you are,” Maude said sarcastically.

Lindsey glanced around as if looking for someone.

“Don’t tell me that the great Maude Laurent came to this dance by herself!” she squealed.

“I came with friends,” Maude answered calmly. She looked fondly at the stage where Jazmine and her band had started to play.

“You poor thing! I couldn’t have shown my face all alone. I’m so glad Matt came with me. I’d be lost without him.”

Maude looked at Matt, who hadn’t bothered to wear a 1970s outfit and was still surrounded by girls.

"He's not even dressed up," she scoffed, trying to hide her discomfort. "And from where I'm standing, it looks like he came with the entire female population of Franklin High."

Lindsey looked like she'd swallowed a wasp. She hissed, "You're just another one-hit wonder, Maude. After this single withers out, no one will ever hear your name again."

"You're just sorry you didn't manage to steal 'Betrayed but Not Broken' instead of 'Paris versus New York City,'" Maude went on, undaunted. "I should thank you. Without your little scam I might never have written my very first hit single. To Lindsey and Thomas," Maude said, raising her glass of punch as if giving a toast. "You say I'm a one-hit wonder when I've already created two," she mused. "If I were you, I'd be worried. How are you ever going to release another Hot 100 hit without me?"

Lindsey swallowed, genuine anguish etched on her face. Maude was confident she'd said aloud exactly what had kept Lindsey awake for the last months.

"Says the nobody who became famous only after singing *my* song. You'd still be stuck in your little French town singing lame opera songs if it wasn't for 'Burning Bridges.'"

"Maybe I used your song to start my career," Maude replied hotly, "but you needed mine to further yours. That means I'm relevant, and you're a has-been."

"I'm planning on collaborating with Matt again soon," Lindsey taunted Maude defiantly. "We'll have an even bigger hit than 'Burning Bridges.'"

"Good luck with that," Maude said, feeling a lot less flippant than she sounded. "The smoke has cleared," she pointed at Matt, who was standing alone, having finished signing autographs. "I don't think we have anything more to say to each other, Lindsey. Enjoy your evening."

She turned but froze as she noticed Thomas entering the gym. He spotted her almost instantly and headed toward her but was stopped, just like Matt had been, by a herd of delighted students. Thomas excused himself, pushed away a few disappointed fans, and walked toward the stage, where the Screaming Angels were starting on "(Shake, Shake, Shake) Shake Your Booty."

"What's he doing?" Maude wondered.

Thomas took the microphone from an equally surprised Stacey and cleared his throat.

"Hi," he started, out of breath. "I'm sorry to interrupt your evening, but this won't take long. I have something very important to say to a very special person."

He looked at Maude and took a deep breath.

"Wow, I've never felt so nervous," he acknowledged frankly. "Maude Laurent, I'm in love with you."

Maude dropped her glass of punch and prayed the ground would open and swallow her alive.

This couldn't be happening.

"I know I acted like a total jerk. I was so wrong, and I'm so sorry. I've been sorry for weeks. I've missed you, your laugh, your sense of humor, and your incredible smile. I want to make things right. Please forgive me. I know you never want to speak to me again, but I won't leave this stage until you do," he finished dramatically.

Maude hid her face behind her hands, wanting it to stop. She slowly peered through her fingers. A whole crowd of students was staring at her, waiting for her answer. Her throat was too dry for her to utter a word so she just looked at Thomas and pointed at the entrance, signifying she wanted to talk outside, away from the bulging eyes and noisy whispers.

As she walked to the entrance, she passed Matt but barely looked at him.

Thomas followed her outside, and the music resumed behind them. Maude heard the crowd cheer.

"I know this is crazy, Maude, but—"

"Crazy?" Maude snorted. "That's the understatement of the year!"

"I didn't know how else to get your attention. You blocked me on PixeLight, you haven't been answering my calls, my text messages—"

"Can you blame me? After what you've done?"

"I know, and I've regretted it ever since. I don't know how to tell you how sorry I am."

"You didn't even tell me yourself, Thomas. I found out while we were at the restaurant. I never felt so humiliated in my entire life! Until this evening, that is."

"I know I never should have stolen your song. I want to make it up to you."

"How? How can you possibly make up for stealing my song and singing with Lindsey?"

"I think we should get back together."

"Ha! I don't understand how that will make up for what you've done."

"I care about you, and I want to help you. If we publicly date we would be the 'hottest teen couple' according to several gossip journals. It'd boost both our singles. Yours could easily reach the top ten on the Billboard 100."

Maude thought of Terence's sad face and how strongly she

wished to make him proud. She'd do anything to show her gratitude to the family who had taken her in and treated her as one of their own. Except pretend to date a boy she didn't like.

"So you want us to date so that I get more streams. How generous of you!" Maude exclaimed sarcastically. "I want to be known for my own achievements. I'd never date a boy just to become famous."

"That's not what I'm saying. I just want to be with you. I want your forgiveness."

Thomas looked at Maude with sorrowful eyes, and she smiled a sad smile.

"Thomas, I've already forgiven you." And when she said it, she realized it was true. She didn't feel the same poisonous sting she had felt the first night she had learned of his betrayal.

"Then there's a chance that we can be together again. Publicly or not, I don't care."

Maude shook her head mournfully.

"I'm sorry, I can't. Besides, I don't need a guy to boost my sales. I want to be judged solely for my music."

"Don't you feel that from the moment we met there was something special between us? We were good together."

"For you, maybe," she insisted. "But we would have broken up eventually," she said softly. *I'm in love with someone else*, she thought, but didn't say.

Suddenly, she realized that she didn't care for Matt's rule. She had to tell him how she felt, and he could decide if he was willing to break his rule. They were more than music partners, so much more. He was incessantly irritating, arrogant, and completely full of himself, but they also had amazing musical chemistry, and he was funny. He made her laugh—when he wasn't laughing at her, that was. And she had feelings for him. Those feelings were there and there wasn't much she could do about them but tell him how she felt. And she hated Lindsey Linton! She hated the fact that he was probably dancing with Lindsey while Maude was here wasting time with Thomas. She needed to speak to him now.

"Thomas, I've got to go!" she cried.

"What, wait!"

It was too late. Maude had dashed back inside.

She spotted Matt almost immediately and ran to him.

"Matt!" she cried breathlessly.

"What do you want?" Matt asked coldly.

Maude faltered slightly, but continued nonetheless.

"I talked to Thomas. I forgave him. And I realized—"

"You forgave him? Now that's a shock," Matt jeered. "Maude, you haven't a single ounce of pride. Do you know that? Thomas just wants to date you again so he can steal more music from us."

"I don't care about that," Maude said hurriedly, trying to stay on track.

"Of course you don't. All you care about are his perfect hair and smile. You couldn't care less that he used you to steal *our* song!"

"You're one to talk!" Maude retorted, feeling her anger rise. "You're the one who came waltzing in with Lindsey when you knew perfectly well I'd be hurt!" she exclaimed.

"Why would you even care about Lindsey? You're stuck in opera land and your Prince Charming just charmed his way back to your heart with some lame, fake romantic gesture. So why the hell would you even give a damn about Lindsey? It's not as if you and I ever had anything going on. I never date my co-workers, remember?" he spat out defensively.

Maude stiffened, and her eyes hardened as she faced him.

"You're right, Matt," she said dryly. "I really am stupid. We won't be seeing each other anytime soon because I'm going back to France and I might never come back to New York."

"That's probably for the best. We'll go to Paris with the Baldwins. Then we'll never see each other again."

Maude turned away from him. She couldn't tell him how she felt anyway, not after what he'd just said. Not after he'd come to the dance with Lindsey. He'd made it perfectly clear he felt nothing for her.

She saw Jazmine hurrying toward them while the band was on a break.

"So how were we?" she asked cheerfully as she reached her friends.

"You were great, Jaz," Maude chirped, trying to sound light-hearted but not quite succeeding.

"Where's Thomas? Did you two talk? That was some speech he gave, huh?"

"Yes, we talked." Maude avoided Matt's gaze. "Everything's fine," she finished limply.

"Maude forgave him," Matt put in, not quite being able to hide his sarcasm.

"Really? Are you two a cou . . ." Jazmine's voice trailed off as she stared into the distance.

"Jaz, what's wrong?" Matt asked worriedly.

Maude looked in the direction Jazmine was looking at and knew what was wrong.

"I can't believe it," she whispered.

Jonathan was on the dance floor kissing a girl.

She was a girl from school named Laura, a loner who hardly

ever spoke to anyone. But she presently looked blissfully happy in Jonathan's arms, and completely unaware of the unintentional distress she was causing.

For the first time Maude saw heartbreak in all its force; its destructive, chaotic sway.

Jazmine stood like a statue. Then her hands shook uncontrollably as one slow tear trickled down her cheek.

"Maude, call an Uber," Matt ordered. "I'll stay and fill in for Jazmine. She can't stay here."

Maude nodded.

There was no way Jonathan would witness her friend falling to pieces because he hadn't been decent enough to tell her that he was going out with someone else.

"Jazmine, let's go. You can't stay here. Come on," she said.

She sheltered Jazmine in her arms. The other girl didn't resist as she was led away.

It was only when they got into the car that she sobbed uncontrollably, overcome with grief, in Maude's arms.

Chapter Thirty-six

The Baldwins and their two French friends sat around a small table on the terrace outside La Cour. The Eiffel Tower shimmered in the distance. Visiting Paris with the Baldwins and Matt was quite different from the first time Maude had been in the city. The first time she'd set foot in Paris, she'd been lonely. Now she was surrounded by people who cared for her. Back then, she'd never left her small, dreary town. Since then, she'd crossed the sea and discovered a whole new country, culture, and language. Maude was a completely different person now. Despite all this, somewhere inside she still felt like she'd failed the only people who had ever trusted her. She had no idea how she'd go back to her life in Carvin. Would she be the laughingstock of the small town?

Victoria and Terence left the kids to take a romantic stroll in the city, and Jazmine, still raw from her heartbreak, wanted to go on a massive shopping spree at the Galeries Lafayette.

Maude's appointment with the CNAOP was the next day, a couple of hours before her live performance on *Terre à Terre. That's tomorrow*, she reminded herself anxiously. This afternoon she was absolutely free to spend time with the Baldwins.

Matt knew exactly what he wanted to do.

“I’m taking Ben with me,” Matt said. “No way we’re spending an entire afternoon in stores.”

Jazmine almost choked.

“Stores?! The Galeries Lafayette aren’t just stores, Matt. They’re literally paradise for anyone with taste. Obviously, I’m wasting my breath talking about taste to someone who *willingly* spends time with Lindsey Linton. I’m not saying you’ve got bad taste, but . . . you’ve got bad taste,” Jazmine declared.

“Whatever.” Matt chuckled, nonplussed. “Ben and I are going to do manly things, right, buddy?”

“Right, we’re men!” Ben cried, thumping his chest and making everyone laugh.

“Say that again in a few years when your voice isn’t squeaking,” Cynthia said, teasing her younger brother.

Maude’s cell buzzed loudly at the edge of the table. She grabbed her phone before it fell and read the incoming text.

Have a nice stay in Paris. Say hello to the Iron Lady for me. Thomas

Maude hid a smile. Ever since the dance Thomas had sent Maude an alarming number of sweet text messages with unwavering constancy.

“That’s Thomas again,” Cynthia observed warily.

Maude nodded. She never answered his texts; nothing would ever happen between her and Thomas after what he’d done. However, his messages were a reminder that she’d been in New York, had lived there, and that someone over there still cared about her.

“We’re going to go check out the outdoor art scene at Place Georges-Pompidou if anyone wants to come,” Matt said, purposely avoiding Maude’s gaze.

"There are some really talented dancers over there," Cynthia gushed.

"A couple of famous imitators too," Matt added.

"And mimes!"

"Breakdancers," Matt put in.

"I'll get my portrait done by a street artist!" Ben exclaimed.

"Well, I'm sticking to shopping. Besides, I really need to get my mind off things," Jazmine murmured.

Cynthia and Maude glanced at each other. Jazmine hadn't quite been herself since the summer dance, and Maude, who had never known Jazmine to be so thoroughly shaken, didn't really know how to handle her.

"Did you get to talk to Jonathan before leaving for France?" Cynthia ventured cautiously.

Jazmine nodded before emitting a small, brittle laugh.

"He's been seeing Laura for three weeks, but he said he didn't know how to tell me." Jazmine's voice shook.

"Mrs. Bonnin, Carvin's main baker and gossip, always used to tell me that men are the worst kind of cowards," Maude recalled, looking directly at Matt. He hadn't even had the decency to warn her he was coming to the dance with Lindsey!

"Maybe guys aren't the problem," Matt interjected sharply. "Perhaps girls should learn to look at what's right in front of them instead of looking for Prince Charming and fairy tales."

"No, I agree with your friend on this one, Maude," Jazmine said. "He's a very good example of how guys can act cowardly. Jonathan told me that even though he cared about me, he didn't want to get hurt. He preferred to be with Laura, a girl he could count on and who's like him in more ways than I am."

"If he means reclusive and klutzy, I guess he's right," Maude uttered dryly. Laura wasn't much better at handling things than Jonathan was.

Jazmine chuckled.

"He *is* right, Maude," she admitted sorrowfully. "I couldn't see that, and the idea is still painful, but I'm glad he made me realize it. He and I are worlds apart. I'm outgoing, fun, sociable. He prefers quiet evenings and is more comfortable in a smaller social circle. He probably would've been unhappy with me. And I'd have been unfulfilled with him."

"He's being too cautious, if you ask me," Matt put in. "He won't take a risk by being in a relationship with someone he genuinely cares about, and instead settles for a relationship with someone he'll never deeply love, because it's safe. He's afraid of exploring uncharted territory."

"I guess some guys don't have the courage to date a beautiful, popular girl while others consider it a risk to date anyone but models or actresses. Probably afraid of losing their coveted spot on Page Six," Maude retorted dryly.

"Models aren't in the music business. When we break up, it's a clean breakup. Not like certain singers who write about their exes betraying them and then continue to see them," Matt fumed.

Maude caught the Baldwin sisters looking at each other dubiously. Cynthia cleared her throat.

"Personally, I can relate to the whole cowardice issue," she declared. "I was afraid to tell Mom and Dad what I truly wanted to do with my life. I'm ready to take risks and step out of my comfort zone a bit. To taking risks!" Cynthia exclaimed, raising her cup of jasmine tea.

"Cheers!" they all cried in unison, with a certain reluctance on Maude's and Matt's parts.

"Now we shop!" cried Jazmine.

The boys grumbled and went their own way.

Chapter Thirty-seven

"How was your day?" Victoria asked.

"I'm exhausted," Maude sighed, as she plopped onto a sofa in the main hall of their hotel that evening.

"Jazmine went crazy at Galeries Lafayette as always," Cynthia moaned, rubbing her feet.

"We had fun!" Ben cried.

"And what are you doing this evening?" Terence asked.

"I'm going to a comedy show. I'm seeing a famous French stand-up comedian called Jamel Djebril," Matt answered.

"Jamel Djebril! I love him!" Maude cried, her frustration regarding Matt subsiding for a moment. "I only saw scraps of his shows on TV because Mrs. Ruchet didn't like him. He's so funny."

"Then you should go with Matt," Victoria urged.

Maude fell back in her seat.

"No, I'm sure you're already going with friends."

"None of my friends were available, but I really wanted to see him while I was here," Matt explained. "You can come if you'd like."

"I'm not sure—" Maude protested, thinking how awkward things were between them.

"Nonsense," Victoria decided firmly. "Matt shouldn't go on his own, and none of us are fluent enough in French to understand the show. And you obviously love this comedian. You're going." Fighting Victoria was useless, and Maude had no intention of trying.

• • •

"He was hilarious!" Maude screeched. "I thought I was going to fall off my seat."

"You almost did. Good thing I caught you." Matt laughed.

They were walking on the Pont des Arts bridge over the glistening waters of the Seine. The rails of the bridge used to be covered with locks that couples from all over the world brought to symbolize their everlasting love. Though the city had taken them down, the bridge still held a remarkably romantic aura. The Eiffel Tower could be seen sparkling in the distance, watching over lovers taking an evening stroll along the peaceful Parisian streets. The tower, impressive in the day, was a superb queen of the night. Her cloak of many colors defied the light of the moon, shining brighter than the stars and making them look pale in comparison, thus confirming that Paris was indeed the one and only true City of Light.

"I'm so glad I saw him!" Maude gushed.

"Getting his autograph was nice too."

"You can thank me for that. Whose idea was it to follow him backstage?"

"We didn't go backstage, Maude. The guards stopped us before we managed that."

"Yes, but he heard us calling his name and came back to give us an autograph and a picture," Maude said, flipping through the pictures in her phone. "Had I listened to you, I wouldn't have this picture to cherish. 'Maude, don't you know how tired artists are after a show?'" Maude mimicked.

"They are!" Matt insisted. "You'll learn that yourself tomorrow after *Terre à Terre*."

"We'll see. It's just two songs, after all, and an interview."

"How are you feeling about that?"

"I'm fine, but I wish everyone would stop asking me that." Maude paused and leaned over to take a closer look at the river.

"Can you believe there were locks all over this bridge?" she mused.

"Lovers are idiots," Matt said bitterly.

Maude laughed and turned to him.

"Matt, have you ever been in love?" she asked, a certain shyness falling over her.

Matt looked away from Maude and gazed intently at the deep water flowing underneath the bridge.

"What was the most foolish thing you ever did for love?" Maude asked, a bit bolder.

"Nothing!" He protested a little too much. "Because I'm not stupid."

"Come on, you have to be honest. Pretend we're playing truth or dare."

"Okay, then I choose dare."

"Pretend we're playing truth and more truth."

"All right." Matt chuckled. He hesitated before admitting in a single breath, "The stupidest thing I did was break my rule: I fell for a girl I was working with."

Maude couldn't help but feel a twinge of envy toward this

unnamed, supernatural creature who had bewitched Matt long enough to make him break his rule.

"You broke that rule? Was it before you made the rule, though? That's why you created it?"

"It was after," Matt went on, looking at Maude intently. "That rule was a great rule, until she came along."

"Who was she?"

"Do you really have to ask?" His gaze fell on her face, and Maude's heart leaped with joy.

Then she kissed him full on the lips only to immediately pull back. But he pulled her into his arms and kissed her; really kissed her. His lips crashed into hers and she felt a fire course through her entire body. His hand tilted her head back and his lips were on her neck and throat as she moaned with pleasure. Then his lips came crashing back on hers, his tongue moving with hers until they were breathless yet so alive. Her hands explored his strong torso, then messed up his hair until they both giggled happily. When his hand moved down to her waist, she pulled him closer, tight against her body, crumpling with pleasure. Their hands strayed, exploring, discovering, uniting as if the rest of the world no longer existed.

When they finally parted Maude pressed her head against his chest; she had never felt happier. They left the bridge and continued their walk, pausing several times to kiss.

They walked in silence for a while, enjoying each other's company, holding hands, the summer night breeze caressing their skin. Finally, Maude spoke.

"You're a liar," she whispered. "You haven't broken your rule at all. We're no longer in business together, so we're not mixing business and pleasure."

"I still fell for you while we worked together. Maybe even on the first day we met. Then I had to watch you date Thomas even after he'd stolen our song."

"I broke up with Thomas after that."

"How come you went to the dance with him?"

"I didn't! You're the one who came with Lindsey."

"Only because she told me at the release party you were going with Thomas!"

"I'd never!"

"It's not as if I hadn't already spent months watching you date the jerk."

"Sorry about that," she said between giggles. "I wasn't trying to rub him in your face. But you were so exasperating those first few weeks remember?"

"Because I didn't know how to talk to you!"

"You, the famous love doctor?"

"You seemed immune to my many charms."

"You repeated your rule over and over. I didn't think I stood a chance."

"Jaz hammered my rule into my brain that night at Silver Spoon. That's why I wasn't planning on seeing you perform *Cenerentola*."

"And you arrived late, only after Jaz called you!" Maude pointed out. "It's so funny to think you cared for so long. Imagine if you'd said something, you'd already be out of your misery." Maude's laughter rang out in the summer night.

"Glad you find my pain amusing," Matt joked. "I should become a stand-up comedian myself and give out dating advice during my shows."

"I'd most definitely pay to see your show." Maude giggled.

"So now it's your turn."

"My turn to do what?"

"Tell me what's the most foolish thing you've done for love."

Maude laughed before saying, "Do I really look like the kind of person who'd kiss and tell?"

"I told you mine. Now you tell me yours!" Matt insisted.

"No one forced you to tell me anything!" Maude protested playfully.

"You dared me to tell you the truth!"

"There is no such thing as *daring* someone to tell the *truth*. You either choose truth or dare, and you chose truth." Maude shrugged. "I admire your honesty, by the way. Can't say I've got a similar moral compass."

"Obviously." Matt snorted.

They neared the Louvre and entered its main courtyard, the Cour Napoléon. The glowing glass pyramid stood in the center of the courtyard surrounded by the adjacent wings of the palace. Maude gazed at the beauty that surrounded her, and thought that no city possessed a more romantic, enchanting charm than Paris.

"Matt," she said turning to him. "Thank you. This is by far the best evening of my life."

Matt looked at Maude under the moonlight and she gazed back, head slightly tilted, eyes shining, and a smile on her lips.

"Who says the night is over?" Matt whispered in her ear, sending shivers down her spine.

"Your aunt says having a good night's rest is very important to avoid stage fright." But Maude's eyes twinkled as she continued, "This is our only night in Paris. Let's make it count."

So the two spent that warm summer night roaming the City of Light, singing, dancing, and kissing in the streets, without a thought for the rest of the world, nor what tomorrow would hold.

Chapter Thirty-eight

The next day, late in the morning, Maude and Matt went to Père Lachaise cemetery.

After walking past the Jim Morrison tomb, they arrived next to a new-looking headstone with a picture of a smiling woman with gray eyes just like Matt's.

"That's where my mother was buried a year ago today."

Maude bowed her head solemnly as Matt placed a bouquet on her grave.

"Mom," he said in French. "This has been the hardest year of my life. This year has been full of firsts. My first grief, your first birthday without you since I was born. First Mother's Day without a mom. First Christmas without you. First fight with Dad where you couldn't play peacemaker." Matt's voice broke. "I know our relationship isn't how you would've wanted. I promise I'll work on that. But with the help of this person standing next to me, I'm going to get through this. I wanted you to meet her. You'd have liked her for sure. She's a crazy opera fan, just like you. Thanks to her, I'm finally ready to sort through your boxes. Mom, meet Maude Laurent."

He took Maude's hand and drew her closer to the grave. Maude bent down and placed a bouquet of white roses.

"Hi, Isabella, I'm Maude Laurent. Though I'm not sure that's even my name. I'm going to discover who my family is today, and I'll come back to tell you. The thing is, I don't know what I would've done without your son here. You should be proud of him. He's the best. I'm going to miss him so much."

Maude," Matt said, turning to her, "I don't think you moving back to France should mean we're over."

"A long-distance relationship?" she said, daring to hope. "People say long distance doesn't work."

"We'll be the exception," he said, taking her hands in his. "Maude, death is the only final good-bye. But long distance doesn't have to be. Not if we don't let it. We'll video chat every day."

"I'll text you every night before I go to sleep."

"I'll tag you in all my PixeLight posts, even if you aren't there."

"I'll send you kisses across the ocean."

"I'll visit you in Carvin as often as I can."

"We'll make it work," they promised in unison.

Together, they sat at the graveside, chatting in Frenglish, dreaming about the future. Soon enough, they did the one thing they were made to do together: they composed a song that they sang for the first time right in front of Isabella Durand's smiling picture.

Then Maude gave Matt privacy with his mother and went to the CNAOP, her heart thumping in her chest, her hands moist, her fear as high as her hope, and a determination to know the truth.

Maude knew France was famous for its slow administration. Waiting hours in administrative lines, even when they had a scheduled appointment, was a skill the French learned at a young age. Unfortunately, it was Maude's first direct encounter with French public administration, and what she thought would take a matter of minutes actually turned out to be a matter of hours.

Her appointment was at two o'clock so she had arrived at one thinking she would be able to leave sooner.

When the clock finally struck two, Maude was getting restless; the line hadn't moved! She hadn't realized that one o'clock was the second hour of the employees' lunch break. As time went by, she began to worry. She had to be at the TV studio at five to check the acoustics and do her makeup and hair.

But she couldn't miss this chance, her only chance to retrieve her box. *Ticktock* went the clock.

Ticktock went Maude's brain, and just as she was about to despair, she was finally called in by a middle-aged woman, Mrs. Rotonde, who looked like she wanted to be anywhere other than where she was. Discontentment was clearly one of the prerequisites for working in French government administration.

In Maude's eyes, the woman appeared to be a plump middle-aged oracle with the key to her identity. Maude followed her eagerly to her office, recording every moment in her mind.

"Your name is Maude Laurent," Mrs. Rotonde stated in a lazy, unconcerned Parisian drawl.

"Yes," Maude answered, as if a pale, floating halo could be seen over the woman's head.

"Can I see some ID? Have you filled in all the forms?" she asked, as if Maude was the least competent person she'd ever encountered.

"Of course," Maude stammered, hurriedly rummaging through her bag. "I'm sorry, I'm terribly nervous because I'm finally—"

"That's nice," the woman interrupted. "Just give me the ID."

Maude handed the woman her ID, questionnaire, and other documents she'd printed from the website. Mrs. Rotonde checked everything, then left the room. When she came back a few minutes later she was carrying the treasured box, which she thrust into Maude's hands.

It was nothing like Maude had imagined. She'd pictured a large golden chest more than an actual box. The box she held in her hands was a medium-sized wooden box with tooled leather on the lid, adorned with exquisite fan motifs. The box was locked with a wrought-iron clasp. Maude searched for the key, but there was none to be seen.

"I'm guessing the key's in here," Mrs. Rotonde indicated, waving a sealed envelope.

Mrs. Rotonde's initial apathy was waning as she looked at the carved box with keen interest. Mothers, she explained, rarely left objects for their children. Letters, documents, yes. Beautifully carved boxes were never among the things she handed to people searching for their biological mothers. Mothers who gave birth anonymously in France were often poor, abandoned young women who had nothing but their own selves. No family, no husband, no friends. They surrendered their child to be brought up by another family, hopeful of giving that child a better chance in life.

"Why don't you open the box right here?" Mrs. Rotonde suggested.

"Thank you so much, Mrs. Rotonde," Maude whispered hoarsely. "It's something I'd rather do alone."

Mrs. Rotonde sighed in disappointment when Maude made a movement to leave.

She had no intention of opening her box in front of a stranger. Besides, she had to leave right away if she wanted to make it in time for her TV performance.

Chapter Thirty-nine

"You're all set, Mademoiselle Laurent," Stephanie said. "Nervous?" she asked kindly.

Stephanie had just finished Maude's makeup, and they had talked a mile a minute, as if they had known each other forever. What a strange delight to speak French again! Weirdly, some words came to her only in English and she had to think twice before finding the word in French.

"A little," she admitted. "It's a good kind of nervous, though. The rehearsal and acoustical checks went well, so everything should be fine."

"The host is very kind and funny. I'm sure you'll have a great time. I'll let you rest now. Don't ruin your makeup, but break a leg!" Stephanie called as she left the room.

Once alone, Maude removed the wooden box from her bag and caressed it fondly. Never had she felt closer to her mother than she did at that very moment. However, she recalled Mme. Tragent's advice about stage fright. "Stay focused! Don't talk to anybody before the show."

But she had waited over sixteen years for this. She couldn't wait a second longer.

Maude ripped open the sealed envelope, took out the key, and unlatched the box.

Click went the clasp, and the carved lid was lifted. There was a letter.

Maude closed her eyes for a second then opened them as she steadied her breath. Her hand trembled slightly as she took the piece of paper, yellowed by time, and read.

My dear Maude,

If you are reading this letter, it means your father and I are no longer of this world and that my dear friend Robert has raised you.

I want you to know that your father and I love you very much. As I look at you sleeping in your crib next to me, I wonder if I will ever have the strength to leave you, my beautiful baby.

I must be strong for I must go save your father if I can. I pray that our family will be reunited soon. But my hope is waning every day that your father remains imprisoned in Nigeria.

I'm writing this letter to you, my beautiful daughter, to explain why I must leave for now.

As Robert has probably explained, I, Danielle Laurent, was born in Guadeloupe, a French Caribbean island. Your father, Aaron Ekenechukwu Okafor, was born in New York to Igbo parents. His parents had to flee Nigeria in 1967 when the war began devastating the country. Everyone calls him Ekene.

The war ended in 1970 but they never went back. Years later your father moved to Nigeria to fight for human rights and the advancement of democracy, and for the preservation of the environment. He had to leave his family behind in New York and was no longer in touch with them when I met him.

We met and married in Nigeria.

I've been a human rights lawyer for a couple of years now, and I've traveled all over the world. But the day I met your father was the most beautiful day of my life. As Robert has probably told you, it was love at first sight. Robert, who is my closest friend as well as the best human rights lawyer I've ever met, introduced us at a party given by Amnesty International. Although Robert returned to France a few months later, I decided to stay in Nigeria with your father.

Since then we've been inseparable. Through all the dangers and trials, we have stayed together, fighting against corruption and trying to conserve the nature in this beautiful country. You see, Nigeria is not only a beautiful country, but it also has many amazing resources, including oil.

The village where Ekene and I settled is far away from Lagos and the vibrant, fancy life that people have on Victoria Island.

In our beautiful village, one of the biggest oil corporations, Stonewell, exploits the oil and does it carelessly too. The oil leaks into rivers, pollutes the water, kills fish, and destroys people's lives and livelihoods. Those who can, leave. Those who can't, live in very poor conditions while Stonewell and the CEO, Mark Burden, make billions. It's so wrong. The governor of the state, Pete Kanu, one of the most corrupt men I've ever come across, refuses to do anything about it. Instead, he benefits from it. Recently, our team has been trying to bring Kanu and Stonewell to trial for ecocide and human rights violations. We were so close to building a strong case against them that Pete Kanu felt threatened, and ready to go to extreme lengths to silence us.

Then I learned I was pregnant. Ekene wanted me to be safe during the pregnancy, so I came back to France five months ago. He was supposed to follow me a month later but he was captured by Kanu's men and has been imprisoned for five months now.

His men have been looking for me as well, which is why I gave birth in anonymity in France a month ago and have given you my maiden name, Laurent, instead of Aaron's name, Okafor. We weren't sure about your Igbo name yet: we thought Adanna was well suited but weren't sure. Now as I look at you, I feel that "father's daughter" is the perfect name for you as you look so much like your father.

I must return to save your father. I have connections in France and Nigeria, and if we work together we should be able to get him out of jail. In the meantime, you'll stay with the Ruchets. I hope to be back in a couple of months, but if that proves impossible, Robert has promised me to care for you as he would his own until we can come back, and I have complete faith that he will. He'll tell you how brave your parents were and how they fought to make this world a better place.

I'll save your father or die trying.

I would like to tell you so much more, but I haven't much time and I must rest.

I will just give you simple advice: follow your heart no matter what. That is the soundest piece of advice a mother can give her child and I hope I will be telling you this in person, that I will get to see you grow up.

Your father made this jewelry box, and I have enclosed a few pictures in it for you. I love you so much it hurts.

Your mother,

Danielle Laurent-Okafor

Maude looked inside the box and took out the pictures, trying to calm the soft tremor in her hand. Through her tears she could see the first picture was of her parents, Danielle and Ekene. Ekene was a tall, dark-skinned man with a soft, serious smile aimed at the camera. He appeared calm but his eyes betrayed a preoccupation as well as a certain sense of alertness. His arm rested around Danielle's shoulders in what appeared a lazy stance, although, as Maude peered more closely at the picture, she saw his fingers fastened to Danielle's shoulder in a protective manner. Danielle seemed happy, almost in a careless way, her arm wrapped around Ekene's waist. She was a petite, brown-skinned woman dressed stylishly in a bright-red dress, wearing a shell necklace around her neck. She was assured, beaming happily at her husband, tugging at his shirt impatiently as if wanting to distract him from the camera.

Maude had her father's nose. She had her mother's round cheekbones. She was a product of their life.

Maude tore her eyes away from the picture and met an unfamiliar reflection in the mirror. She could no longer recognize herself. Where was the girl, happy, content, and hopelessly optimistic about life? She was no longer there. She was gone, murdered like her parents. She would never be the same again. But she had wanted this hadn't she? Her conversation with Victoria that night in the kitchen in New York came back to her. Was it easier to not know?

Horrific images flashed through Maude's mind as she pictured her parents, Ekene and Danielle. They had names and faces now. She now understood why the Ruchets had been so reluctant to tell her the truth. How could she bear it?

Suddenly she laughed a laugh she didn't recognize. It resembled a savage growl.

She hated her parents. How could they save the world and not save her? They had dumped her on their "friends."

Robert Ruchet was her mother's best friend. How was this even possible? It didn't make any sense. How could Robert be anyone's friend, let alone her mother's? Maude stopped laughing. Her hands shook uncontrollably. She couldn't stop shaking all over as if possessed.

There was a light knock on the door and Matt entered the dressing room. He must have realized something was wrong because he rushed toward her.

"Maude, what's going on?" he asked.

She didn't answer, couldn't answer. She couldn't speak, and she wanted her brain to shut down.

Stop thinking, brain, she told herself as she shook like a leaf being blown around in a storm.

"Stop thinking," she whispered hoarsely. "Stop thinking."

"Maude, what's the matter? What's this?" he asked, picking up the letter that had fallen to the floor.

He read it and looked at her in utter shock.

"Maude." He shook her lightly.

"My parents are dead, Matt," she whispered hoarsely. "My parents were murdered."

"Maude, I'm so sorry. I'm so sorry," he repeated, taking her in his arms. His warm embrace acted like a catalyst and Maude wailed helplessly against his chest. Her cries came from deep within, and he rocked her gently, stroking her hair, wrapping her in his arms. When she finally lifted her head, she looked calm though still in pain.

"Your shirt," she moaned, pointing at the mascara-stained patch on his chest.

"It doesn't matter," he said, smiling softly at her. He handed her a tissue.

"I'm a mess," she observed miserably between sniffles.

"You're beautiful," Matt replied.

Maude couldn't help but laugh.

"Thank you, Matt. For everything."

"I'm not finished yet," Matt said.

Maude wiped her face and turned to him.

"I wasn't by your side for *Cenerentola* but I'm here now, and I'll help you get through this."

"I'm a wreck."

"You still have to play this evening," Matt said gently.

"Matt—" She started to protest.

"You will play this evening." Matt silenced her.

Maude turned to the mirror.

"You'll play for them," he added softly. "Just like I play for my mother every time I compose alone in my creation room."

Maude looked at him, her eyes filled with sadness.

"You'll play beautifully for your parents because it will be the first time that they hear you. They'll be sitting in the front row. They'll be looking at their daughter, their only daughter, and they'll beam with pride."

She nodded slowly.

"Look at these hands," Matt said, taking her hands in his. "Your hands are a gift. Your voice is a gift. Your parents will listen to you tonight. Do you hear me, Maude?"

Maude nodded more firmly, a look of determination slowly replacing her distress.

"I'll play for them."

"For Ekene and Danielle," he whispered, taking her face in his hands.

She nodded, feeling his hands on her skin.

"For Ekene and Danielle," she echoed.

The door opened wide and Stephanie popped her head.

"You're up in five . . . " Her voice trailed off as she looked at Matt and Maude.

He let go of Maude abruptly. "Umm, I was just leaving."

Stephanie looked past him. "What happened to your face?!" she shrieked.

She hurried to Maude to repair her makeup. Matt headed for the door, but Maude stopped him. "Stay, please," she asked, almost shyly.

"I'm not going anywhere."

Stephanie huffed and puffed and fixed Maude's makeup with a few expert strokes, muttering that boyfriends should never be allowed into dressing rooms before concerts because they always made girls cry, and she had to repair the damage.

"Okay, I'm done. Now hurry!" the makeup artist cried.

"You're up in two minutes. Don't you dare mess up your makeup again!"

Maude ran out, keeping her hands away from her recently rouged cheeks. Matt hurried after her.

She stood right behind the curtain and listened to the host's cheerful voice, announcing her. *"Now, ladies and gentlemen, we have a new artist with us tonight. She's spent the last six months in New York working on songs. Her latest single is a hit . . ."*

"Maude," Matt whispered, tugging her sleeve.

"Yes?" She looked back at him, smiling.

"I just wanted to tell you, to let you know that you can always count on me."

"I know, Matt." Maude smiled gratefully.

"Her voice will take your breath away, her music is amazing . . ."

"No, I'm serious. Whichever part of the world you find yourself in, you can always count on me if you need me."

Maude nodded.

"Give a round of applause for Maude Laurent!" the host cried.

"That's your cue! Go!" Matt urged.

Maude reluctantly turned away from him and hurried on stage.

The blaring lights blinded her as she entered and faced the cheering crowd. She had to restrain her impulse to shield her eyes, and continued steadily toward the dark Steinway.

She had played it earlier, but then she hadn't felt nervous. Her hands hadn't been trembling, and her voice hadn't been shaky. Maude sat on the piano stool and looked at the crowd. They were all there.

Terence and Victoria were holding hands and beaming at her. Cynthia, dignified as always, was trying to keep Ben from falling off his seat while he was waving madly at Maude. Jazmine, hands clasped, looked like she was sending all the positive energy she could muster from her seat.

Maude turned to the piano and sang her first song. *For Danielle and Ekene*, she thought.

She had played this song many times before, but this time was different. She had grown. Maude wasn't the same person she'd been six months ago, and her performance wasn't that of a mere teenager—it was that of a young woman who had looked life in the eye and refused to buckle. She finished her first song and prepared herself for the second.

She had planned to sing "Sunrise," but now she knew she couldn't play that song, not after all she'd just been through.

Maude dedicated her second song, the song she and Matt had created at the cemetery, "Coming Home," to her parents.

She took a deep breath and sang:

"There is nothing left for me to do

"But to live without you

"To bear the pain and misery

"Of your silent memory."

As she played, she released the pain she had been holding back for years. Her parents were dead. They were gone forever, but she was still alive. Though her pain was severe, it also gave her strength. Strength to sing in a clear voice, strength to overcome her fears, strength to master her initially shaky fingers, and strength to let her notes reverberate through the audience.

"Our souls will meet again

"Oh yes, we'll smile again

"I won't ever be alone

"The day that I'll be coming home."

Her voice rang out as clear as water from a fountain, and wavered with deep emotion as the song washed away her doubt, drowned her insecurities, and melted her pain into a beautiful, calm river of hope.

Maude ended her song and carefully folded her hands on her knees.

"I did it," she muttered softly to herself.

The crowd broke into thunderous applause. She could hear whistling and thumping. As she walked toward the host, she squinted to avoid the glaring lights, and saw the crowd on its feet, cheering and calling her name.

She smiled and greeted the host, a man with a bulbous nose and a large, kind smile.

"Wow, wow, wow," he exclaimed. This host was known for his exuberance. But then, TV hosts were rarely known for being discreet. "That was incredible, Maude!"

Maude laughed, relieved to be breathing at a normal pace again.

"Just tell me, Maude," he started in a conversational tone. "How does a sixteen-year-old teenager, raised in the north of France, end up spending six months in New York recording with the world's hottest pop star?"

"That, my friend, is a very interesting question," she answered, her dark-brown eyes twinkling mischievously. "It was all thanks to Paris. It inspired me to sing. The video went viral, and the rest is history."

"You're one lucky girl, Maude Laurent! I have another question for you. I'm sure you've heard Lindsey Linton and Thomas Bradfield's duet 'Paris versus New York City.' I think you have a unique position to answer this question. Which city do you prefer: Paris or New York?"

Maude laughed again and knew without seeing him that Matt was chuckling behind the scenes.

"Had you asked me this question six months ago, I would've said Paris without a doubt. Paris will always be the city where I was discovered, and it's the most romantic city in the world," Maude started. "Now, I honestly can't imagine living anywhere other than New York," she admitted, startled at her own admission.

She knew now New York was where she truly felt alive. She'd go back one day, back to her father's birthplace.

Back to where she truly belonged.

Chapter Forty

Everything has happened so fast, Maude thought regretfully, a heaviness building in her chest.

She had barely had time to say proper good-byes to Matt and Ben, who were due to take an early flight. She had hugged Ben warmly, and he'd promised to let her know which instrument he chose for his twelfth birthday.

"Just don't choose bagpipes," Maude had murmured between hugs.

Then she'd turned to Matt. They had looked at each other a little awkwardly, sensing five pairs of Baldwin eyeballs staring curiously at them. They had already said their good-byes far from the others and renewed their promises of seeing each other again soon.

"It was a pleasure working with you," Matt said simply, stretching out his hand.

"The pleasure was all mine," Maude replied in an even tone. She took his hand and shook it just as awkwardly as she felt.

They had parted ways. He was flying back to New York and she was back in Carvin. Not much had changed here since she'd left. The Grand Place was animated, everyone wanting to enjoy the few precious rays of summer sun. Couples were walking hand in hand, and from afar Maude could see Mrs. Bonnin eyeing them curiously from behind her counter, storing mental notes under her immaculately clean white baker's hat.

While the Baldwins checked in at the Belle Etoile hotel, Maude went to see her old friend.

"Maude," Mrs. Bonnin cried. "How you've grown! And so stylish, oh my! I almost didn't recognize you."

Maude hugged her warmly with one arm, the other holding her cherished box. She'd never let it go. She inhaled the delicious aromas that emanated from the oven. How she'd missed this bakery!

"I'm sure you were too busy spying on Carvin's newest couples. Is it just me, or does Mr. Martin finally have a girlfriend?" Maude asked utterly baffled. "Please tell me she isn't a mail-order bride."

"No, honey." Mrs. Bonnin laughed. "She's the new girl in town. Her name's Abby, and she's always dreamed of living in a big city."

"She should visit New York some time," Maude replied, taking a bite of the warm croissant that the baker had insisted on giving her.

"Honey, you don't understand. *This* is the big city for her," Mrs. Bonnin explained, an amused twinkle in her eye. Maude nearly choked.

"*Whaaat?* Where does she come from?"

"Avesnes-le-Comte."

That was self-explanatory.

"So, I want to know everything about your trip to New York," Mrs. Bonnin said eagerly. In her accent it sounded more like "Neu Yorque," but Maude understood nevertheless.

"I'll tell you everything, just not now. I've got a few things to do first," Maude replied, smiling.

"Okay, come back as soon as you can," Mrs. Bonnin called as Maude left.

Maude met the Baldwins in the middle of the plaza and they followed her to the Ruchets' house.

"I'd go crazy in a small town," Jazmine observed as they strolled away from the city center.

"Jazmine, don't be rude," Victoria warned.

"I wasn't being rude. The town doesn't look too bad. There's just one huge problem."

"What's that?" Maude asked innocently.

"There isn't a decent shop in sight."

"I'm surprised you waited this long to make that observation." Cynthia chided her.

"I'm so glad I got to know you two," Maude said suddenly.

She was going to miss their bickering.

"Just wait until you hear Jazmine whine about her small-town itch," Cynthia replied.

"It's a *real* condition," Jazmine protested. "I went on an online chat where people described the same symptoms I had."

"That just means they'd escaped from the same psychiatric ward you were held in," her sister snorted.

"STI is a condition that even famous people have, apparently. Don't you find it weird that celebrities are always born in small towns and die in big cities?" Jazmine mused.

"Martians have small-town itch, too, that's why they leave their tiny planet and come visit us on Earth," Cynthia said with a wicked grin.

Maude laughed. "You two can stop now. We're almost there."

Maude paused at the door of a little red-bricked coron-styled house and rang the bell.

When Mr. Ruchet opened the door, she wondered about the startled look on his face. His baffled expression deepened upon seeing Victoria. It was as if he'd seen a ghost. He mustn't have read Maude's email warning them about her return date. It was just like Mr. Ruchet to forget details that didn't revolve around laws, briefs, and legal codes.

Maude's thoughts wandered back to her mother's letter. How could Mr. Ruchet have been her friend? Some friend. He'd never bothered to tell Maude what had happened to her parents. Sure he'd taken care of her, but he'd never shown her the affection that she deserved as the child of his close friend. Was there more to this story? How close had her mom and Robert been?

Had he told her about her mother, Maude could've found her real family years ago. Instead, she'd lived in a lie all those years. Sure, it might have been to protect her, but she'd have preferred the truth. She wished she could tell him just that. But she didn't want to broach the topic in front of the Baldwins. What would they think of her if they knew?

She entered the house. Little had changed.

It was as if time had stopped. Same boring plants, same ornaments, same paintings, same furniture. The twins had grown a few inches but were still the same mischievous, little monsters they had always been as they played loudly in the living room. And of course, Mrs. Ruchet was still comfortably seated on her couch. She probably hadn't moved a single inch in six months.

She noticed that the china vase on the chimney was no longer there, no doubt a victim of the boys' terrible habit of playing soccer in the living room when no one was there to watch them.

She wondered if those extra gray hairs on Mr. Ruchet's temple came from having to take care of his own children.

Mr. Ruchet was explaining that the family had refused to hire a nanny while Maude was abroad and were eagerly waiting for her return. With Maude gone, Mr. Ruchet had been obliged to pick up the twins from school every weekday. It had been an immense task indeed.

Maude noticed that Mrs. Ruchet looked a little green in the face and decided she must have started on a new diet. *Perhaps only green fruit and vegetables*, Maude thought, trying to control irrepressible laughter.

The house seemed smaller now, or perhaps it was Maude who had grown. She couldn't tell.

The family took their seats. Jazmine and Cynthia on the couch next to Mrs. Ruchet, while Terence and Victoria sat on chairs and Maude, after hiding her box behind one of the plants, followed Mr. Ruchet to the kitchen to help with tea and coffee for their guests.

Once alone at the kitchen counter, while the water boiled in the kettle, Mr. Ruchet cleared his throat.

"It's a shame your career didn't take off. The whole town will know that you failed. That we failed."

Mr. Ruchet poured piping hot water into the teapot. As the green tea infused, Maude recalled her conversation with Cynthia at the Landmark and smiled. How could she ever have thought she was a failure if her singles didn't become hits? Now she knew that she was happy she'd even tried.

Mr. Ruchet poured tea into one of the teacups, though Maude thought he could've let it infuse a little longer. He seemed in a hurry to get rid of his guests.

"I did my best," Maude finally replied. "So I can't say I failed because I tried. Which is more than what most people do in a lifetime. I learned so much about music, and myself. And—" Maude couldn't hold the truth back any longer.

"I know my father's name," she blurted. "I know it's Aaron Ekene Okafor."

Mr. Ruchet blanched. The teacup in his hand shook, and he put it on the counter with a *bang*, spilling half the contents.

"Who told you?"

"My mother," Maude replied. "She wrote a letter. She says you were her friend. Imagine that."

"Your mom wrote you a letter? Give it to me right now."

"What? No, it's—"

At that instant, the twins' screams interrupted her sentence.

"Give me the box!" one shouted.

Then Mrs. Ruchet's voice shouted over the brawl, "Boys, stop!"

Maude rushed to the living room, closely followed by Mr. Ruchet.

To Maude's horror the boys were fighting over her mother's box, each tugging on one side of the precious item.

"I was born four minutes before you! I get to keep it!" Leo shouted.

"You were born with only four neurons. I should keep it!" Louis shouted.

"Leave that alone!" she cried as she rushed over to the boys.

Leo pulled with all his might and managed to wrench the box from his brother's grasp. The strength of his tug made him fall over backward. The box flew out of his grip and crashed at Victoria's feet. The pictures and letter scattered everywhere.

Leo rubbed his scratched elbow, looking like he was about to cry. Maude rushed over to the box but Victoria was already kneeling.

"Boys," Victoria said. "You really shouldn't take what doesn't belong to you—"

Picking up the Polaroids, she gasped and dropped the photos. Terence hurried to her side.

She let out a small cry and picked up one of the pictures with a trembling hand.

"Ekene," she said faintly.

"Mom, what's wrong?" Cynthia asked worriedly.

Her daughters knelt beside her.

"That's Ekene," she explained shakily. "My brother. Where did you get this picture, Maude?"

"Your brother?" Maude puzzled. "But these belonged to my mother. She was married to Aaron Ekene Okafor, my father."

"This isn't possible," Victoria stammered. "You can't be—"

Victoria looked up and then back at the picture, astounded.

"You're my brother's baby girl," Victoria said, her voice quivering with emotion, lifting her eyes to look into Maude's.

"You're my aunt?" Maude ventured in utter disbelief. She'd never pronounced any word that came close to designating anyone as family.

Victoria grabbed Maude and hugged her so tightly that Maude thought her bones would pop out of her body, but she clung to her aunt, never wanting to let go.

"She's our niece," an astonished Terence whispered. He sat in the nearest seat, as if his legs could no longer support him.

"How is this possible?" Cynthia asked, eyes shining. "Dad, you didn't suspect anything when you decided to come see her?"

"Not at all, I loved her song, and Saul just kept insisting I sign her."

"My father?" Victoria gasped. "He insisted? He must have known something. I'm sure he did."

"Now, now," Terence cautioned. "We can't just assume he's behind this."

"Really? I can," Victoria spat. "My father's the one who forbade us from speaking to Ekene after he returned to Nigeria."

Cynthia's phone buzzed. "Gotta take this," she said swiftly. She answered the phone and rushed out of the room.

"It's gotta be him," Victoria continued. "Let me start from the beginning. You need to hear the whole story." Victoria's voice shook. It didn't matter that they were standing in the Ruchets' living room. The story was out and needed to be told.

Victoria took a deep breath. "My parents fled the Biafran War in the sixties. When Ekene was a young man and years after the war ended, he wanted to go back to Nigeria as a human rights activist. My father, Saul Okafor, forbade him from leaving. He said our lives were in New York, and he also looked down on Ekene's job, he didn't even consider it a profession. My father warned him that if he left, he was to never contact our family again. I loved Ekene so much. I had two brothers, but Ekene was my best friend, my protector, my hero. He used to call me Queen, which I thought was totally appropriate." Victoria laughed then sighed painfully. "I'm ashamed to say I selfishly begged him to stay."

Victoria paused and shook her head sadly.

"I remember that night like it was yesterday. I cried and pleaded. I told him I needed him more than any of the unnamed people he would be trying to save. He smiled sadly and told me,

'If I stand by and watch what is going on without doing anything, Queen, I am as guilty as the perpetrators. I hope someday you will understand.' I think of those words all the time. That was the last time I saw him or heard from him. Until that day when my father received that fateful letter. Ekene had been killed."

A tear rolled down Victoria's cheek.

"I hadn't known he'd married let alone had a baby," she said in a hoarse whisper. "My father took his death very badly. My mother died not long after, blaming my father for Ekene's death. I never fully got over it myself, but I can say that today I understand Ekene's choice. I fight for women's rights, and there isn't a single day that passes in which I don't thank Ekene for showing me that we all have our part to play in making this world a better place. Your father was a hero—I'm sure your mother was, too, Maude. They helped a lot of people, and you should be proud of that."

"Even if it means I never got to know them?" Maude asked, bitterness choking her voice.

Victoria smiled sadly.

"I don't expect you to understand now, just like I clung to Ekene years ago. I hope one day you will." She took Maude's hand and pressed it affectionately.

"*You're* my redemption, Maude. I never got to thank my brother for everything he'd done for me, but now that you're here I know I'll find peace once more. I had no idea you existed, but I'm pretty sure my father did. You're coming back home with us immediately." She grabbed Maude's luggage.

"Robert, do something!" Mrs. Ruchet urged.

"You aren't leaving with ze girl. There is absolutely no proof of zis!" Mr. Ruchet exclaimed.

"Oh come on," Jazmine exclaimed. "Don't you see the

resemblance between Mom, Uncle Ekene, and Maude? Geez, Mom, were you and your brother twins?"

"Resemblance won't work in court, young lady," Mr. Ruchet stated curtly.

"Aren't you ashamed of yourselves?" Victoria hissed. "You hid Maude's parents from her. She had a right to know."

Mr. Ruchet swallowed. "It was Marie-Antoinette who didn't want to tell Maude." All eyes turned to Mrs. Ruchet. She looked down at the coffee table and sighed.

This was the first time that Maude had ever seen her foster mother at a loss for words.

Finally, Mrs. Ruchet spoke, her voice, hoarse, her eyes downcast.

"Robert was once in love with Danielle. Don't know what he saw in her. She wasn't so pretty after all. All brains, no beauty," Mrs. Ruchet said, stumbling over the English words. "When he arrived with the baby, I only agreed to let her stay if Robert never interfered in her upbringing. She could not know about her parents, or she'd have bothered us about that."

"I felt guilty," Mr. Ruchet admitted shamefacedly. "I'm the one who convinced Danielle to go to Nigeria. After she met Ekene, Danielle and I remained close friends. Marie-Antoinette never believed that I no longer loved your mother. When I met you, Marie-Antoinette, there never was another woman for me. Your spirit, your beautiful curves, your passion: I loved them all."

"Loved?" Mrs. Ruchet croaked.

"Love," he answered. He gazed at his wife with tenderness.

Just then, Cynthia burst inside the living room, holding out her phone.

"Maude!" she squealed. "We did it! Your performance from

Terre à Terre! It's trending. Your streams are up! 'Betrayed but Not Broken' is *number two* on Musicfy Top 100!"

Maude stumbled, grabbing Victoria's arm for support and holding on to her for dear life. She couldn't believe it. All her hard work. Their work. She gazed at the whole family, *her* family, her heart brimming with joy and gratitude.

"We did it!" Maude cried, pumping her fist in the air.

The Baldwins hugged Maude and jumped up and down, screaming in the living room. The Ruchets from the eldest to the little twins eyed the celebration warily.

"You can work on a full album!" Jazmine said.

"She's right," Terence said, fishing his phone out. "I'll call Alan and Travis right away—"

"Don't." Mrs. Ruchet's authoritative tone startled the entire family. Terence's finger hung over his phone.

"I told you, Maude stays here. Her mother entrusted us with her care. We won't let her go."

Victoria and Terence exchanged worried glances.

But Cynthia took a defiant step toward Robert Ruchet and his wife.

"If you don't let us leave with Maude today," Cynthia threatened, "we'll sue you on Maude's behalf for the emotional distress that your silence caused. I'll learn the entire French civil code if I have to, and once we're done, you won't have a roof left over your heads."

Seeing Cynthia's determined stance, Mr. Ruchet took a step back. Holding up his hands, he said, "No need to sue, young lady. You'll make an excellent lawyer one day. But today, I won't stand in your way. Danielle would've wanted this. You can leave with Maude. She deserves to be with her family."

The Baldwins were stunned, but, quickly gathering their wits, gladly took Maude's things and rushed out of the house.

Outside, the Baldwins celebrated their victory.

They headed back to the Grand Place, but before leaving, Maude had just one more stop to make.

"Back already?" Mrs. Bonnin asked when Maude entered the bakery. She was humming a tune while cleaning her counter.

"I'm leaving," Maude answered solemnly. "For good."

Mrs. Bonnin paused and smiled a sad, tired smile. "I'm happy for you. They seem like kind people."

"They are."

As a parting gift, Maude gave Mrs. Bonnin the greatest gift of all.

"They're my biological family: aunt, uncle, and cousins."

Mrs. Bonnin's eyes almost fell out of their sockets as she choked on this delicious piece of news. This gourmet gossip would last her for months!

Maude hugged a stunned Mrs. Bonnin and kissed her good-bye.

Then she left Carvin "for good" as she had so elegantly put it.

Chapter Forty-one

When Maude stepped into her grandfather's house in Brooklyn for the first time, she felt a shiver of apprehension run down her spine. The house had a gloomy air about it, and even the colorful Igbo masks couldn't cheer the place up.

Saul had decorated the living room with Igbo statuettes and masks neatly displayed in every corner, on the walls, and on pieces of furniture. The most interesting mask, however, was the old man's grim demeanor that, Maude felt certain, was intended to ward off the faint of heart.

Victoria hadn't told Maude much about her father. Maude had imagined him as tall, muscular, with an imposing, booming, thunderous voice like a djinn from Arabian tales. Instead she found a frail but healthy seventy-year-old leaning on an exquisite wooden cane. The only sound was a steady *clump*, *clump*, *clump* from the stick that was more like a scepter than a cane. He sat in the middle of the living room wearing a regal isiagu. The cloth was patterned with the faces of lions and lined with gold buttons. On his head, instead of a crown, he wore a leopard cap, and he wore it well.

Maude followed Victoria's lead but didn't say a word. Victoria curtsied in the Igbo manner reserved for elders, but Maude did not.

“Pa, this is Maude Laurent. Ekene’s daughter.” Victoria’s voice shook. “But you know that don’t you?”

Maude knew how hard it was for Victoria to speak with a steady, respectful voice when rage boiled inside her. Maude was glad Victoria was the one speaking and not her.

“I know who she is,” Saul said. He hit the ground with his cane. “Why are you bringing her here?”

“Aren’t you the one who insisted Terence bring her to America?” Victoria countered.

Her father retreated into silence.

“I know you were angry with Ekene, but why? Why did you not take Maude in when her parents died? She was your son’s daughter.”

“He was no longer my son,” Saul interjected. “The night he left for Nigeria, I told him he was no longer my son and that if he left I would reject him forever. He left. I kept tabs on that foolish boy. His wife. He married that silly woman.”

“My mother wasn’t silly,” Maude blurted, but he didn’t look at her. It was as if she didn’t exist.

“I spoke to him once before he was imprisoned. I told him to come home. I gave him one more chance. But he pushed me away. He told me to ‘stay away.’ So I did. After your brother died, I stayed away. Left that girl with that French family. You know me, once I’ve decided, I don’t change my mind. I wanted nothing to do with her until her face began to haunt me after my heart attack. I’m dying, and I can’t die without righting what your brother did wrong.”

“My brother did nothing wrong,” Victoria countered softly.

Saul finally looked at Maude, and it was to her that he spoke.

“You will never understand my position unless you’ve seen

what I've seen. Blood, death, massacres. You will never understand me, a man who did everything to give his children a better life, a safe life, a peaceful life. You will never understand the pain of seeing Ekene walk away from it all. He did not respect his elders, his parents, his family. I will never forgive him. But you will never understand. I don't expect you to."

Chapter Forty-two

"Maude Adanna Okafor-Laurent, you are officially welcomed to your new room!" Jazmine cried. Maude had finished unpacking her belongings in the sisters' room, and the girls wanted to celebrate with a girls' night out. She had come a long way since January. Back then, she had wanted her own space. Now she knew she wanted to spend as much time with her newfound cousins as she possibly could.

"Jaz, you still haven't cleaned up your side!" Cynthia admonished. "You're such a slob! You know what, Maude? We should kick Jaz out of this room."

"You'd miss me too much," Jaz answered. "Anyway! Three cheers for Maude, for the upcoming release of her latest single 'Coming Home' and finally being able to compose a full album with Matt!"

"Hip-hip-hurray!" the girls shouted in unison.

"I'm just grateful I'll be allowed to sing at my own release party this time." Maude smiled.

"After seeing your live performance in Paris, Alan couldn't wait to have you on stage again. Your performance was breathtaking. I almost cried when you sang 'Coming Home.' It's a good thing Matt was there before you performed," Cynthia observed, with a side glance at Jazmine.

"He was there when I needed him the most. He's amazing, and we were so enthusiastic about making our long-distance relationship work! But we haven't discussed if we're going to stay together now that we're going to work together again." Maude sighed.

At that moment Victoria appeared at the girls' door.

"Maude, can I speak to you alone?" she asked. "And Jazmine?"

"Yes?" Jazmine asked sweetly.

"Clean this room before I come back, or you're the one who's going to need a human rights lawyer."

Maude followed Victoria to her bedroom where photo albums and pictures were scattered on her bed. "We haven't had time to talk since we came back from my father's, but I think you must have a lot of questions."

"I don't want you to wreck your relationship with your father because of me," Maude admitted with a heavy sigh.

"How do you feel?"

"I can't believe how his pride kept him from me all this time."

"We respect our elders, but honestly sometimes I think there must be some limit to their hold over us."

"I don't know, I don't feel as angry as I should be. I don't know if I'll go over to his place anytime soon, but he looked like he was in so much pain. I can't imagine what it's like to lose a child."

"Neither can I. But I'd never turn away from my grandchild. I don't know if I'll ever forgive him."

"I'm just glad that we're reunited now. I mean, if you knew how badly I wanted a family, you'd understand how much I don't want to cause a rift in yours."

Victoria took her in her arms.

"My dear girl, you really are your father's daughter."

Chapter Forty-three

"Thank you! Thank you very much!" Maude gushed, breathless as she waved to the cheering crowd. The Mood was packed for Maude's first show in New York, and the atmosphere was thick.

Maude had performed "Coming Home" and "Betrayed but Not Broken," and the feeling was exhilarating. Her fear, her anxieties were gone. The only thing that mattered was communicating with the crowd. And as she watched the crowd applaud and cheer energetically, she felt an indescribable sense of empowerment.

She noticed Matt in the crowd, talking earnestly to a reporter, and sighed. With everything she'd had to do to return to life in New York, she and Matt hadn't had a moment to themselves, let alone a chance to talk about where they stood now that she was back and ready to work on an album.

Maude went back to her piano and started her last song.

"How many of you have felt utmost joy and bewilderment when discovering you're falling in love?" she asked as she began the introduction. The crowd screamed its answer.

"Yeah," Maude agreed. "I know the feeling. How many of you don't know how to voice that feeling?"

Again the crowd cheered, and a female voice rose out from the crowd and said, "Show us how it's done, girl!"

"I'm going to show you how it's done." Maude laughed.

"How long have we been friends?

"It feels like forever

"Will this phase come to an end?

"Or become something stronger?"

Maude sang her heart out, secretly dedicating the song to all the lovers in the world, including the boy who had inspired the lyrics.

Once she'd finished, Maude ran backstage and straight into her uncle's arms.

"Are you comfortable with the choice you made seven months ago?" Maude asked.

"I remember arguing with Alan when we signed you," Terence said. "'What more does she have?' Alan asked me. 'Why do you want her and not Thomas Bradfield?' Do you know what I told him, Maude?"

"That you felt deep down I was your long-lost niece?"

Terence chuckled.

"I said, 'She's got soul, Alan. She'll put the soul in Soulville. Thomas won't.' Today as I watched you perform, I knew I'd been right all along."

"I've got to hand it to you, Terence," Alan said, coming up from behind him. "You know how to spot a shooting star in the midst of a starlit sky."

"That's because I don't just look for dollar bills in that starlit sky."

Alan just laughed, a slow cynical laugh.

"Your uncle's company needs someone like me, or it would be a sinking ship," he said, looking at Maude.

Maude held her uncle closer, peering at Alan through narrowed eyes. "So Matt's finally ready to work on his new album," Alan droned on, ignoring Maude's reaction.

"He's reached the last stage of grief: acceptance," Terence answered. "I thought Maude could work with him on his album. They make a great team."

"That's undeniable. The best I've seen in a long time," Alan agreed, before walking away. "Maude, Rita Hems wants you to answer a few questions. Go to her now."

"She'll do no such thing," Terence answered back.

Terence shook his head. "If it was up to Alan, you wouldn't get a moment's rest."

Maude left the backstage and went to the rooftop to get some fresh air.

The city was filled with shining lights, and she wanted to breathe in the night air.

"Am I interrupting?" Matt asked as he came up behind her.

"You know you're not," she answered.

"That's not what you would've said seven months ago," he reminded her. "If I recall, you told me we'd never be friends."

"I *was* right, though," Maude acknowledged, a smile creeping on her lips. "What we are has nothing to do with friendship."

"And now?"

"When we started dating I was supposed to be going back to Carvin," Maude answered, shyly. "We were going to do long distance. I don't want to hold you to any promises. You never said we'd be together here," she added flustered. "Alan and Terence want us to work together on your new album as well as mine. I know your rule: you don't mix business and pleasure."

Matt smiled a slow, satisfied smile.

"Rules were meant to be broken."

Then he kissed her, and the bright, shimmering lights that illuminated the city exploded like a joyous, dancing fireworks display.

Chapter Forty-four

July's summer glory had taken over the city and with it came long, warm summer nights and hot, dry summer days.

Ben's twelfth birthday had finally arrived, and it was difficult to decide who was the most excited Baldwin. Victoria loved traditions, and this was to be her last twelfth birthday tradition, so she wanted everything to be perfect. Maude couldn't wait to find out which instrument Ben had chosen. As for Ben, he enjoyed being the center of so much attention and speculation. Even Matt, who always managed to wiggle secrets out of Ben, hadn't the faintest idea, as he confessed to Maude that evening when she asked him.

"Mrs. Bonnin was right: men are useless," Maude huffed in mock despair.

Matt just laughed and followed her into the living room where the rest of the family was gathered. The lights were dimmed, and candles had been lit all over the room. Ben was sitting on a chair in the center. At his feet was a large, dark case.

"We're gathered here to celebrate Benjamin's twelfth birthday," Victoria announced. "This is a very special birthday for you. You've spent the last months discovering and exploring all sorts of instruments. We'll soon discover which instrument you've chosen, but first you must hear the birthday chant especially written for you."

Victoria stood up and recited:

"On this special day
"We're all gathered here
"To light the way
"To your twelfth year."

Terence rose and continued:

"A boy no longer
"You're now a man
"But as your father
"I'll always hold your hand."

Right on cue Cynthia followed with a grin:

"Music is a gift
"And throughout this year
"You've tried all sorts of beats
"And strained our poor ears."

Jazmine laughed and added:

"Now you've made your choice
"Now you will reveal
"The instrument you feel
"Will complement your voice."

Matt said simply:

"Be good to it
"Entertain ears and soul
"Never part from it."

Finally, Maude took a deep breath and ended the chant:

"Have tons of fun
"Play from night til dawn
"Happy Birthday, Ben

"*This party's just begun.*"

They all clapped and hugged a beaming Ben with several echoing "Happy birthdays."

"I know you're all dying to know which instrument I've chosen, and you won't have to wait much longer," Ben started once the room quieted.

"Oh come on, Ben, just tell us," Jazmine exclaimed impatiently.

"If I recall correctly, you made us wait quite some time, Jaz," her father observed.

"I remember," Ben put in. "We waited so long the ice-cream cake started to melt."

"That didn't stop you from downing two-thirds of it all by yourself," Cynthia chided.

"I didn't want it to go to waste!" Ben protested.

"This is beside the point. Ben, please proceed," Victoria urged.

He opened his case and took out his instrument. It had a long sticklike neck, at the top of which were two large tuning pegs, and, at the bottom, a small sound box covered with python skin on the front. Two strings were attached from the pegs to the base.

"What's this?" Jazmine asked.

"It looks like a very thin violin," Cynthia observed.

"This is an *erhu*," Benjamin said. "I've been taking lessons with Yu Jong, my teacher at school, for a couple of months now, and she says I'm a natural." Ben grinned sheepishly.

"What are you going to play?" Victoria asked, her eyes sparkling. She loved discovering new instruments.

"It's called 'Ballad of North Henan Province,' which is a province in China."

He placed the erhu carefully on his lap in an upright position and started playing. Although not played the same way, its sound was close to that of a violin.

Maude watched Ben as he used his left hand to alter the tone of the strings while his right hand skillfully led the bow across the strings. The ballad varied from slow to faster rhythms, retaining a peaceful melody that refreshed the mind, lifted the spirit, and could soothe the most restless disposition. It enthralled its audience, who listened in stunned silence and breathed in the enchanting notes of an instrument that had awed and amazed audiences for centuries.

Maude curled up on the sofa, a faint smile on her lips. Ever since she'd set foot in New York City she had discovered so much about herself. When she'd arrived, she was just a French girl in New York who spoke faltering English, had no family, no real identity, and only a limited knowledge of music. As she looked at her new family and listened to Ben's erhu she felt alive. She was a French girl of Nigerian and Caribbean descent who loved France and America. Furthermore, she belonged to the entire world and the entire world waited out there for her. She knew who she was, where she came from, and that the world was rich with different beats, instruments, and rhythms that she would spend her entire life discovering.

Maude also felt something she had never felt before, an acute certainty she had never before experienced, a knowledge that made her feel warm inside.

She was home.

Acknowledgments

Writing *A French Girl in New York* has been a labor of love. I wish to thank all the people I met along one of the most important journeys of my life.

First and foremost, I'd like to mention the invaluable Sarah Audu. Thank you for your creativity, your multiple talents as a consultant, your essential professional input, your keen eye, and incredible love and patience. Thank you, my loving sister Deborah for your infallible support and insights on life in New York. A huge thank-you to the talented multi-instrumentalist Saë for your instrumental virtuosity and for giving me access to the music industry. What fun we've had together!

There are two amazing ladies who believed in this novel way back when they read its first drafts: thank you Maya Rock and I-Yana Tucker for believing in this story and for being a part of this journey from the start!

As the journey continued, I felt lucky to meet more awesome people along the way!

A heartfelt *merci* to my wonderful agent Mary Darby, who championed this novel and helped me bring it to a new level. Thank you, Fiona Simpson, for your editorial work and for making this manuscript ready for the world.

A big thank-you to all my literature teachers in France who encouraged me to write.

Last but not least, a warm thank-you to my family, including my beloved Tatie Maguy and my two honorary grandmothers on both sides of the Atlantic, Winona Ducille and Nicole.

About the Author

Anna Adams is a French-American lawyer turned author. Born in France and raised partly in the United States and in France, Anna grew up loving stories in French and English. She currently lives in the beautiful city of Paris. And when not in France, Anna enjoys writing in libraries all over the world. *A French Girl in New York* is her first novel.

Want more of Maude's story?

Turn the page for a preview of book 2

A French Star in New York

Coming soon from Wattpad Books!

Chapter One

Maude Laurent had been on lockdown in Manhattan for the past twenty-four hours.

She pondered for some time the awful chain of events that had led her to this situation.

During the twenty-third hour, she rested. And on the twenty-fourth, she woke, famished for edible forms of French sanity. French rolls, French somethings, French anythings.

Manhattan was madness. Maude was in Manhattan. Maude was in madness.

Peering out the window of her bedroom, she threw an irate "Humpf!" at the sky and at the herd of paparazzi scrambling below. Teasing her misery by displaying a large, sunny grin, the sky refused to dissolve into raindrops to satisfy Maude's stormy mood.

After brushing her luxuriant natural hair into a bun, Maude let her reflection peer back at her in the oval mirror. Her smooth, chocolate-brown skin glowed under the flirtatious ray of light dancing around the room, and her dark-brown eyes glowered with defiance at her reflection.

"Today, I'm breaking free," she stated, like many optimistic celebrities under siege had done before her. She slammed the door to her bedroom, hurried down the stairs of the Baldwin home, and swung the front door open.

Breaking free was easier said than done. When she stared into the face of the gathered crowd, Maude had to muster all her courage. The paparazzi had microphones and cameras that they shoved in her face with unhinged eagerness. They'd waited hours on the brownstone's steps and now demanded answers to their questions.

"Maude! Did you steal Matt from Lindsey Linton?" one journalist cried.

"Are you and Matt together?" another yelled.

"What is Matt's relationship to Lindsey Linton?"

"Are you going out with Thomas Bradfield? With Matt? With both?"

"Are you in an open relationship?"

"Is Matt coming on tour with you?"

"Are you and Lindsey Linton fighting over Matt?"

Maude was pretty sure these reporters thought teenage celebrities like her were supposed to enjoy basking in the limelight. Her own meteoric rise had, after all, started with a cover song that had gone viral on social media.

They were licking their lips with anticipation for the next potential celebrity feud headline. Fingers snapped. Cameras zoomed. Beads of sweat glistened like shards of glass.

She heard the journalist closest to her, a woman with piercing blue eyes and a messy ponytail, shout, "Zoom in on her face! Don't stop filming, we might get an outburst on camera."

Maude pushed through the crowd and elbowed her way to the dark sedan waiting for her in front of the house. She jumped in and shut the door, while the journalists banged on the roof.

She straightened her sunglasses. They made her face small

but she wished they had the ability to render her invisible from prying eyes.

She locked the door firmly, leaned her head against the window, and rubbed her temples, trying to ease her weariness with the simple gesture.

"Soulville?" Rob, her driver, asked.

Maude didn't hesitate a second.

"Soulville."

Rob pressed the accelerator and the car tore away, scattering the crowd of disappointed journalists.

Three days ago, Maude's life had been perfect. She'd reveled in the joy of discovering her long-lost family. She'd celebrated her cousin's birthday. Her hit song had been playing everywhere. Three days ago, she'd been preparing to leave for her tour with Matt and Terence Baldwin. Three days ago, Matt and she were planning on making their first public outing in New York. They'd spent hours planning their first American date and deciding how they'd be photographed by one of Matt's reporter friends. She'd insisted on just a few shots, not too many, just enough so that their fans—and exes—knew they were an item. They'd also decided to go official on their favorite social media, PixeLight. Three days ago, New York had been her home, her haven, her heaven.

Today, this French girl couldn't wait to get out of New York.

Her phone buzzed with new notifications from PixeLight. Dozens poured in every minute. She turned on airplane mode and her phone went silent. She remembered a time when going viral on social media had been a good thing, when her classical cover of pop star Lindsey Linton's song had propelled her into the limelight. A prelude to the recent success of her latest single "Betrayed but Not Broken."

Could she, Maude Laurent, be accused of cowardice? She often boasted she never ran away from a challenge. But then, that was before her love life had started trending. Of course she was ecstatic her third single was a hit, thrilled when people recognized her and stopped her in the street. She'd been called "the voice of today's generation" and "a teen phenomenon." So many flattering associations, metaphors, and superlatives placed next to her name, she couldn't remember them all.

Until scandal halted her momentum.

She'd quite involuntarily stepped into a muddy puddle she hadn't even known lay on her sunny path.

Upon reaching Soulville Tower, Maude thanked Rob and hurried inside the building.

She'd spent countless hours in Soulville, her second home, working on her first three singles. She'd had legendary fights with Matt, storming out whenever she deemed it necessary to make a point. *But I'm not a diva*, Maude thought ruefully. If she was, she'd be enjoying the unwanted attention.

She ran across the lobby, caressed the grand concert piano with distracted fondness, and stopped in front of the half-open door to Matt's Creation Room. She pushed it slightly, enlarging the triangular scope, through which she peered at him unseen.

He was strumming his acoustic guitar with one hand while the other tousled his dark-blond hair with frustration. His guitar pick was stuck between his clenched teeth. She couldn't see his eyes but knew how gray they shone when bent over his guitar, his mind roaming in search of musical creativity.

Maude's resolve wavered. They had shared so much. She'd argued with him, laughed with him, and derided his Parisian arrogance. She tilted her head, overcome with sadness. He had been there for her when she'd learned the truth about her parents' tragic deaths. He'd held her in his arms when she'd welcomed tears as a delivery from her blinding pain.

She gave herself a mental jolt and walked inside the room.

She laid the fateful edition of *Hollywood Buzz* on the coffee table without saying a word.

Its title popped off the page, CAN THE LOVE DOCTOR CURE THIS LOVE TRIANGLE?, by Lexie Staz, followed by a large photo of Matt and Lindsey kissing.

Matt took the magazine, scanned the cover quickly, and threw the magazine back on the coffee table.

"It was just one kiss," Matt said calmly, looking straight into her eyes. "At the summer dance, way before you and I got together in Paris."

Looking at the magazine cover again, Maude felt her head spin as a wave of nausea assaulted her.

She knew he was telling the truth. She could see the disco ball from the 1970s-themed summer dance she had attended weeks ago at her high school. The same one where her ex, Thomas Bradfield, had made a passionate declaration. The one where she'd almost told Matt her feelings for him before losing her nerve.

It was one thing to know that Matt hadn't betrayed her, and another to wrap her head around the image of him kissing her arch nemesis.

That wasn't the worst part.

Maude picked up the magazine, went to the folded page and read the article aloud.

"'A couple of weeks ago, a source spotted Matt making out with Lindsey Linton.

"'When I interviewed Maude Laurent for the release of her

single "Betrayed but Not Broken," she assured me she and Matt were just friends. But their eyes blatantly said otherwise.

"'Now rumor has it that Matt is preparing to accompany Maude on her tour as the singer's boyfriend.

"'What about Lindsey?

"'"Maude stole him from me," Lindsey Linton told me herself when I asked her. "Ever since she started working with him, she's been after him. She's doing it just so she can use him. Every girl Matt went out with benefited from his fame."

"'Maude wouldn't be the first singer to date a celebrity just to further her career. But wasn't her label selling her as the ordinary girl next door?

"'According to Lindsey, things went from bad to worse after the iconic pop star was asked to replace Maude in an opera performance of *La Cenerentola*.

"'A source confided to me: "Maude choked. They had to replace her with Lindsey, and Maude's hated her ever since."

"'But Maude isn't satisfied until she has them all. Not only has she skillfully maneuvered herself to steal Matt from Lindsey, she now also has Thomas Bradfield, a rising pop star, wrapped around her little finger.

"'The young pop singer, made famous after his "Paris versus New York City" duet with Lindsey, isn't hiding his feelings for Maude, whom he calls his "ideal girlfriend."

"'Soulville tried to sell Maude Laurent as a sweet French girl. Boy, were they wrong . . .'"

"She goes on and on and on," Maude finished, throwing the magazine aside.

"I was angry with you," Matt explained. "You'd left with Jazmine, and I thought you were in love with Bradfield. I danced with Lindsey, we kissed, but I stopped it there. Nothing else happened."

"I believe you," Maude repeated wanly. "I mean"—she sighed—"we weren't a couple back then. But somehow, I don't know why, it's still hard to digest. And these words. This article." Maude squeezed her arms around her waist, seeking comfort and finding none.

"Don't let this get to you," Matt said. He took her hand and gently pulled her into his arms. "Lexie must have sensed there was something going on between us during the interview at the release party so she investigated. Her 'source' is probably some dumb kid at your school." He cupped Maude's face in his hands. "It would have been hard not to notice the lingering looks the two of us shared when we spoke about our work during the interview."

Maude couldn't shake the image of Matt and Lindsey kissing. Seeing him with another girl was one thing, but she and Lindsey had an acrimonious relationship. The words in the article kept ringing in her head.

"Don't worry, Maude. We can wait a little before we go public. We'll do that while we're on tour together," Matt said.

Maude shook her head and took a step back, untangling herself from his embrace and warmth.

"You're not coming with me on tour, and we can't—we can't be together," Maude blurted. She'd thought about it long and hard. Staying holed up in her room had given her ample time to think. She winced when Matt took a step back as if he'd received a blow.

"You're overreacting."

"I'm described as some sort of man-eater who steals guys from other girls, *and* as someone who's *sleeping* her way to fame. I don't need more time to think, Matt. I gave this a great deal of thought. If we go public my reputation will be ruined. I'll only be seen as 'Matt's girlfriend.' My success will be tied to yours."

"Your song cover went viral last year. And then you released another hit with a label. You became famous on your *own*."

"These rumors about us dating have added a million new followers to my PixeLight account. And counting." Maude turned off airplane mode on her phone and it immediately started hissing with new PixeLight notifications.

"Seriously?" Matt said. He took out his own phone and went straight to Maude's PixeLight account. He scrolled up and down in disbelief.

"You're a way bigger star than I am," she pointed out.

"I know, but—"

"Your ex, Stella, managed to launch a whole makeup brand after you dated. Tiana, a whole clothing line, and—"

"No need to remind me of all my exes." Matt stopped her.

"I'm not like them, Matt. I want to be my own person."

"That's why I'm crazy about you, Maude." He took her hand in his and enveloped it with care. "Don't ruin everything because of this. We just need to wait a little and deny that there was anything going on between me and Lindsey."

"Nobody will believe what we say if Lindsey and Thomas keep saying the opposite. Lindsey is more famous than I am. She's been in the game way longer than me. And, like you just mentioned, my career started only because my cover of *her* song went viral. Everybody will think I'm out to get her!"

"You can't live your life for everybody else," Matt said. "If you let gossip dictate your life, you'll never truly live."

"You don't understand. I grew up without parents. The one thing that I had was dignity. Making sure that I never did something that I felt was contrary to my principles. I wanted my parents to be proud."

"They are, Maude."

"I'd never forgive myself if my career success was linked to dating you or a scandal involving me fighting another girl over a guy. My success has to be the result of my own hard work. Not who I date."

"So you're just going to give up on us? We'd promised each other that even distance wouldn't separate us when you thought you were going to live in France."

"That was different." Maude faltered. She pulled away from Matt. "Dignity and honesty are the only things I can hold on to. I'd be miserable any other way."

"So, you've made up your mind. Nothing I say can change that?" he asked, bitterly.

"I'm just an ordinary girl at heart. From a little French town nobody knows."

"You're a star now. You can't expect to hide your love life forever."

"I want to be appreciated for my music, *not* for who I may or may not be dating," Maude said. "I'm sorry, Matt. It's over.""

Maude turned around and left the room, tears streaming down her cheeks while her phone kept buzzing.